PRAISE FOR DENNIS LEHANE'S

MOONLIGHT MILE

"*Moonlight Mile* is yet more proof that the author is as much social historian as mystery writer, and that his true literary forefathers include John Steinbeck as well as Raymond Chandler. . . . Nobody pokes his nose into the crummy apartments and seedy bars and trash-packed alleys and emotional messes of lower-class life with more observational rigor than Lehane."　　　　　　　*—Chicago Tribune*

"Throughout, Lehane's writing mixes the streetwise and the lyrical. . . . Lehane is a writer bringing new confidence and an easy prowess to a new chapter in an epic story—the Kenzie-Gennaro saga."　　　　　　　　　　*—Washington Post*

"*Moonlight Mile* is everything that Lehane readers have come to expect: a tight story filled with unexpected turns, delivered in prose that goes down easily. Compulsively readable, the duo at its heart is well worth spending time with."

—Denver Post

"[*Moonlight Mile*] zooms along the express track without sacrificing the emotional punch of Lehane's previous works."　　　*—Los Angeles Times Book Review*

"Given that this is Lehane writing, the novel offers intense and violent action, brilliantly evoked Boston and surrounding locales, an assortment of finely etched individuals skilled in thuggery, various awful parents, and a complicated knot of a plot with surprise twists to spare."　　　　　　　*—Houston Chronicle*

"*Moonlight Mile* is the kind of detective novel that brings out the reviewer's clichés—mesmerizing, page-turning, pulsating—but they're all true. I regretted putting it down at night and had to stop myself from dismissing my own work to read it the very next morning. . . . But I can honestly say you'll love this novel—if you like smart dialogue, compelling characters and plot, and thought-provoking ideas."　　　　　　　　　　　　　　　　　*—Virginian Pilot*

"For fans of the Boston-based detective couple—a blue-collar Nick and Nora Charles—. . . the return is more than welcome. . . . Mapped out with Hammett-like precision, but as with Hammett (and Raymond Chandler and Ross Macdonald and Charles Willeford), when Lehane's on his game, it isn't the plot that matters. It's the characters, and the smart, hard-boiled prose." —*Philadelphia Inquirer*

"You always learn something new when reading Lehane. Here, he'll have you flipping pages as fast as you can, loving the pace and danger, all the while pondering how far your own moral compass might wobble away from true north under the right circumstances." —*Dallas Morning News*

"Streamlined and fast-paced, the novel cruises through a well-designed and executed plot. But at the same time, Lehane uses the form to give a twist of his own to hard-boiled detective fiction, employing it as a lens to magnify the moral consequences of choices that his characters make. He knows how to get equally valid chills and laughs out of the same situation, throwing the reader for a welcome loop. . . . The dialogue pops with energy." —*Columbus Dispatch*

"Lehane delivers an emotional story that connects with the characters' capacity to grow. . . . *Moonlight Mile* is a worthy return for Lehane's iconic characters." —*Kansas City Star*

"Lehane is one of America's best crime novelists; this book could easily become as memorable a film as two of his other spellbinding novels, *Mystic River* and *Shutter Island*." —*Lansing State Journal*

"It will send Lehane first-timers to the stacks searching for earlier titles." —*Florida Times-Union*

"Big-hearted, sometimes heartbreaking, and always compelling." —*Seattle Times*

"Dennis Lehane is one of the best in the business of writing in the hard-boiled detective form. . . . Lehane is a master of the genre's lean, propulsive style and its sharply observed descriptions." —*St. Petersburg Times*

"Lehane's interest in investigating moral ambiguity and a genuine affection for his characters makes *Moonlight Mile* a satisfying send-off." —*Christian Science Monitor*

"*Moonlight Mile* reflects the national zeitgeist—resentful, fearful, and angry—like few other novels I've read this year. Lehane, always a populist, nails it." —*Oregonian*

MOONLIGHT MILE

ALSO BY DENNIS LEHANE

A Drink Before the War
Darkness, Take My Hand
Sacred
Gone, Baby, Gone
Prayers for Rain
Mystic River
Shutter Island
Coronado: Stories
The Given Day

MOONLIGHT MILE

DENNIS LEHANE

wm

WILLIAM MORROW
An Imprint of HarperCollins*Publishers*

"Moonlight Mile." Words and Music by Mick Jagger and Keith Richards. Copyright © 1971 (Renewed) ABKCO Music, Inc., 85 Fifth Avenue, New York, NY 10003. All Rights Reserved. Used by Permission of Alfred Music Publishing Co., Inc.

A hardcover edition of this book was published in 2010 by William Morrow, an imprint of Harper Collins Publishers.

FIRST WILLIAM MORROW PAPERBACK EDITION PUBLISHED 2012.

Designed by Jamie Lynn Kerner

The Library of Congress has catalogued the hardcover edition as follows:

Lehane, Dennis.
   Moonlight mile / Dennis Lehane. — 1st ed.
     p. cm.
   Sequel to: Gone, baby, gone.
   ISBN 978-0-06-183692-3 (hardcover)
   ISBN 978-0-06-201584-6 (international edition)
   1. Kenzie, Patrick (Fictitious character)—Fiction. 2. Gennaro, Angela (Fictitious character)—Fiction. 3. Private investigators— Fiction. 4. Missing persons—Investigation—Fiction. 5. Innercities—Massachusetts—Boston—Fiction. 6. Boston (Mass.)— Fiction. I. Title.
    PS3562.E426M66 2010
    813'.54—dc22

                                     2010025883

ISBN 978-0-06-207242-9 (pbk.)

12 13 14 15 16 OV/RRD 10 9 8 7 6 5 4 3 2

For Gianna Malia
Welcome, Little G

I am just living to be lying by your side
But I'm just about a moonlight mile on
*   down the road*

—MICK JAGGER/KEITH RICHARDS, "MOONLIGHT MILE"

PART I
YOU SEEMED SO REAL

CHAPTER ONE

ON A BRIGHT, UNSEASONABLY WARM AFTERNOON in early December, Brandon Trescott walked out of the spa at the Chatham Bars Inn on Cape Cod and got into a taxi. A pesky series of DUIs had cost him the right to operate a motor vehicle in the Commonwealth of Massachusetts for the next thirty-three months, so Brandon always took cabs. The twenty-five-year-old trust-fund baby of a superior court judge mother and a local media mogul father, Brandon wasn't your run-of-the-mill rich kid asshole. He worked double shifts at it. By the time the state finally suspended his license, he was on his fourth DUI. The first two had been pled down to reckless driving, the third had brought him a stern warning, but the fourth had resulted in injury to someone besides Brandon, who escaped without a scratch.

This winter afternoon, with the temperature hanging just below forty degrees, Brandon wore a manufacturer-stained, manufacturer-faded hoodie that retailed for around $900 over a white silk T with a collar dragged down by a pair of $600 shades. His baggy shorts also had little rips in them, compliments of whichever nine-year-old Indonesian had been poorly paid to put them there. He wore flip-flops in December, and he sported an insouciant mop of blond surfer's hair with an adorable habit of drooping helplessly over his eyes.

After drinking his weight in Crown Royal one night, he'd flipped his Dodge Viper coming back from Foxwoods with his girlfriend riding shotgun. She'd only been his girlfriend two weeks, but it was unlikely she'd be anyone's girlfriend ever again. Her name was Ashten Mayles and she'd been in a persistent vegetative state ever since the top of the car compacted against the top of her skull. One of the last acts she'd attempted to perform while she'd still had use of her arms and legs was to try and take Brandon's keys from him in the casino parking lot. According to witnesses, Brandon had rewarded her concern by flicking a lit cigarette at her.

In possibly the first brush with actual consequence that Brandon had ever known, Ashten's parents, not wealthy but politically connected, had decided to do everything in their power to ensure that Brandon paid for his mistakes. Hence the Suffolk County DA's prosecution on DUI and reckless endangerment. Brandon spent the entire trial looking shocked and morally outraged that anyone could get away with expecting personal responsibility of him. In the end, he was convicted and served four months' house arrest. In a really nice house.

During the subsequent civil trial, it was revealed that the trust-fund baby had no trust fund. He had no car, had no house. As far as anyone could tell, he didn't own so much as an iPod.

Nothing was in his name. Things had once *been* in his name, but he'd fortuitously signed them all over to his parents one day before the car accident. It was the *before* part that killed people, but no one could prove otherwise. When the jury in the civil trial awarded damages in the amount of $7.5 million to the Mayles family, Brandon Trescott emptied his pockets of the nothing that was in them and shrugged.

I had a list of all the things Brandon had once owned and was legally prohibited from using. Use of said items, it was deemed by the court, would constitute not just the appearance of ownership but the fact of it. The Trescotts protested the court's definition of "ownership," but the press beat the shit out of them, the public outcry was loud enough to lead ships ashore through night fog, and they ultimately signed off on the deal.

The next day, in a wonderful "fuck you" to both the Mayles family and those loud voices of the great unwashed, Layton and Susan Trescott purchased their son a condominium in Harwich Port, since the Mayles' attorneys had not covered future earnings or future possessions in the agreement. And it was to Harwich Port that I followed Brandon early on a December afternoon.

The condo smelled of mold and rug beer and food left rotting in the sink on crusted plates. I knew this because I'd been in there twice to plant bugs and swipe all the passwords off his computer and generally do all the snoopy, sneaky shit clients pay top dollar to pretend they don't know guys like me get up to. I'd gone through what little paperwork I could find and hadn't found any bank accounts we didn't know about or any stock reports that hadn't been reported. I hacked his computer and found pretty much the same—nothing but his self-serving rants to ex-frat buddies and some pathetic, never sent, letter-to-the-editor screeds rife with misspellings. He visited a lot of porn sites and a lot of gaming sites and he read every article ever written about himself.

When the cab dropped him off, I pulled my digital recorder out of the glove compartment. The day I'd broken into his place and hacked his computer, I'd placed an audio transmitter the size of a grain of sea salt under his media console and another in his bedroom. I listened to him let out a bunch of small groans as he prepared for the shower, then the sound of him shower-ing, drying off, changing into fresh clothes, pouring himself a drink, flicking on his flat screen, turning it to some soul-crushing reality show about stupid people, and settling onto the couch to scratch himself.

I slapped my own cheeks a couple times to stay awake and flipped through the newspaper on the car seat. Another spike in unemployment was predicted. A dog had rescued his owners from a fire in Randolph even though he'd just had hip surgery and his two hind legs were strapped to a doggie wheelchair. Our local Russian mob boss got charged with DUI after he stranded his Porsche on Tinean Beach at high tide. The Bruins won at a sport that made me sleepy when I watched it, and a Major League third baseman with a twenty-six-inch neck reacted with self-righteous fury when questioned about his al-leged steroid use.

Brandon's cell rang. He talked to some guy he kept calling "bro," except it came out "bra." They talked about *World of Warcraft* and *Fallout 4* on PS2 and Lil Wayne and T.I. and some chick they knew from the gym whose Facebook page mentioned how much extra working out she did on her Wii Fit even though she, like, lived across from a park, and I looked out the window and felt old. It was a feeling I had a lot lately, but not in a rueful way. If this was how twenty-somethings spent their twenties these days, they could have their twenties. Their thirties, too. I tilted my seat back and closed my eyes. After a while, Brandon and his bra signed off with:

"So, a'ight, bra, you keep it tight."

"You keep it tight, too, bra, you keep it real tight."

"Hey, bra."

"What?"

"Nothing. I forgot. Shit's fucked up."

"What?"

"Forgetting."

"Yeah."

"A'ight."

"A'ight."

And they hung up.

I searched for reasons not to blow my brains out. I came up with two or three dozen real fast, but I still wasn't certain I could listen to many more conversations between Brandon and one of his "bras."

Dominique was another issue entirely. Dominique was a blue-chip working girl who'd entered Brandon's life ten days earlier via Facebook. That first night, they'd IM'd back and forth for two hours. Since then, they'd Skyped three times. Dominique had remained fully clothed but wildly descriptive about what would happen should (a) she ever deign to sleep with him and (b) he came up with the sizable cash allotment necessary to make that happen. Two days ago, they'd traded cell phone numbers. And, God bless her, she called about thirty seconds after he clicked off with bra. This, by the way, was how the asshole answered a phone:

Brandon:	Talk to me.
	(**Really. And people continued to contact him.**)
Dominique:	Hey.
Brandon:	Oh, *hey*. Shit. Hey! You around?
Dominique:	I will be.
Brandon:	Well, come here.
Dominique:	You forget we Skyped. I wouldn't sleep with you there wearing a hazmat suit.
Brandon:	So you're thinking about sleeping with me finally. I never met a whore decided who she'd do it with.
Dominique:	You ever meet one who looked like me?
Brandon:	No. And you're, like, near my mom's age. And still. Shit. You're the hottest chick I ever—
Dominique:	How sweet. And let's clarify something— I'm not a whore. I'm a carnal service provider.
Brandon:	I don't even know what that means.
Dominique:	I'm totally unsurprised. Now go cash a bond or a check or whatever you do and meet me.
Brandon:	When?
Dominique:	Now.
Brandon:	Now now?

Dominique:	Now now. I'm in town this afternoon and this afternoon only. I won't go to a hotel, so you better have another place, and I won't wait long.
Brandon:	What if it's a real nice hotel?
Dominique:	I'm hanging up now.
Brandon:	You're not hang—

She hung up.

Brandon cursed. He threw his remote into a wall. He kicked something. He said, "Only overpriced whore you'll ever meet? You know what, bra? You can buy ten of her. And some blow. Go to Vegas."

Yes, he actually called himself "bra."

The phone rang. He must have tossed it along with the remote, because the ringtone was distant and I heard him scramble across the room to get to it. By the time he reached it, the ringtone had died.

"Fuck!" It was a loud scream. If I'd had my window rolled down, I could have heard it from the car.

It took him another thirty seconds before he prayed.

"Look, bra, I know I did some shit, but I promise, you get her to call back again? I'll go to church and I'll deposit a boat-load of the green in one of those baskets. And I'll be better. Just have her call back, bra."

Yes, he actually called God "bra."

Twice.

His ringtone had barely burped before he flipped his phone open. "Yeah?"

"You get one shot here."

"I know it."

"Give me an address."

"Shit. I—"

"Okay, I'm hanging—"

"Seven seventy-three Marlborough Street, between Dart-mouth and Exeter."

"Which unit?"

"No unit. I own the whole thing."

"I'll be there in ninety minutes."

"I can't get a cab that fast around here, and it's rush hour soon."

"Then get the power of flight. See you in ninety. Ninety-one? I'm gone."

THE CAR WAS A 2009 ASTON Martin DB9. Retailed for two hundred thousand. Dollars. When Brandon pulled it out of the garage two town houses over, I checked it off the list on the seat beside me. I also snapped five photos of him in it while he waited for traffic to thin so he could enter it.

He hit the gas like he was launching an expedition to the Milky Way, and I didn't even bother chasing him. The way he weaved in and out of traffic, even someone with the aware-ness of meat loaf, like Brandon, would see me riding his ass. I didn't need to follow him anyway—I knew exactly where he was going and I knew a shortcut.

He arrived eighty-nine minutes after the phone call. He ran up the stairs and used a key on the door, and I caught it on film. He ran up the interior stairs, and I entered behind him. I followed him from fifteen feet away, and he was so wired that he didn't even notice me for a good two minutes. In the kitchen on the second floor, as he opened the fridge, he turned when I snapped off a few shots on the SLR and he fell back against the tall window behind him.

"Who the fuck're you?"

"Doesn't much matter," I said.

"You paparazzi?"

"Why would paparazzi give a shit about you?" I snapped a few more shots.

He leaned back to get a good look at me. He grew past the fear of a stranger popping up in his kitchen and moved on to threat-assessment. "You're not that big." He cocked his surfer's head. "I could kick your bitch ass out of here."

"I'm not that big," I agreed, "but you definitely couldn't kick my bitch ass out of anywhere." I lowered the camera. "Seriously. Just look in my eyes."

He did.

"Know what I'm saying?"

He half-nodded.

I slung the camera onto my shoulder and gave him a wave. "I'm leaving anyway. So, hey, have a good one, and try not to brain-damage any more people."

"What're you going to do with the pictures?"

I said the words that broke my heart. "Pretty much nothing."

He looked confused, which was hardly uncommon for him. "You work for the Mayles family. Right?"

My heart broke just a tiny bit more. "No. I do not." I sighed. "I work for Duhamel-Standiford."

"A law firm?"

I shook my head. "Security. Investigations."

He stared back at me, mouth open, eyes narrowed.

"Your parents hired us, you dumb shit. They figured you'd

eventually do something moronic because, well, you're a moron, Brandon. This little incident today should confirm all their fears."

"I'm not a moron," he said. "I went to BC."

In place of a dozen comebacks, a shiver of exhaustion rippled through me.

This was my life these days. This.

I left the kitchen. "Best of luck, Brandon." Halfway down the stairs, I stopped. "By the way, Dominique's not coming." I turned back toward the top of the stairs and leaned my elbow on the railing. "And, oh yeah, her name's not Dominique."

His flip-flops made a sloppy-wet-kiss noise as he crossed the floorboards and appeared in the doorway above me. "How do you know?"

"Because she works for me, dumbass."

CHAPTER TWO

AFTER I LEFT BRANDON, I MET Dominique at the Neptune Oyster in the North End.

When I sat down, she said, "That was fun," her eyes a bit wider than usual. "Tell me everything that happened when you got to his house."

"Can we order first?"

"Drinks are already on their way. Dish, dish."

I told her. Our drinks came, and we found time to scan the menu and decide on lobster rolls. She drank a light beer. I drank sparkling water. I reminded myself it was better for me than beer, particularly in the afternoon. But part of me still felt like a sellout. What I was selling out was less clear to me, but I felt it all the same.

When I finished recounting the tale of my encounter with Brandon Flip-Flops, she clapped her hands and said, "Did you really call him a moron?"

"Called him a few other things, too. Most weren't complimentary."

As our lobster rolls arrived, I removed my suit jacket, folded it, and laid it over the arm of the chair to my left.

"I'll never get used to it," she said. "You, all dressed up."

"Yeah, well, it's not like the old days." I bit into my lobster roll. Maybe the best lobster roll in Boston, which made it, arguably, the best lobster roll in the world. "It's not the dressing-up I have a hard time with. It's the hair care."

"It's a nice suit, though." She touched the sleeve. "Very nice." She bit into her roll and appraised the rest of me. "Nice tie, too. Your mom pick it out?"

"My wife, actually."

"That's *right,* you're married," she said. "Shame."

"Why's it a shame?"

"Well, maybe not for you."

"Or my wife."

"Or your wife," she acknowledged. "But some of us remember when you were a lot more, um, playful, Patrick. 'Member those days?"

"I do."

"And?"

"They seem a lot more fun to remember than they were to live."

"I don't know." She raised one soft eyebrow and took a sip of beer. "I remember you living them pretty well."

I drank some water. Drained the glass, actually. I refilled it from the overpriced blue bottle they'd left on the table. Not for the first time, I wondered why it was socially acceptable to leave a bottle of water or wine on the table but not a bottle of whiskey or gin.

She said, "You're not a very polished staller."

"I wasn't aware I was stalling."

"Trust me, you were."

It's odd how fast a beautiful woman can turn a guy's mind into lint storage. Just by being a beautiful woman.

I reached into the inside pocket of my suit jacket. I pulled out an envelope and handed it across the table. "Your payment. Duhamel-Standiford already took out taxes."

"Thoughtful of them." She placed it in her purse.

"I don't know if it's thoughtful. They're sticklers for the rules, though."

"You never were," she said.

"Things change."

She considered that and her dark eyes grew darker, sadder. Then her face lit up. She reached into her purse and pulled the check back out. She laid it on the table between us. "I have an idea."

"No, you don't."

"Sure I do. Let's flip a coin. Heads—you pay for lunch."

"I'm already paying for lunch."

"Tails . . ." She tapped a fingernail on the side of her pilsner glass. "Tails—I cash this check and we walk over to the Millennium, get a room, and blow the rest of the afternoon damaging the structural integrity of a box spring."

I took another drink of water. "I don't have any change."

She frowned. "Me, either."

"Oh, well."

"Excuse me," she said to our waiter. "Would you have a quarter we could borrow? Give it right back."

He handed it to her, a tiny tremor in his fingers for a woman almost twice his age. She could do that, though, unsettle a guy of most any age.

When he walked away, she said, "He was kinda cute."

"For a zygote."

"Now now." She perched the coin on her thumbnail and spring-loaded the thumb against the tip of her index finger. "Call it."

"I'm not playing," I said.

"Come on. Call it."

"I have to get back to work."

"Play hooky. They won't know the difference."

"I'll know the difference."

"Integrity," she said. "How overrated."

She flicked her thumb and the quarter tumbled toward the ceiling, then tumbled back to the table. It landed on the paycheck, equidistant between my water and her beer.

Heads.

"Shit," she said.

When the waiter passed, I gave him his quarter back and asked for the check. While he rang up the bill, we didn't say a word. She finished her light beer. I finished my water. The waiter ran my credit card and I did the math for a good tip. The next time he passed, I handed him the bill.

I looked across the table into her large, almond eyes. Her lips were parted; if you knew where to look you would see a small chip at the bottom of her upper left incisor.

"Let's do it anyway," I said.

"The room."

"Yes."

"The box spring."

"*Sí.*"

"Sheets so wrinkled they'll never be ironed out."

"Let's not set the bar too high."

She flipped open her cell and called the hotel. After a few moments, she said to me, "They have a room."

"Book it."

"This is so decadent."

"It was your idea."

My wife spoke into the phone. "We'll take that one if it's available now." She gave me another giddy look, as if we were sixteen and borrowing her father's car without his knowledge. She tilted her jaw back toward the phone. "Last name is Kenzie." She spelled it out. "Yes. K as in 'kangaroo.' First name is Angie."

In the room, I said, "Would you prefer I call you Angie? Or Dominique?"

"The question is which one do *you* prefer?"

"I like 'em both."

"Both it is."

"Hey."

"Yeah?"

"How can we wreck the sheets from over here on the dresser?"

"Good point. You got me?"

"I got you."

After we'd dozed to the distant honks and beeps of rush-hour traffic ten stories below, Angie propped herself up on her elbow and said, "This was crazy."

"It was."

"Can we afford it?"

She knew the answer, but I said it anyway. "Probably not."

"Shit." She looked down at the white sheets with their high thread count.

I touched her shoulder. "Every now and then, we should get to live a little. D-S pretty much assured me they'd hire me on permanent after this job."

She looked up at me, then back at the sheets. " 'Pretty much' isn't ironclad."

"I know that."

"They've been dangling this fucking *permanence* in front of you for—"

"I know."

"—too long. It's not right."

"I know it's not. But what am I going to do?"

She scowled. "What if they don't make a real offer?"

I shrugged. "I don't know."

"We're almost out of money."

"I know."

"And we have an insurance bill coming up."

"I know."

"Is that all you can say? 'I know'?"

I realized my teeth were gritted hard enough to snap. "I'm sucking it up, Ange, and doing jobs I don't like for a company I'm not terribly in love with so that eventually I can get hired permanent and we can get insurance and benefits and a paid vacation. I don't *like it* any more than you do but until you finish school and get a job again, I don't know what else I can do or fucking say that will change things."

We each took a breath, our faces a little too red, the walls a little too close.

"I'm just talking about it," she said softly.

I looked out the window for a minute, felt all the black fear and stress of the last couple of years crowding my skull and revving my heart.

Eventually, I said, "This is the best option I see on the table right now. If Duhamel-Standiford keeps playing carrot-on-a-stick, *then*, yeah, we'll have to reconsider what I'm doing. Let's hope they don't."

"Okay," she said and it came out riding a long, slow exhalation.

"Look at it this way," I said, "the debt's so big and we're so financially fucked that the bonus money we just blew on the hotel room wouldn't have made a dent."

She tapped her fingers lightly on my chest. "Ain't you sweet to say?"

"Oh, I'm a helluva guy. You didn't know?"

"I knew." She hooked a leg over mine.

"Pshaw," I said.

Outside, the horns grew more insistent. I pictured the strangled traffic. Nothing moving, nothing even appearing to.

I said, "We leave now or we leave an hour from now, we'll get home the same time."

"What do you have in mind?"

"Shameful, shameful things."

She rolled on top of me. "We have the sitter till seven-thirty."

"Ample time."

She lowered her head until our foreheads touched. I kissed her. It was the kind of kiss we'd taken for granted a few years ago—deep and unhurried. When we broke it, she took a slow breath and then leaned back in and we tried another one.

Angie said, "Let's have a few dozen more of those . . ."

"Okay."

"And then a bit more of that thing we tried an hour ago . . ."

"That was interesting, wasn't it?"

"And then a long hot shower . . ."

"I'm sold."

"And then go home and see our daughter."

"Deal."

CHAPTER THREE

THE PHONE CALL CAME AT THREE the next morning.

"You remember me?" A woman's voice.

"What?" I was still half-asleep. I checked the caller ID: PRIVATE NUMBER.

"You found her once. Find her again."

"Who is this?"

Her words slushed through the phone line. "You owe me."

"Sleep it off," I said. "I'm hanging up."

"You owe me." She hung up.

THE NEXT MORNING, I WONDERED if I'd dreamed the call. If I hadn't, I already had trouble remembering if it was last night or the night before. By tomorrow, I assumed, I'd forget the whole thing. On the walk to the subway, I drank my cup of Dunkin's under a low, clay sky and ragged clouds. Brittle gray leaves stirred in the gutter, waiting to fossilize in the first snow. The trees were bare along Crescent Avenue, and cold air off the ocean hunted the gaps in my clothes. Between the end of Crescent Avenue and the harbor itself was JFK/UMass Station and the parking lot beyond. The stairs leading up to the subway station were already thick with commuters.

Even so, a face appeared at the top of the stairs that I couldn't help but be drawn to. A face I'd hoped never to see again. The weary, embattled face of a woman who'd been passed by when life was handing out luck. As I drew close to her, she tried a hesitant smile and raised a hand.

Beatrice McCready.

"Hey, Patrick." The breeze was sharper up top and she dealt with it by burrowing into a flimsy jean jacket, the collar pulled up to her earlobes.

"Hi, Beatrice."

"I'm sorry about the call last night. I . . ." She gave a helpless shrug and looked at the commuters for a moment.

"Don't mention it."

People jostled us as they headed for the turnstiles. Beatrice and I stepped off to the side, close to a white metal wall with a six-by-six subway map painted on it.

"You look good," she said.

"You, too."

"It's nice of you to lie," she said.

"I wasn't," I lied.

I did some quick math and guessed she was about fifty. These days, fifty might be the new forty, but in her case it was the new sixty. Her once-strawberry hair was white. The lines in her face were deep enough to hide gravel in. She had the air of someone clinging to a wall of soap.

A long time ago—a lifetime ago—her niece had been kid-napped. I'd found her and returned her to the home she shared with her mother, Bea's sister-in-law, Helene, even though Helene was not what you'd call a natural-born mother.

"How're the kids?"

"Kids?" she said. "I only have one."

Jesus.

I searched my memory. A boy. I remembered that. He'd been five or six, shit, maybe seven, at the time. Mark. No. Matt. No. Martin. Definitely Martin.

I considered rolling the dice again, saying his name, but I'd already let the silence drag on too long.

"Matt," she said, careful eyes on me, "is eighteen now. He's a senior up the Monument."

Monument High was the kind of school where kids studied math by counting their shell casings.

"Oh," I said. "He like it?"

"He's . . . under the circumstances, he's a, ya know, he needs direction sometimes, but he turned out better than a lot of kids would."

"That's great." I regretted the word as soon as it left my mouth. It was such a bullshit, knee-jerk modifier to use.

Her green eyes flashed for just a second, like she wanted to explain in precise detail just how fucking *great* her life had been since I'd had a hand in sending her husband to prison. His name was Lionel and he was a decent man who'd done a bad thing for good reasons and flailed helplessly while it all transformed into carnage around him. I'd liked him a lot. It was one of the more cutting ironies of the Amanda Mc-Cready case that I'd liked the bad guys a hell of a lot more than the good ones. One exception had been Beatrice. She and Amanda had been the only blameless players in the entire clusterfuck.

She stared at me now, as if searching for a me behind the me I projected. A more worthy, more authentic me.

A group of teenage boys came through the turnstiles wearing letter jackets—varsity athletes heading to BC High a ten-minute walk down Morrissey Boulevard.

"Amanda was, what, four when you found her?" Bea said.

"Yeah."

"She's sixteen now. Almost seventeen." Her chin tipped at the athletes as they descended the stairs toward Morrissey Boulevard. "Their age."

That stung. Somehow I'd lived in denial that Amanda Mc-Cready had aged. That she was anything but the same four-year-old I'd last seen in her mother's apartment, staring at a TV as a dog-food commercial played in the cathode rays bathing her face.

"Sixteen," I said.

"You believe it?" Beatrice smiled. "Where's it go, the time?"

"Into somebody else's gas tank."

"Ain't that the truth."

Another group of athletes and a few studious-looking kids came toward us.

"You said on the phone she was gone again."

"Yeah."

"Runaway?"

"With Helene for a mother, you can't rule it out."

"Any reason to think it's more, I dunno, dire than that?"

"Well, for one, Helene won't admit she's gone."

"You call the cops?"

She nodded. "Of course. They asked Helene about her. Helene said Amanda was fine. The cops left it at that."

"Why would they leave it at that?"

"*Why?* It was city employees who took Amanda in '98. Helene's lawyer sued the cops, sued their union, sued the city. He got three million. He pocketed a million, and two million went into a trust for Amanda. The cops are terrified of Helene, Amanda, the whole thing. If Helene looks them in the eye and says, 'My kid's fine, now go away,' guess what they do?"

"You talk to anybody in the media?"

"Sure," she said. "They didn't want to touch it either."

"Why not?"

She shrugged. "Bigger fish, I guess."

That didn't make sense. I couldn't imagine what it was but she wasn't telling me something.

"What do you think I can do here, Beatrice?"

"I don't know," she said. "What can you do?"

The softening breeze moved her white hair around. There was zero doubt that she blamed me for her husband getting shot and being charged with a grocery list of crimes while he lay in his hospital bed. He'd left his house to meet me at a bar in South Boston. From there, the hospital. From the hospital, jail. From jail, prison. He'd walked out of his house one Thursday afternoon and never walked back in.

Beatrice kept looking at me the way nuns used to look at me in grammar school. I hadn't liked it then, I didn't like it now.

"Beatrice?" I said. "I'm real sorry your husband kidnapped his niece because he thought his sister was a shitty parent."

"*Thought?*"

"But he did, in fact, kidnap her."

"For her own good."

"Okay. So we should just let anybody decide what's good for a kid who doesn't belong to them. I mean, why not? Every kid with an asshole parent, line up at the nearest subway station. We'll ship you all to Wonkaville where you'll live happily ever after."

"You through?"

"No, I'm not." I could feel a rage building in me that got closer to the surface of my skin every year. "I've eaten a lot of shit over the years for doing my job with Amanda. That's what I did, Bea, what I was hired to do."

"Poor guy," she said. "All misunderstood."

"What *you* hired me to do. You said, 'Find my niece.' And I found her. So you want to give me the arched eyebrow of guilt for the next ten years, knock yourself out. I did my job."

"And a lot of people got hurt."

"*I* didn't hurt 'em, though. I just found her and brought her back."

"That's how you live with it?"

I leaned back against the wall and exhaled a long burst of air and frustration. I reached into my coat and pulled out my Charlie Card to slide through the turnstile. "I gotta go to work, Bea. A pleasure seeing you. Sorry I can't help."

She said, "Is it about money?"

"What?"

"I know we never paid your bill from the first time you found her, but—"

"What? No," I said. "It has nothing to do with money."

"Then what?"

"Look," I said as softly as I could, "I'm hurting just as bad as anyone in this economy. It's not *about* the money, no, but I can't afford to take on any job that doesn't pay, either. And I'm about to go in for an interview with someone who *might* give me a permanent job, so I couldn't take side cases anyway. Do you understand?"

"Helene's got this boyfriend," she said. "Her latest? Been in prison, of course. Guess what for."

I shook my head in frustration and tried to wave her off.

"Sex crimes."

Twelve years ago, Amanda McCready had been kidnapped by her uncle Lionel and some rogue cops who'd had no interest in ransoming or hurting her. What they'd wanted was to put that child in a home with a mother who didn't drink like she owned stock in London gin or pick her boy toys from the Sex Freaks Shopping Network. When I found Amanda, she was living with a couple who loved her. They'd been determined to give her health, stability, and happiness. Instead, they'd gone to prison, and Amanda had been returned to Helene's home. By me.

"You owe, Patrick."

"What?"

"I said you owe."

I could feel the rage again, a *tick-tick* turning into a tom-tom beat. I had done the right thing. I knew it. I had no doubt. What I had in place of doubt, though, was this rage—murky and illogical and growing deeper every day of the last twelve years. I put my hands in my pockets so I wouldn't punch the wall with the white subway map on it. "I don't owe anyone anything. I don't owe you, I don't owe Helene, I don't owe Lionel."

"What about Amanda? You don't think you owe her?" She held her thumb and index finger a whisker from touching. "Just a little bit?"

"No," I said. "Take care, Bea." I walked toward the turnstiles.

"You never asked about him."

I stopped. I dug my hands deeper into my pockets. I sighed. I turned back to her.

She shifted her weight from her left foot to her right. "Lionel. He should have been out by now, you know, a normal guy like him. The lawyer told us when we pled guilty that he'd be sentenced to twelve years but only do six. Well, that was the sentence. They told the truth about that." She took a step toward me. She stopped. She took two steps back. The crowd streamed between us, a few people giving us looks. "He gets beat up a lot in there. Worse things, too, but he won't talk about that. He isn't meant for a place like that. He's just a sweetie, you know?" She took another step back. "He got in a fight, some guy trying to take whatever my husband didn't want to give? And Lionel, he's a big guy, and he hurt this guy. So now he has to do the full twelve and he's almost done. But they're talking about new charges maybe unless he turns rat. Helps the feds with some gang that's running drugs and things in and out of there? They say if Lionel doesn't help them, they'll mess with his sentence. We thought he'd get out in *six years*." Her lips got caught between a broken smile and a hopeless frown. "I don't know sometimes anymore, you know? I don't."

There was no place for me to hide. I held her eyes as best I could but I eventually dropped my gaze to the black rubber flooring.

Another group of students walked behind her. They were

laughing about something, oblivious. Beatrice watched them go and their happiness shrank her. She looked light enough for the breeze to toss her down the stairs.

I held out my hands. "I don't do independent work anymore."

She nodded at my left hand. "You're married, uh?"

"Yeah." I took a step back in her direction. "Bea, look—"

She held up a hard hand. "Kids?"

I stopped. I didn't say anything. I couldn't find the words suddenly.

"You don't have to answer. I'm sorry. I am. I was stupid to come. I just thought, I dunno, I just . . ." She glanced off to her right for a moment. "You're good at it I bet."

"Huh?"

"I bet you're a real good father." She gave me a wadded-up smile. "I always thought you would be."

She turned into the crowd exiting the station and vanished from my view. I went through the turnstile and down the stairs to the subway platform. From there I could see the parking lot that led out to Morrissey Boulevard. The crowd streamed from the stairwell onto the asphalt, and for a moment, I saw Bea again, but just for a moment. Then I lost sight of her. The crowd was thick with high school kids, and most were taller than her.

CHAPTER FOUR

MY COMMUTE WAS ONLY FOUR STOPS on the Red Line. Still, when you're crammed into a moving can with a hundred other people, four stops can wrinkle a suit pretty good. I exited South Station and shook my arms and legs in a futile attempt to restore luster to my suit and topcoat, and then I walked over to Two International Place, a skyscraper as sleek and heartless as an ice pick. Here, on the twenty-eighth floor, sat the offices of Duhamel-Standiford Global.

Duhamel-Standiford didn't tweet. They didn't have a blog or pop up on the right side of a Google screen when someone typed in "private investigation greater boston." Not to be found in the Yellow Pages, on the back of *Security and You* magazine, or begging for your business at two A.M. between commercials for Thighmaster 6000 and 888-GALPALS. Most of the city had never heard of them. Their advertising budget amounted to the same number every quarter: 0.

And they'd been in business for 170 years.

They occupied half of the twenty-eighth floor of Two International. The windows facing east overlooked the harbor. Those facing north peered down on the city. None of the windows had blinds. All doors and cubicles were constructed of frosted glass. Sometimes, in the dead of summer, it made you want to put your coat on. The typeface on the glass entrance door was smaller than the door handle:

DUHAMEL-STANDIFORD
SUFFOLK COUNTY, MA
ESTAB. 1840

After I was buzzed through that door, I entered a wide anteroom with ice-white walls. The only things hanging on the walls were squares and rectangles of frosted glass, none more than a foot wide or tall and most in the seven-by-nine range. It was impossible to sit or stand in that room and not suspect you were being watched.

Behind the sole desk in that vast anteroom sat a man who'd outlived everyone who could remember a time when he hadn't sat there. His name was Bertrand Wilbraham. He was of indefinable age—could have been a weathered fifty-five or a sprightly eighty. His flesh reminded me of the brown bar soap my father used to keep in the basement washroom and, except for two very thin and very black eyebrows, his head was hairless. He never even sported a five-o'clock shadow. All male employees and subcontractors of Duhamel-Standiford were required to wear a suit and tie. The style of said suit and tie was up to you—although pastels and floral prints were frowned upon—but the shirt had to be white. Pure white, no pinstripes, however subtle. Bertrand Wilbraham, however, always wore a light gray shirt. His suits and ties changed, hard as it might have been to tell, from solid grays to solid blacks to solid navies, but the gray, protocol-busting shirts remained the same, as if to say, The revolution will be dour.

Mr. Wilbraham did not seem terribly fond of me, but I took comfort in knowing he didn't seem terribly fond of anyone. As soon as he buzzed me in that morning, he raised a small pink phone memo from his immaculate desktop.

"Mr. Dent requests your presence in his office as soon as you've arrived."

"I've arrived."

"Duly noted." Mr. Wilbraham opened his fingers. The pink sheet of paper dropped from his hand and floated into the wastebasket.

He buzzed me through the next set of doors and I went down a hallway with a dove-gray carpet. Halfway down, there was an office used by subcontractors like me when we had to log office hours on behalf of the company. It was empty this morning, which meant I had squatter's rights. I entered and allowed myself the brief fantasy that it would be mine, permanently, by day's end. I cleared the thought from my head and dropped my bags on the desk. The gym bag held my camera and most of my surveillance equipment from the Trescott job. The laptop bag held a laptop and a photo of my daughter. I unholstered my gun and placed it in my desk drawer. It would stay there until day's end, because I like carrying a gun about as much as I like eating kale.

I left the glass box and walked the dove-gray hallway up to Jeremy Dent's office. Dent was vice president of labor relations and the man who'd first subbed work out to me two years ago.

Before that, I'd worked independently. I'd had a rent-free office stuffed in the belfry of St. Bartholomew's Church. It was a thoroughly illegal arrangement between me and Father Drummond, the pastor. When the Archdiocese of Boston had to start paying the piper for decades of covering up child rape by sick priests, they sent an appraiser to St. Bart's. Whereupon my rent-free office vanished as completely as the bell that had once resided in the belfry but hadn't been seen since the Carter presidency.

Dent came from a long line of Virginia gentlemen soldiers and had graduated third in his class at West Point. Vietnam, War College, and a quick climb up the armed forces career ladder had ensued. He drew command duty in Lebanon in the mid-eighties, came back home, and pulled the plug. Walked away from the whole deal at thirty-six and the rank of lieutenant colonel, for reasons never fully understood. He crossed paths with old family friends in Boston, the kind whose ancestors had carved their names in the galley planks of the *Mayflower*, and they mentioned an opening in a firm that few in their circle ever mentioned until things got dire.

Twenty-five years later, Dent was a full partner. He had the white colonial in Dover and the summer place in Vineyard Haven. He had the beautiful wife as well as the firm-jawed son, two willowy daughters, and four grandkids who looked like they spent after-school time posing for Abercrombie ads. And yet he carried whatever had chased him out of the service like a nail in the back of his neck. Charming as he was, you never felt fully comfortable with the guy, because he never seemed fully comfortable with himself.

"Come on in, Patrick," he said after his secretary deposited me at his door.

I entered and shook his hand. The Custom House peeked

over his right shoulder while a Logan runway jutted out from
under his left elbow.

"Have a seat, have a seat."

I did, and Jeremy Dent sat back in his, looked out at the city
for a minute from his corner office chair. "Layton and Susan
Trescott called me last night. They said you took care of the
Brandon thing. Got him to show his hand and all that."

I nodded. "Wasn't hard."

He raised a glass of water to that, took a sip. "They said
they were thinking of sending him to Europe."

"That'd go over well with his probation officer."

He raised his eyebrows to his own reflection. "That's what
I said. And his mother a judge, too. She seemed genuinely surprised. Parenting, Jesus—a million ways to fuck it up, about
three ways to do it right. And that's for the mothers. As a father,
I always felt the best I could hope for was to rise to the level of
the eunuch with the biggest sac." He finished his water, and his
feet came off the edge of his desk. "Want a juice or something?
I can't drink coffee anymore."

"Sure."

He went to the bar beneath a flat-screen TV and pulled
out a bottle of cranberry juice, went fishing for some ice. He
brought the glasses over, clinked his off mine, and we both
drank cranberry juice from heavy Waterford crystal. He returned his ass to his chair, his heels to the desk, and his gaze
to the city.

"So you're probably wondering about your status around
here."

I gave him a soft raise of the eyebrows. I hoped it conveyed
I was interested but not pushy.

"You've done great work for us, and I did say we'd revisit

the idea of bringing you on full-time after you wrapped up the Trescott case."

"I do recall that, yeah."

He smiled, took another drink. "How do you think that went?"

"With Brandon Trescott?"

He nodded.

"About as good as we could hope. I mean, we got the kid to tip his hand to us before he could tip it to some tabloid journalist posing as a stripper. I'm sure the Trescotts have already begun re-hiding the assets."

He chuckled. "They started around five o'clock last night."

"So, okay, then. I'd say the whole thing went pretty well."

He nodded. "It did. You saved them a ton of dough and made us look good."

I waited for the "but."

"But," he said, "Brandon Trescott also told his parents you threatened him in his kitchen and cursed him."

"I called him a moron, if I remember right."

He lifted a piece of paper off his desk, consulted it. "And a dumbass. And a dumb shit. And joked about his giving people brain damage."

"He put that girl in a wheelchair," I said. "For life."

He shrugged. "We're not paid to care about her or her family. We're paid to keep *them* from taking our clients to the cleaners. The victim? Not our concern."

"I never said she was."

"You just said, I quote, 'He put that girl in a wheelchair.' "

"For which I harbor him no ill will. Like you said, it's a job. And I did it."

"But you insulted him, Patrick."

I tried each word out. "I. Insulted. Him."

"Yeah. And his parents help keep the lights on around here."

I placed my drink on his desk. "I confirmed for them what we all know—that their son is, functionally speaking, a sub-idiot. I left them all the information they need to go about protecting him from himself so he can keep the parents of a paraplegic from getting their greedy hands on his two-hundred-thousand-dollar car."

His eyes widened for a sec. "That's what that thing cost? The Aston Martin?"

I nodded.

"Two hundred thousand." He whistled. "For a British car."

We sat in silence for a bit. I left my drink where it was and eventually said, "So, no permanent job offer, I take it."

"No." He shook his head slowly. "You're not comprehending the culture here yet, Patrick. You're a great investigator. But this chip you've got on your shoulder—"

"What chip?"

"What . . . ?" He chuckled and gave that a small toast of his glass. "You think you're wearing that nice suit, but all I see you wearing is class rage. It's draped over you. And our clients see it, too. Why do you think you've never met Big D?"

Big D was the companywide nickname for Morgan Duhamel, the seventy-year-old CEO. He was the last of the Duhamels—he had four daughters, all married to men whose names they'd taken—but he'd outlasted the Standifords. The last one of them hadn't been seen since the mid-fifties. Morgan Duhamel's office remained, along with those of several of the older partners, in the original headquarters of Duhamel-Standiford, a discreet chocolate bowfront tucked away on Acorn Street at the foot of Beacon Hill. The old-money clients were directed there to discuss cases; their offspring and the nouveaux riches came to International Place.

"I always assumed Big D didn't take much interest in the subcontractors."

Dent shook his head. "He's got encyclopedic knowledge of this place. All its employees, all their spouses and relatives. *And* all the subcontractors. It was Duhamel who told me about your association with a weapons dealer." He raised his eyebrows at me. "The old man doesn't miss shit."

"So he knows about me."

"Mmm-hmm. And he likes what he sees. He'd love to hire you full-time. So would I. Put you on a partner track. But if, and only if, you lose the attitude. You think clients like sitting in a room with a guy they feel is judging them?"

"I don't—"

"Remember last year? The CEO of Branch Federated came up here from headquarters in Houston, specifically to thank you. He's never flown in to thank a partner and he flew in to thank a *sub*. You remember that?"

Not an easy one to forget. The bonus on that case paid for my family's health insurance last year. Branch Federated owned a few hundred companies, and one of the most profitable was Downeast Lumber Incorporated. DLI operated out of Bangor and Sebago Lake, Maine, and was the country's largest producer of TSCs, or temporary support columns, which construction crews used to stand in for support beams that were being restructured or built off-site. I'd been inserted into the Sebago Lake offices of Downeast Lumber. My job had been to get close to a woman with the wonderfully alliterative name of Peri Pyper. Branch Federated suspected her of selling trade secrets to competitors. Or so we'd been told. After I had worked with Peri Pyper for a month, it became apparent to me that she was gathering evidence to prove that Branch Federated was tampering with its mills' pollution-monitoring equipment. By the time I got close to her, Peri Pyper had gathered clear evidence that Downeast Lumber and Branch Federated had knowingly violated both the Clean Air Act and the False Statement Act. She could prove Branch Federated had ordered its managers to miscalibrate pollution monitors in eight states, had lied to the department of health in four states, and had fabricated the results of its own quality-assurance testing in every single plant, bar none.

Peri Pyper knew she was being watched, so she couldn't remove anything from the building or transfer it to her home computer. But Patrick Kendall, her drinking buddy and a lowly marketing accounts manager—he could. After two months, she finally asked for my help at a Chili's in South Portland. I agreed. We toasted our pact with margaritas and ordered another Triple Dipper platter. The next night, I helped her right into the waiting arms of Branch Federated security.

She was sued for breach of contract, breach of fiduciary responsibility, and breach of her confidentiality agreement. She was prosecuted for grand theft and convicted. She lost her house. She also lost her husband, who bailed while she was under house arrest. Her daughter was bounced from private school. Her son was forced to drop out of college. Last I heard, Peri Pyper worked days answering phones at a used-car dealership in Lewiston, worked nights cleaning floors at a BJ's Wholesale in nearby Auburn.

She'd thought I was her drinking buddy, her harmless flirtation, her political soul mate. As they'd placed the cuffs on her, she'd looked into my face and seen my duplicity. Her eyes widened. Her lips formed a perfect O.

"Wow, Patrick," she said, just before they led her away, "you seemed so real."

I'm pretty sure it's the worst compliment I've ever received.

So when her boss, a doughy dickhead with a 7 handicap and an American flag painted on the tail fin of his Gulfstream, came to Boston to thank me personally, I shook his hand firmly enough to make his man boobs shake. I answered his questions and even had a drink with him. I had done all that was asked of me. Branch Federated and Downeast Lumber could continue shipping its TSCs to construction sites all over North America, Mexico, and Canada. And the groundwater and top soil in the communities in which its mills operated could continue to poison the dinner tables of everyone within a twenty-mile radius. When the meeting was over, I went back home and chased a Zantac 150 with liquid Maalox.

"I was perfectly polite to that guy," I said.

"Polite the way I'm polite to my wife's sister with the fucking herpes sore under her right nostril."

"You swear a lot for a blue blood," I said.

"You're fucking right I do." He held up a finger. "But only behind closed doors, Patrick. That's the difference. I modulate my personality for the room I'm in. You do not." He paced a circle around his desk. "Sure, we snuffed out a whistle-blower in DLC, and Branch Federated compensated us regally. But what about next time? Who's going to get their business next time? Because it isn't going to be us."

I didn't say anything. The view was nice. A sky caught between gray and blue. A thin film of cold mist turning the air pearl. Far off beyond the center of the city, I could see trees that were black and bare.

Jeremy Dent came around the desk and leaned against it, his ankles crossed.

"You fill out your 479s on the Trescott case?"

"No."

"Well, take the sub office and do that. Fill out your expense reports and don't forget to file your 692s as well. See Barnes in equipment so he can clear you on the gear you used—what'd you go with, the Canon and the Sony?"

I nodded. "I used those new Taranti bugs in the kid's place, too."

"I heard they were glitchy."

I shook my head. "Worked like a charm."

He finished his drink and leveled his gaze at me. "Look, we'll find a new case for you. And if you can just get through *that one* without pissing anybody off, we'll hire you permanent, okay? You can tell your wife I gave you my word."

I nodded, a hole in my stomach.

BACK IN THE EMPTY OFFICE, I considered my options.

I didn't have many. I was working one case and it was far from a cash cow. An old friend, Mike Colette, had asked me to help figure out which employee was embezzling from his freight company. It took me a few days with the paperwork to narrow it down to his night-shift supervisor and one or two of his short-haul truckers, but then I did some further digging and they didn't look as right for it as I'd originally thought. So now I'd turned my attention to his accounts-payable manager, a woman he'd promised me was a trusted confidante, beyond reproach.

I could expect to bill another five, maybe six, hours for that job.

At day's end, I'd walk out of Duhamel-Standiford and wait for their next call, their next trial. In the meantime, the bills arrived in the mailbox every day. The food in the fridge got eaten and the shelves didn't miraculously fill back up. I had a Blue Cross Blue Shield bill due at the end of the month and not enough money to pay it.

I sat back in my chair. Welcome to adulthood.

I had half a dozen files to update and three Brandon Trescott reports to write, but I picked up the phone instead and called Richie Colgan, the Whitest Black Man in America.

He answered the phone, "*Tribune,* Metro Desk."

"Not an ounce of you sounds like a brother."

"My people don't have a sound, just a proud and royal legacy temporarily interrupted by racist crackers with whips."

"You telling me if Dave Chappelle answers one phone and George Will answers the other, I'm gonna have trouble guessing which is the white guy?"

"No, but to discuss it in polite company is still *verboten.*"

"Now you're German," I said.

"Only on my French racist father's side," he said. "What up?"

"Remember Amanda McCready? Little girl went—"

"Missing, what, five years ago?"

"Twelve."

"Shit. Years? How old *are* we?"

"'Member how we felt in college about old geezers who talked about, like, the Dave Clark Five and Buddy Holly?"

"Yeah?"

"That's how kids today feel when we talk about Prince and Nirvana."

"Naw."

"Believe it, bitch. So anyway, Amanda McCready."

"Yeah, yeah. You found her with the cop's family, brought her back, everyone on the force hates your guts, you need a favor from me."

"No."

"You don't need a favor?"

"Well, I do, but it's directly connected to Amanda Mc-Cready. She went missing again."

"No shit."

"No shit. And her aunt says no one cares. Not the cops, not you guys."

"Hard to believe. Twenty-four-hour news cycle and all? These days we can make a story out of anything."

"Explains Paris Hilton."

"Nothing explains that," he said. "Point is—a girl disappears again twelve years after her first disappearance brought down a gang of cops and cost the city a few mil during a bad budget year? Shit, that's news, white boy."

"That's what I thought. You almost sounded black there, by the way."

"Racist. What's the aunt's name, uh, bitch?"

"Bea. Well, Beatrice McCready."

"Aunt Bea, uh? Well, this ain't Mayberry."

HE CALLED ME BACK TWENTY MINUTES later. "That was simple."

"What happened?"

"I talked to the investigating officer, a Detective Chuck Hitchcock. He said they investigated the aunt's claim, went to the mother's house, poked around, and talked to the girl."

"Talked to the girl? Amanda?"

"Yeah. It was all a hoax."

"Why would Bea make up a—?"

"Oh, Bea's a champ, what she is. You know Amanda's mother—what's it, Helene?—she's had to take out a couple restraining orders on this woman. Ever since her kid died, she left the reser—"

"Wait, whose kid?"

"Beatrice McCready's."

"Her kid didn't die. He's at Monument High."

"No," Richie said slowly, "he's not at Monument High. He's dead. Him and a few other kids were in a car last year, none of them old enough to drive, none of them old enough to drink, but they did both anyway. They blew a stop sign at the bottom of that big-ass hill where St. Margaret's Hospital used to be? Got pancaked by a bus on Stoughton Street. Two kids dead, two kids talking funny for the rest of their lives but not walking while they're doing it. One of the dead was this Matthew McCready. I'm looking at it in our Web archives right now. June 15, last year. You want the link?"

CHAPTER FIVE

EXITED JFK/UMASS STATION AND HEADED for home, my head still buzzing. I'd hung up the phone and clicked on the link Richie sent me, and there it was—a page 4 story from last June about four boys who took a joyride in a stolen car and came flying down a hill stoked on pot and Jager. The bus driver never had time to hit his horn. Paralyzed from the waist down, Harold Endalis, 15. Paralyzed from the neck down, Stuart Burrfield, 15. Dead on arrival at the Carney ER, Mark McGrath, 16. Dead on scene, Matthew McCready, 16. I descended the station stairs and headed up Crescent Avenue toward home, thinking about all the stupid shit I'd done at sixteen, ten or twelve ways I could have died—probably should have died—before seventeen.

The first two houses on the south side of Crescent, a matching pair of small white Capes, were abandoned, victims of the wonderful mortgage crisis that had spread such cheer across the land of late. A homeless guy approached me in front of the second one.

"Yo, bro, you got a minute to hear me out? I'm not looking for a handout."

He was a small guy, wiry and bearded. His baseball cap, cotton hoodie, and battered jeans were streaked with grime. The ripe odor coming off him told me it had been a while since he'd bathed. He didn't have nut-bag eyes, though; there was no meanness in him, no crackhead edge.

I stopped. "What's up?"

"I'm not a beggar." He held out his hands to ward off my assumptions. "I want to make that clear."

"Cool."

"I'm not."

"Okay."

"But I got a kid, you know? And there ain't no jobs. My old lady, she's sick, and my baby boy he just needs some formula. Shit's, like, seven bucks and I—"

I never saw his arm move, but he snatched my laptop bag off my shoulder just the same. He took off with it, tear-assing for the back of the nearest abandoned house. The bag held my case notes, my laptop, and a picture of my daughter.

"You dumb shit," I said, not sure if I was talking to myself or to the homeless guy, maybe to both of us. Who knew the fucker had such long arms?

I pursued him down the side of the house through knee-high weeds and crushed beer cans, empty Styrofoam egg containers, and broken bottles. It was probably a squatters' house these days. When I was a kid, it was the Cowans' house, then the Ursinis'. A Vietnamese family bought it next and did a lot of rehab on it. Just before the father lost his job and then the mother lost hers, they'd begun remodeling the kitchen.

It was still missing the back wall there; some of the plastic tarps nailed to the framing flapped in the afternoon breeze. As I reached the backyard, the homeless guy was only a few feet ahead and about to be slowed by a chain-link fence. I sensed movement to my left. A plastic tarp parted and a dark-haired guy swung a length of pipe into the side of my face and I spun into the plastic and fell into the unfinished kitchen.

I'm not sure how long I lay there—long enough to notice, as the room shook behind watery waves of air, that all the copper had been stripped from beneath the sink and behind the walls. Long enough to feel reasonably certain my jaw wasn't broken, though the left side of my face was simultaneously numb and on fire, and blood leaked steadily from it. I got to my knees and a nail bomb detonated in my skull. Everything that wasn't directly in front of my nose vanished behind black cloaks. The floor shimmied.

Someone helped me to my feet and then pushed me into a wall, and someone else laughed. A third person, farther away, said, "Bring him in here."

"I don't think he can walk."

"Lead him, then."

Fingers vise-gripped the back of my neck and guided me into what had once been the living room. The black cloaks receded from view. I could make out a small fireplace, the mantel torn away and probably used as firewood. I'd been in this room once before, when a bunch of us sixteen-year-olds followed Brian Cowan in here to raid his father's liquor cabinet. A couch had sat under the windows facing the street. A garden bench sat there now and a man sat on it, his eyes on me. I was dropped on the couch across from him, a ratty orange thing that smelled like the Dumpster behind a Red Lobster.

"You gonna puke?"

"Curious about that myself," I said.

"I told him to trip you, not hit you with a pipe, but he got a little excited."

I could see the guy with the pipe now—a slim, dark-haired Latino in khaki cargo pants and a wife-beater. He gave me a shrug as he tapped the pipe back and forth in his palm. "Oops."

"Oops," I said. "I'll remember that."

"You won't remember shit, *pendejo,* I hit you again."

Hard to argue with logic. I took my eyes off the help and considered the boss on the bench. I would have expected prison-lean and prison-mean, gin-pale eyes. Instead, the guy wore a yellow-and-green-plaid shirt under a black wool sweater and a pair of tan corduroys. On his feet were a pair of canvas Vans with a pattern of black and gold squares. His red hair was a little on the longish side and flyaway. He didn't look gangsta; he looked like a science teacher at a prep school.

He said, "I know you got some rough friends and I know you've been in some serious scrapes, so you don't scare easy."

News to me. I was scared shitless. Pissed off, instinctively memorizing every detail I could about the two guys I could see, and thinking about ways to get the Latino's pipe into my hands and straight up his ass—but scared out of my mind, just the same.

"Your first instinct is going to be to come after us, if we let you live." He unwrapped a piece of bubble gum and popped it in his mouth.

If.

"Tadeo, give him a towel for his face." The science teacher gave me a cocked eyebrow. "Yeah, I said his name. Know why, Patrick? Because you won't come after us. You know why you won't come after us?"

It would hurt too much to shake my head, so I simply said, "No."

"Because we're bad fucking guys and you're a soft fucking guy. Maybe not once, but this isn't 'once.' I hear your business went to shit because you started bailing on anything that smelled like a rough case. Understandable for a guy who got shot a bunch of times, almost bled out and shit. Still, the word's out you don't have the stones to do this at our level anymore. You're not part of this life. And you don't want to be."

Tadeo came back from the kitchen area and put two paper towels in my hand. I fumbled for them, listing to my left, and he ran the end of the pipe along the side of my neck with a soft chuckle.

I snatched the pipe out of his hand and drove a foot into his knee at the same time. Tadeo fell backward and I came off the couch. The science teacher yelled, "Hey!" and pointed a pistol at me and I froze. Tadeo scrambled backward on his ass until he reached the wall. He stood, favoring his good leg. I remained frozen, the pipe in my hand, my arm cocked. Science Teacher lowered the gun as an indication I should lower the pipe. I gave him a tiny nod of agreement. Then I flicked my wrist. The pipe tomahawked across the room and hit Tadeo between his eyebrows. He let out a yelp and bounced off the wall. The gash above his nose opened and flooded his eyes. He took two steps toward the center of the room and then three more steps to the side. He took a few more steps and walked into the wall. He put his hands on the wall and gulped for air.

"Oops," I said.

Science Teacher dug the gun barrel into my neck. "Sit," he hissed, "the fuck down."

The third guy came into the room now—huge, maybe six-four, three-eighty. He was breathing heavy, waddling.

"Take Tadeo upstairs," the redhead said. "Put him in the shower, throw some cold water on him, see if he has a concussion."

"How do I see if he has a concussion?" the big guy asked.

"Look into his eyes, I don't fucking know. Ask him to count to ten."

I asked, "Will you learn anything new if he can't?"

"I told you to shut up."

"No. You told me to sit the fuck down, and you're already running out of options."

The fat guy led Tadeo out of the room. Tadeo kept polishing the air in front of him, like a dog having a dream.

I lifted the paper towels off the floor. One side of them was clean, and I pressed that side to my face, came back with a red Rorschach test. "I'm going to need stitches."

Science Teacher leaned forward on his bench, the gun pointed at my stomach. He had an open face with a light dusting of freckles the same color as his hair. His smile was bland and eager, like he was acting the community-theater role of someone who wanted to be helpful. "What makes you think you're walking out of here?"

"Like I said, your option-clock is ticking down to nothing. There were people on the street when that guy boosted my bag. Someone's already called the cops. The house next door isn't occupied, but the house behind you is, you dumb shit, and there's a good chance someone saw Tadeo pop me with the pipe. So whoever hired you to deliver whatever message you're supposed to deliver, I'd get kinda peppy about delivering it."

Science Teacher didn't strike me as stupid. If he'd wanted to kill me, he would have put two in the back of my head when I'd been kneeling on the floor of the unfinished kitchen.

"Stay away from Helene McCready." He squatted in front of me, the gun dangling between his thighs as he gazed up into my face. "You snoop around her or her kid, you ask any questions, I'll bullet-fuck your entire life."

"Gotcha," I said with a nonchalance I didn't feel.

"*You* got a kid now, Patrick, a wife. A nice life. Go back to it and stay in it. And we'll all forget this."

He stood and stepped back as I made it to my feet. I walked into the kitchen and found the roll of paper towels on the floor. I pulled off a wad and pressed it to my face. He stood in the doorway, staring at me, the gun in his waistband. My own gun sat back in the desk at Duhamel-Standiford. Not that it would have done me any good after Tadeo hit me in the head with a pipe. Then they would have just taken the gun, and I'd be out a laptop, a laptop bag, and a gun.

I looked over at him. "I gotta go to an ER and get my face stitched up, but don't worry, I don't take it personally."

"Gosh," he said, "you promise?"

"You threatened my life, but I'm cool with that, too."

"Darn white of you, too." He blew a bubble and let it snap.

"But," I said, "you stole my laptop and I really can't afford to buy a new one. Don't suppose you'd give that back to me?"

He shook his head. "Finders keepers."

"I mean, that fucks me up, man, but I'm not going to turn it into something it ain't. Because it's just business. Right?"

"If it ain't, 'business' will do until the right word shows up."

I pulled the paper towels from my face. They were a mess. I folded them over and put the wad back to the side of my head for a minute, looked again at the redheaded science teacher standing in the doorway.

"So be it," I said and dropped the red wad of paper towels on the floor, tore off a fresh batch, and let myself out of the house.

CHAPTER SIX

WHEN WE SAT DOWN TO EAT, Angie looked across the table at me with the same controlled fury she'd been wearing since she got a good look at my face, heard about my trip to the health center, and ascertained that I was, in fact, not going to die tonight.

"So," she said, "let's start at the beginning." She speared a few pieces of lettuce. "Beatrice McCready finds you at JFK Station."

"Yes, ma'am."

"And she tells you her smutty sister-in-law misplaced her daughter again."

"Helene's smutty?" I said. "I hadn't noticed."

My wife smiled. Not the nice smile. The other one.

"Daddy?"

I looked over at our daughter, Gabriella. "Yeah, honey?"

"What's smutty?"

"It's like kooky," I said, "only it rhymes with slutty."

"What's slutty?"

"It's like ooky," I said, "except it doesn't rhyme with kooky. Why aren't you eating your carrots?"

"You look funny."

"I wear big bandages on my face every Thursday."

"No suh." Gabriella's eyes grew wide and solemn. She had her mother's big brown eyes. She also had her olive skin and wide mouth and dark hair. From me she'd gotten curls, a thin nose, and a love of silliness and wordplay.

"Why aren't you eating your carrots?" I asked again.

"I don't like carrots."

"You did last week."

"No suh."

"Uh-huh."

Angie put her fork down. "Don't start this, the both of you. Do not."

"No suh."

"Uh-huh."

"No suh."

"Uh-huh. I got pictures."

"No suh."

"Uh-huh. I'll get my camera."

Angie reached for her wineglass. "Please?" She fixed me with eyes as huge as our daughter's. "For me?"

I looked back at Gabriella. "Eat your carrots."

"Okay." Gabby dug a fork into one and plopped it in her mouth, chewed. Her face lit up around the chewing.

I raised my eyebrows at her.

"It's good," she said.

"Right?"

She speared another one and munched away.

Angie said, "I've been watching it for four years and I still don't know how you do that."

"Ancient Chinese secret." Very slowly, I chewed a tiny chunk of chicken breast. "By the way, not sure what you've heard, but it's kinda hard eating when you can't use the left side of your mouth."

"You know what's funny?" Angie asked in a voice that suggested something wasn't.

"I do not," I assured her.

"Most private investigators don't get kidnapped and assaulted."

"The practice is rumored to be trending upward, however."

She frowned and I could feel both of us trapped inside ourselves, not sure what to do with today's violence. There was a time we would have been experts at it. She would have tossed me an ice pack on her way to the gym, expected me to be raring to get back to work by the time she got back. Those days were long gone, though, and today's return to easy bloodshed drove us into our protective shells. Her shell is made of quiet fury and wary disconnection. Mine is made of humor and sarcasm. Together we resemble a comedian failing an anger-management class.

"It looks awful," she said with a tenderness that surprised me.

"It only feels four or five times as bad as it looks. Really. I'm fine."

"That's the Percocet."

"And the beer."

"I thought you weren't supposed to mix the two."

"I refuse to bow to conventional wisdom. I'm a decider. And I've decided I want to feel no pain."

"How's that working out?"

I toasted her with my beer. "Mission accomplished."

"Daddy?"

"Yeah, sweetie?"

"I like trees."

"I like trees, too, honey."

"They're tall."

"They sure are."

"Do you like *all* trees?"

"Every one."

"Even short ones?"

"Sure, honey."

"But why?" My daughter held her hands out, palms-up, a sign that she found this line of questioning of global importance and—lucky us—quite possibly endless.

Angie shot me a look that said: Welcome to my day.

FOR THE LAST THREE YEARS, I'd spent the days at work, or, as opportunities dwindled, trying to hustle up work. Three nights a week, I watched Gabby while Angie took classes. Christmas break was approaching, however, and Angie would take finals next week. After the New Year, she'd begin an internship with Blue Sky Learning Center, a nonprofit specializing in educating teens with Down syndrome. When that was finished, in May, she'd receive her master's in applied sociology. But until then, we were a one-income family. More than one friend had suggested we move to the suburbs—homes were cheaper, schools were safer, property taxes and car insurance premiums were lower.

Angie and I grew up together in the city, though. We took to picket fences and split-level ranches like we took to shag carpeting and Ultimate Fighting. Which is to say, not so much. I once owned a nice car, but I'd sold it to start a college fund for Gabby, and now my beater Jeep sat in front of my house, without moving, for weeks at a time. I prefer subways—you pop down the hole on one side of the city, pop back up on the other side, and you never have to hit your horn, not once. I don't like mowing lawns or trimming hedges or raking the mowed lawns or the hedge trimmings. I don't like going to malls or eating in chain restaurants. In fact, the appeal of the suburban ideal—both in a general and a particular sense—escapes me.

I like the sound of jackhammers, the bleat of sirens in the night, twenty-four-hour diners, graffiti, coffee served in cardboard cups, steam exhaled through manhole covers, cobblestone, tabloid newspapers, the Citgo sign, someone yelling "Tax-*i*" on a cold night, corner boys, sidewalk art, Irish pubs, and guys named Sal.

Not much of which I can find in the suburbs, at least not to the degree I've grown accustomed to. And Angie is, if anything, worse.

So we decided to raise our child in the city. We bought a small house on a decent street. It has a tiny yard and it's a short walk to a playground (short walk to a pretty hairy housing project, too, but that's another matter). We know most of our neighbors and Gabriella can already name five subway stops on the Red Line, in order, a feat which fills her old man with bottomless pride.

"She asleep?" Angie looked up from her textbook as I came into the living room. She'd changed into sweats and one of my T-shirts, a white one from The Hold Steady's *Stay Positive* tour. It swam on her, and I worried she wasn't eating enough.

"Our gabby Gabby took a breath during a discourse on trees—"

"Arghh." Angie threw her head back against the couch cushion. "What's with the trees?"

"—and promptly drifted off to sleep." I dropped onto the couch beside her, took her hand in mine, gave it a kiss.

"Besides getting beat up," she said, "did anything else happen today?"

"You mean with Duhamel-Standiford."

"With them, yes."

I took a deep breath. "I didn't get a permanent job, no."

"Shit!" She shouted it so loudly that I had to hold up a hand and she glanced in the direction of Gabby's room and cringed.

"They said I shouldn't have called Brandon Trescott names. They suggested I am uncouth and in need of an adjustment in my manners before I partake of their benefits program."

"Shit," she said, softer this time and with more despair than shock. "What are we going to do?"

"I don't know."

We sat there for a bit. There was nothing much to say. We were getting numb to it, the fear, the weight of worry.

"I'll leave school."

"No, you won't."

"Yeah, I will. I can go back in—"

"You're this close," I said. "Finals next week, one internship, and then you're bringing home the bacon by summer, at which point—"

"*If* I can even find a job."

"—at which point, I can *afford* to freelance. You're not packing it in this close to the finish line. You're top of your class. You'll find a job no problem." I gave her a smile of confidence I didn't feel. "We'll make it work."

She leaned back a bit to study my face again.

"Okay," I said to change the subject, "lay into me."

"About what?" All mock-innocence.

"We made a pact when we married that we were done with this shit."

"We did."

"No more violence, no more—"

"Patrick." She took my hands in hers. "Just tell me what happened."

I did.

When I finished, Angie said, "So the upshot is that in addition to not getting the job with Duhamel-Standiford, the world's worst mother lost her child again, you didn't agree to help, but someone mugged you, threatened you, and beat the shit out of you anyway. You're out a hospital co-pay and a really nice laptop."

"I know, right? I loved that thing. Weighed less than your wineglass. A smiley face popped on-screen and said, 'Hello,' every time I opened it up, too."

"You're pissed."

"Yeah, I'm pissed."

"But you're not going to go into crusade mode just because you lost a laptop, am I right?"

"Did I mention the smiley face?"

"You can get yourself another computer with another smiley face."

"With what money?"

There was no answer for that.

We sat quietly for a bit, her legs on my lap. I'd left Gabby's bedroom door slightly ajar, and in the silence we could hear her breathing, the exhalations carrying a tiny whistle at their backs. The sound of her breathing reminded me, as it so often did, of how vulnerable she was. And how vulnerable we were because of how much we loved her. The fear—that something could happen to her at any moment, something I'd be helpless to stop—had become so omnipresent in my life that I sometimes pictured it growing, like a third arm, out of the center of my chest.

"Do you remember much of the day you got shot?" Angie asked, throwing another fun topic into the ring.

I tipped my hand back and forth. "Bits and pieces. I remember the noise."

"No kidding, uh?" She smiled, her eyes going back to it. "It was loud down there—all those guns, the cement walls. Man."

"Yeah." I let loose a soft sigh.

"Your blood," she said, "it just splattered the walls. You were out when the EMTs got there and I just remember looking at it. That was your blood—that was *you*—and it wasn't in your body, where it belonged. It was all over the floor and all over the walls. You weren't the white of a ghost, you were light blue, like your eyes. You were lying there but you were gone, you know? It was like you were already halfway to Heaven with your foot on the gas."

I closed my eyes and raised my hand. I hated hearing about that day and she knew it.

"I know, I know," she said. "I just want us both to remember why we got out of the rough-stuff business. It wasn't just because you got shot. It was because we were junkies to it. We loved it. We still love it." She ran a hand through her hair. "I was not put on this earth just to read *Goodnight, Moon* three times a day and have fifteen-minute discussions about sippy cups."

"I know," I said.

And I did. No one was less built to be a stay-at-home mom than Angie. It wasn't that she wasn't good at it—she was—it was that she had no desire to define herself by the role. But then she went back to school and the money got tight and it made the most sense to save on day care for a few months, so she could go to school nights and watch Gabby days. And just like that—gradually and then suddenly, as the man said—we found ourselves here.

"I'm going crazy at this." Her eyes indicated the coloring books and toys on our living-room floor.

"I gather."

"Bat-shit fucking crazy."

"That would be the approved medical terminology, sure. You're great at it."

She rolled her eyes in my direction. "You're sweet. But, baby? I might be doing a great job faking it, but I am faking it."

"Isn't every parent?"

She cocked her head at me with a grimace.

"No," I said. "Really. Who in their right mind wants to have fourteen conversations about trees? Ever? Never mind in one twenty-four-hour period. That little girl, I adore her, but she's an anarchist. She wakes us up whenever she feels like it, she thinks high-energy at seven in the morning is a positive, sometimes she screams for no reason, she decides on a second-to-second basis which foods she'll eat and which she'll fight you over, she puts her hands and face into truly disgusting places, and she's attached to our hips for at least another fourteen years, if we're lucky enough for a college we can't afford to take her off our hands."

"But that old life was killing us."

"It was."

"I miss it so much," she said. "That old life that was killing us."

"Me, too. One thing I learned today, though, is that I've turned into a bit of a pussy."

She smiled. "You have, uh?"

I nodded.

She cocked her head at me. "You were never *that* tough to begin with."

"I know," I said, "so imagine what a lightweight I am now."

"Shit," she said, "I just love the hell out of you sometimes."

"Love you, too."

She slid her legs back and forth across my thighs. "But you really want your laptop back, don't you?"

"I do."

"You're going to go get it back, aren't you?"

"The thought had occurred to me."

She nodded. "On one condition."

I hadn't expected her to agree with me. And the small part of me that had sure hadn't expected it this quickly. I sat up, as attentive and obsequious as an Irish setter. "Name it."

"Take Bubba."

Bubba wasn't only the ideal wingman on this because he

was built like a bank-vault door and had not even a passing acquaintance with fear. (Truly. He once asked me what the emotion felt like. He was also baffled by the whole empathy concept.) No, what made him particularly ideal for this evening's festivities was that he'd spent the last several years diversifying his business to include black-market health care. It started as a simple investment—he'd bankrolled a doctor who'd recently lost his license and wanted to set up a practice servicing the kind of people who couldn't report their bullet wounds, knife wounds, head wounds, and broken bones to hospitals. One, of course, needs drugs for such patients, and Bubba was forced to find a supply for illegal "legal" drugs. This supply came from Canada, and even with all the post-9/11 noise about increased border control, Bubba got dozens of thirty-gallon bags of pills delivered every month. Thus far, he hadn't lost a load. If an insurance company refused to cover a drug or if the pharmaceutical companies priced the drug out of wallet-range of working- and lower-class folk in the neighborhoods, street whispers usually led the patient to one of Bubba's network of bartenders, florists, lunch-cart drivers, or corner-store cashiers. Pretty soon anyone living off the health-care grid or near the edge of it owed a debt to Bubba. He was no Robin Hood—he cleared a profit. But he was no Pfizer, either—his profit was in the fair range of 15 to 20 percent, not in the anal-rape range of 1,000 percent.

Using Bubba's people in the homeless community, it took us about twenty minutes to identify a guy who matched the description of the guy who stole my laptop.

"You mean Webster?" the dishwasher at a soup kitchen in Fields Corner said.

"The little black kid from '90s TV?" Bubba said. "Why would we be looking for him?"

"Nah, man, I most definitely do not mean the little black kid from '90s TV. We in the oh-tens now, or ain't you heard?" The dishwasher scowled. "Webster's a white boy, on the small side, got a beard."

I said, "That's the Webster we're looking for."

"Don't know if it's his first name or last, but he cribbed up at a place on Sydney round—"

"No, he blew out of there today."

Another scowl. For a dishwasher, he was kind of prickly. "Place on Sydney up by Savin Hill Ave.?"

"No, I was thinking of the other end, the place by Crescent."

"You ain't thinking then. You ain't know shit. Clear? So just shush it, boy."

"Yeah," Bubba said, "just shush it, boy."

I wasn't close enough to kick him, so I shut up.

"Yeah, the place he staying is at the end of Sydney. Where it meet Bay Street? There. Second floor, yellow house, got one of them AC units in the window stopped working during Reagan, look like it gonna fall out on someone's head."

"Thanks," I said.

"Little black kid from '90s TV," he said to Bubba. "Man, if I wasn't fifty-nine and a half years old? I'd profoundly whoop your ass over that shit."

CHAPTER SEVEN

WHERE SYDNEY STREET CROSSES SAVIN HILL Avenue, it becomes Bay Street and sits on top of a subway tunnel. About every five minutes, the whole block shudders as a train rumbles beneath it. Bubba and I had sat through five of these shudders so far, which meant we'd been sitting in Bubba's Escalade for nearly half an hour.

Bubba does not do sitting still very well. It reminds him too much of group homes and orphanages and prisons, places he's called home for roughly half his time on earth. He'd already fiddled with the GPS—punching in random addresses in random cities to see if Amarillo, Texas, had a Groin Street or Toronto sent tourists traipsing along Rogowski Avenue. When he exhausted the entertainment value of searching for nonexistent streets in cities he never intended to visit, he played with the satellite radio, rarely landing on a station for more than thirty seconds before he'd let loose a half-sigh, half-snort and change the channel. After a while, he dug a bottle of Polish potato vodka out from under the seat and took a swig.

He offered me the bottle. I declined. He shrugged and took another pull. "Let's just kick the door in."

"We don't even know if he's in there."

"Let's just do it anyway."

"And if he comes home while we're in there, sees his door kicked down and takes off running, what do we do then?"

"Shoot him from the window."

I looked over at him. He peered up at the second story of the condemned three-decker where Webster allegedly lived. His deranged cherub's face was serene, a look it usually got when it contemplated violence.

"We're not shooting anyone. We're not going to lay a glove on this guy."

"He stole from you."

"He's harmless."

"He stole from you."

"He's homeless."

"Yeah, but he stole from you. You should set an example."

"For who—all the other homeless guys lining up to steal my bag so I'll chase them into a house where I'll get the shit kicked out of me?"

"Them, yeah." He took another swig of vodka. "And don't give me this 'He's homeless' shit." He pointed the bottle at the condemned building across the street. "He's living there, ain't he?"

"He's squatting."

"Still a home," Bubba said. "Can't call someone homeless if they have, ya know, a fucking home."

On some purely Bubba level, he had me there.

On the other side of Savin Hill Avenue, the door to Donovan's bar opened. I nudged Bubba, pointed across the avenue as Webster crossed toward us.

"He's homeless, but he's in a bar. This guy has a better life than me. Probably has a fucking plasma and a Brazilian chick comes Tuesdays to clean and vacuum."

Bubba threw open his door as Webster was about to pass the SUV. Webster paused and, in that second, forfeited any chance to escape. Bubba towered over him and I came around from the other side and Bubba said, "Remember him?"

Webster had adopted a position of half-cringe. When he recognized me, he closed his eyes to slits.

"I'm not going to hit you, man."

"I will, though." Bubba slapped Webster on the side of his head.

"Hey!" Webster said.

"I'll do it again."

"Webster," I said, "where's my bag?"

"What bag?"

I said, "Really?"

Webster looked at Bubba.

"My bag," I said.

"I gave it back."

"To who?"

"Max."

"Who's Max?"

"He's Max. He's the guy paid me to take your bag."

"Red-haired dude?" I said.

"No. Dude's got, like, black hair."

Bubba slapped the side of Webster's head again.

"What the hell you do that for?"

Bubba shrugged.

"He bores easily," I said.

"I didn't *do* nothing."

"You didn't what?" I pointed at my face.

"I didn't know they were going to do that. They just told me to steal your bag."

"Where's the redheaded guy?" I said.

"I don't know any redheaded guy."

"Fine, where's Max?"

"I don't know."

"Where'd you take the bag? You wouldn't take it back to the same house where I chased you."

"No, man, I took it to a garage."

"What kind of garage?"

"Huh? Like a place that fixes cars and shit. Has a few for sale out front."

"Where?"

"On Dot Ave., just before Freeport, on the right."

"I know that place," Bubba said. "It's, like, Castle Automotive or something."

"Kestle. With a K," Webster said.

Bubba slapped him upside the head again.

"Ow. Shit."

"You take anything out of the bag?" I said. "Anything?"

"Nah, man. Max told me not to, so I didn't."

"But you looked in there."

"Yeah. No." He rolled his eyes. "Yeah."

"There was a picture of a little girl in there."

"Yeah, I saw it."

"You put it back?"

"Yeah, man, I promise."

"If it ain't there when I find the bag, we'll come back, Webster. And we won't be all sweet and shit."

"You call this sweet?" Webster said.

Bubba slapped the side of his head a fourth time.

"Sweet as it'll ever get," I said.

KESTLE CARS & REPAIR SAT ACROSS from a Burger King in the part of my neighborhood the locals call Ho Chi Minh Trail, a seven-block section of Dorchester Avenue, where waves of Vietnamese, Cambodian, and Laotian immigrants settled. There were six cars on the lot, all in dubious condition, all with MAKE AN OFFER painted in yellow on their windshields. The garage bay doors were closed and the lights were off, but we could hear loud chatter from the back. There was a dark green door to the left of the bay doors. I stepped aside and looked at Bubba.

"What?"

"It's locked."

"You can't pick a lock no more?"

"Sure, but I don't carry a kit on me. Cops frown on that shit."

He grimaced and pulled a small leather case from his pocket. He unrolled it and selected a pick. "Is there anything you *can do* anymore?"

"I cook a mean swordfish Provençal," I said.

He gave that a mild shake of his head. "Last two times it was pretty dry."

"I don't make dry fish."

He popped the lock. "Then a guy who looks like you does, and he served it last two times I was at your house."

"Shit's cold," I said.

The back office smelled of trapped heat, burned motor oil, stale gusts of ganja and menthol cigarettes. We found four guys back there. Two I'd met before—the fat guy with the audible breathing and Tadeo, sporting a ridiculous bandage over his nose and forehead that made my own bandage look just a little less ridiculous. The fat guy stood to the far left side of the room. Tadeo stood directly in front of us, half his body behind a metal desk the color of eggshell. A third guy, in a mechanic's overalls, was passing a joint when we walked in. He wasn't yet drinking age and fear seized his face when Bubba entered behind me; unless the fear made him stupid ballsy (it happens), he'd be the least of our problems.

The fourth guy sat slightly to our right, behind the desk. He had dark hair. His skin was covered in a sheen of sweat, fresh droplets popping through the pores as we watched. He was about thirty-going-on-a-coronary, and you could smell the crank singeing his veins from Newfoundland. His left knee jackhammered under the desk, his right hand patted a steady bongo beat on the top. My laptop sat in front of him. He stared at us with bright eyes pinned to the rear wall of his skull. "This one of the guys?"

The fat guy pointed at me. "That's the one fucked up Tadeo's face."

Tadeo said to me, "The re-up's coming on that shit, homes. Believe it," but there was a hollow catch in his voice that came from trying not to look at Bubba.

"I'm Max." The tweeker behind my laptop gave me a broad smile. He sucked oxygen into his nostrils and gave me a wink. "I'm the IT guy up in this shit. Nice laptop."

I nodded at the table. "My laptop."

"Huh?" He look wildly confused. "This is my laptop."

"Funny. Looks a lot like mine."

"That's called a model." His eyes popped against their sockets. "If they all looked different, they'd be kind of hard to manufacture, don't you think?"

"Yeah," Tadeo said, "you fucking retarded and shit?"

I said, "I'm just a girl standing before a boy looking for his laptop."

"I heard you'd got your head in the right place about this," Max said. "We were never supposed to see you again. No harm, no foul. You want to bring us into your life, you don't *fucking* understand how bad that will be." He closed my laptop and placed it in the drawer to his right.

"Look," I said, "I can't afford a replacement."

He rocked forward into the desk, his whole endoskeleton surging against his skin. "Call a fucking insurance company."

"It's not insured."

"This fucking guy, bro," he said to Bubba, then checked the position of his men. He looked back at me. "You're out of this. Just let it go and you'll stay out of it. Run back to your little life."

"I'm going. I just want to take my laptop back with me. And the picture of my daughter that was in my bag. Bag's yours."

Tadeo moved all the way out from behind the desk. The fat guy stayed against the wall, breathing heavy. The kid mechanic was breathing heavy, too, and blinking like crazy.

"I know the bag's mine." Max got to his feet. "I know this office is mine, that ceiling, the O-ring in your ass, if I feel like it."

"Uh, okay," I said. "Hey, who hired you, by the way?"

"Man, you with the *questions*." He flung his hands at me like he was auditioning for a Lil Weezy video and then scratched the back of his head furiously. "You don't make demands. You go the fuck home." He shooed me with his fingers. "Bro, I say one word and you're fucking—"

Bubba's shot spun him in place. Max let out a sharp shout and fell back into his chair. The chair slammed off the wall and dumped Max to the floor. He lay there for a bit with blood pouring from the vicinity of his waistline.

"What's with all this 'bro' shit lately?" Bubba lowered his gun. It was his new favorite, a Steyr 9mm. Austrian. Hideous-looking.

"Ho, shit!" Tadeo said. "Holy fucking shit."

Bubba pointed the Steyr at Tadeo and then the fat guy. Tadeo put his hands on his head. The fat guy did too. They both stood there shaking and awaiting further instruction.

Bubba didn't even bother with the kid. He'd dropped to his knees and lowered his head to the floor and kept whispering, "Please, please."

"You fucking shoot the guy?" I said. "A bit harsh, no?"

"Don't bring me out on this shit if you're going to leave your pair at home." Bubba frowned. "Goddamn embarrassing what a civilian you've become, man."

I got a closer look at Max as a burst of air left his mouth. He ground his forehead into the cement floor and pounded a fist on it.

"He's fucked up," I said.

"I barely hit him."

"You blew one of his hips off."

Bubba said, "He's got two."

Max began to shake. The shakes quickly turned to convulsions. Tadeo took a step toward him and Bubba took two steps toward Tadeo, the Steyr aimed at his chest.

"I'll kill you just for being short," Bubba said.

"I'm sorry." Tadeo raised his hands as high as they could go.

Max flopped onto his back. Kettle hisses preceded his gulps of air.

"I'll kill you for wearing that deodorant," Bubba told Tadeo. "I'll kill your friend for being your friend."

Tadeo lowered his hands until they shook in front of his face. He closed his eyes.

His friend said, "We're not friends. He gives me shit about my weight."

Bubba raised an eyebrow. "You could lose a few but you're not an orca or anything. Shit, man, just lay off the white bread and the cheese."

"I'm thinking Atkins," the guy said.

"I tried that."

"Yeah?"

"You gotta give up alcohol for two weeks." Bubba grimaced. "Two *weeks*."

The guy nodded. "That's what I told the wife."

Max kicked the desk. The back of his head rattled off the floor. Then he was still.

"He dead?" Bubba asked.

"No," I said. "But he's heading there, he don't get a doctor."

Bubba produced a business card. He asked the big guy, "What's your name?"

"Augustan."

"Well . . . No, really?"

"Yeah. Why?"

Bubba looked over at me and shrugged before looking back at Augustan. He handed him the card. "Call this guy. He works for me. He'll fix your friend up. The fixing's free, but the drugs'll cost you."

"That's fair."

Bubba rolled his eyes at me and let loose a sigh. "Grab your laptop, would you?"

I did.

"Tadeo," I said.

Tadeo lowered his shaking hands from his face.

"Who hired you?"

"What?" Tadeo blinked several times. "Uh, a friend of Max's. Kenny."

"*Kenny?*" Bubba said. "You got me out of bed so I could shoot some prick over a *Kenny*? That's fucking humiliating."

I ignored him. "Redheaded guy from the house, Tadeo?"

"Kenny Hendricks, yeah. He said you knew his old lady. Said you found her kid once when she went missing."

Helene. If it smelled of stupid, Helene just had to be somewhere nearby.

"*Kenny,*" Bubba repeated with a bitter sigh.

"Where's my bag?" I said.

"Other drawer," Tadeo said.

Augustan said to Bubba, "I can call your doc now?"

"Augustan always?" Bubba asked. "Never Gus?"

"Never Gus," the big guy said.

Bubba gave that some thought, then nodded. "Go ahead. Call the number."

Augustan flipped open a cell and dialed. I found my bag in the desk drawer, found Gabby's picture and my case files, too. As Augustan told the doctor his buddy was losing a lot of blood, I put the laptop in my bag and walked to the door. Bubba pocketed his weapon and followed me out of the garage.

CHAPTER EIGHT

IN MY DREAM, AMANDA MCCREADY WAS ten, maybe eleven. She sat on the porch of a yellow bungalow with stone steps, a white bulldog snoring at her feet. Tall ancient trees sprouted from a strip of grass between the sidewalk and the street. We were somewhere down South, Charleston maybe. Spanish moss hung from the trees, and the house had a tin roof.

Jack and Tricia Doyle sat behind Amanda in wicker armchairs, a chess table between them. They hadn't aged at all.

I came up the walk in my postal outfit, and the dog raised its head and stared at me with sad black eyes. Its left ear bore a spot the same black as its nose. It licked its nose and then rolled on its back.

Jack and Tricia Doyle looked up from their chess game and stared at me.

"I'm just delivering the mail," I said. "I'm just the mailman."

They stared. They didn't say a word.

I handed Amanda the mail and stood waiting for my tip. She leafed through the envelopes, tossing them aside one by one. They landed in the bushes and turned yellow and wet.

She looked up at me, her hands empty. "You didn't bring anything we can use."

THE NEXT MORNING I COULD BARELY lift my head off the pillow. When I did, the bones near my left temple crunched. My cheekbones ached and my skull throbbed. While I'd slept, someone had seeded the folds of my brain with red pepper and glass.

And that wasn't all—none of my limbs or joints were pleased when I rolled over, sat up, or breathed. In the shower, the water hurt. The soap hurt. When I tried to scrub my head with shampoo, I accidentally pressed my fingertips into the left side of my skull and produced a bolt of agony that nearly put me on my knees.

Drying off, I looked in the mirror. The upper left side of my face, one half of the eye included, was purple marble. The only part that wasn't purple was the part that was covered in black sutures. Gray streaked my hair; it had even found my chest since the last time I'd paid attention. I ran a comb carefully over my head, then turned to reach for the razor and my swollen knee yelped. I'd barely moved—a minor shift of weight, nothing more—but my kneecap felt like I'd swung the claw end of a hammer into it.

I just fucking love aging.

When I entered the kitchen, my wife and daughter clasped their hands to their cheeks and shrieked, eyes wide. It was so perfectly timed, I knew it had been planned, and I gave them a big thumbs-up as I poured myself a cup of coffee. They exchanged a fist bump and then Angie opened her morning paper again and said, "That looks suspiciously like the laptop bag I got you last Christmas."

I slung it over the back of my chair as I sat at the table. "One and the same."

"And its contents?" She turned a page of the *Herald*.

"Fully recovered," I said.

She raised appreciative eyebrows. Appreciative and maybe a little envious. She glanced at our daughter, who was temporarily fascinated by the pattern of her plastic place mat. "Was there any, um, collateral damage?"

"One gentleman may have a bit of difficulty entering a potato-sack race anytime soon. Or, I dunno"—I sipped some coffee—"strolling."

"And this is because?"

"Bubba decided to speed the process along."

At his name, Gabriella raised her head. The smile that spread across her face was her mother's—so wide and warm it hugged your whole body. "Uncle Bubba?" she said. "You saw Uncle Bubba?"

"I did. He said to say hello to you and Mr. Lubble."

"I'll go get him." She burst out of her chair and out of the room and the next sound we heard was her scrambling through the toys on the floor of her bedroom.

Mr. Lubble was a stuffed animal bigger than Gabby. Bubba had given it to her on her second birthday. Mr. Lubble was, as best we could figure, some kind of a cross between a chimpanzee and an orangutan, though it's possible he represented a primate we were wholly unfamiliar with. For some reason, he was dressed in a lime-green tuxedo with a yellow tie and matching yellow tennis shoes. Gabby had given him the name Mr. Lubble, but none of us could recall why except to assume she'd been trying to say "Bubba," but, at two, Lubble was the closest she could get.

"Mr. Lubble," she called from her bedroom, "come out, come out."

Angie lowered her paper and ran a hand over mine. She was a bit shocked at my second-day appearance, which was worse than my first-day appearance when I'd returned from the health center. "Should we worry about reprisals?"

It was a fair question. With any act of violence, you have to assume reprisal is a given. You hurt someone, most times they will try to hurt you back.

"I don't think so," I said, realizing it was true. "They'd mess with me, but not with Bubba. Plus, I didn't take anything from them but what belonged to me."

"In their minds, it didn't belong to you anymore."

"True."

We shared a careful look.

"I've got that cute little Beretta," she said. "Fits right in my pocket."

"Been a while since you fired it."

She shook her head. "Sometimes when I take those 'Mommy time' drives?"

"Yeah?"

"I go to the range on Freeport."

I smiled. "You do?"

"Oh, I do." She smiled back. "Some girls relieve stress with yoga. I prefer emptying a clip or two."

"Well, you always were the better shot in the family."

"Better?" She opened her paper again.

Truth was I couldn't hit sand on a beach. "Fine. Only."

Gabby came back in the room dragging Mr. Lubble by one lime-green arm. She placed him on the seat beside her and climbed up into her own.

"Did Uncle Bubba kiss Mr. Lubble good night?" she asked.

"He did." I would have felt worse about lying to my child if I hadn't already set the precedent with Santa Claus, the Easter Bunny, and the Tooth Fairy.

"Did he kiss me good night?"

"He did."

"I remember." Apparently the lying starts early and we call it creativity. "And he told me a story."

"About what?"

"Trees."

"Of course."

"He also said Mr. Lubble should get more ice cream."

"And chocolate?" Angie said.

"And chocolate?" Gabby considered the pros and cons. "Okay, I guess."

"You *guess*, huh?" I chuckled, looked over at Angie. "That's all you, by the way."

Angie lowered her paper. She was pale suddenly, her jaw too loose.

"Mommy?" Even Gabby noticed. "What's wrong?"

Angie gave her a weak smile and handed the paper to me. "Nothing, honey. Mommy's just tired."

"Too much reading," our daughter said.

"No such thing as too much reading," I said. I looked at the paper and then back at Ange, gave her a confused look.

"Lower-right-hand side of the page," she said.

It was the Crime Blotter, an if-it-bleeds-it-leads section they served up on the last page of the metro section. The last item read: "Maine Woman Slain in Car-Jack." I saw the lede then and put the paper down for a moment. Angie reached across the table and ran her warm palm along my forearm.

> A mother of two was gunned down in an apparent carjacking in the early hours of Tuesday morning as she left work at BJ's Wholesaler in Auburn. Peri Pyper, 34, of Lewiston, was approached by the suspect as she tried to start her 2008 Honda Accord. Witnesses reported hearing signs of a struggle followed by a gunshot. The suspect, Taylor Biggins, 22, of Auburn, was arrested a mile away after a police pursuit and surrendered without a struggle. Mrs. Pyper was flown by medevac to Maine Medical Center but was pronounced dead at 6:34 A.M., according to MMC spokesperson Pamela Dunn. Mrs. Pyper is survived by a son and a daughter.

Angie said, "It's not your fault."

"I don't know that. I don't know anything."

"Patrick."

"I don't know anything," I said again.

IT WAS A THREE-HOUR DRIVE to Auburn, Maine, and in that time, my attorney, Cheswick Hartman, arranged everything. I arrived at the law offices of Dufresne, Barrett and McGrath

and was led into an office with James Mayfield, a junior partner in the firm, who handled most of their defense litigation.

James Mayfield was a black man with salt-and-pepper hair,
a matching mustache, and considerable height and girth. He
had a bear of a handshake and an easy way about him that
seemed authentic and unforced.

"Thanks for seeing me, Mr. Mayfield."

"You can call me Coach, Mr. Kenzie."

"Coach?"

"I coach baseball, basketball, golf, football, and soccer in
this town. People call me Coach."

"And why wouldn't they?" I said. "Coach it is."

"When an attorney of Cheswick Hartman's stature calls
me up and says he'll cochair my litigation on a case, pro bono,
I sit up in my seat."

"Yes."

"He said you are a man who never breaks his word."

"That was kind of him."

"Kind or not, I want your word in writing."

"Understandable," I said. "I brought my own pen."

Coach Mayfield pushed a stack of papers across the desk
and I began to sign. He picked up the phone. "Come on in now,
Janice, and bring the stamp."

When I was finished signing a page, Janice notarized it.
By the time I was done, she'd notarized fourteen pages. The
contract was, in its essence, quite simple—I agreed that I was
working for the firm of Dufresne, Barrett and McGrath as an
investigator on behalf of Taylor Biggins. In that capacity, anything Mr. Biggins said to me fell under attorney-client privi-
lege. I could be charged, tried, and convicted if I ever discussed
our conversation with anyone.

I rode out to the courthouse with Coach Mayfield. The sky had that milky blue cast it got sometimes before a nor'easter, but the air was mild. The town smelled of chimney smoke and wet asphalt.

The holding cells sat in the bowels of the courthouse. Coach Mayfield and I met Taylor Biggins on the other side of the bars, where the jailers had left a wooden bench for us.

"Yo, Coach," Taylor Biggins said. He looked younger than twenty-two, a stringy black kid wearing an extra-large white T that draped his body like a dinner bell over a toothpick, and drooping jeans he kept pulling up over his bunched-up boxers, because they'd taken his belt.

"Bigs," Coach Mayfield said and then to me: "Bigs played Pop Warner for me. Baseball and football."

"Who's this?"

Mayfield explained.

"And he can't say nothing to nobody?"

"Not a word."

"Throw his ass in a hole if he does?"

"Without a flashlight, Bigs."

"A'ight, a'ight." Bigs wandered around his cell for a minute, his thumbs hooked into his belt loops. "What you need to know?"

"Did someone pay you to kill the woman?" I asked.

"Nigger, what?"

"You heard me."

Bigs cocked his head. "You saying, was I *put up* to this dumb shit?"

"Yeah."

"Who the fuck would do what I did if they was thinking straight? I was high as a motherfucker, man. I been whaling on the clear for three days."

"The clear?"

"The clear," Bigs said. "Meth, cheese, crank, whatever you want to call it."

"Oh," I said. "So why'd you shoot her?"

"I wasn't *trying* to shoot nobody. Ain't you been listening? She just wouldn't give up the keys. When she grab my arm— *pop*. And she stop grabbing my arm. I just wanted to take her car. I got a friend, Edward, he buy cars. That's all it was."

He looked out through the bars at me, already heading down a dark corridor's worth of DTs, his skin shiny with sweat, eyes wider than his head, mouth taking quick, desperate breaths.

"Walk me through it," I said.

He gave me an injured, incredulous look, like I was putting him out.

"Hey, Bigs," I said, "besides Coach here, you've got one of the best criminal defense lawyers in the country looking into your case because I asked him to. He's capable of cutting your sentence in half. You understand?"

Bigs eventually nodded.

"So answer my questions, dickhead, or I'll make him go away."

He wrapped his arms around his abdomen and hissed several times. Once the cramps had subsided, he straightened and looked back through the bars at me. "Ain't nothing to walk you through. I needed a car that's easy to chop. A Honda or a Toyota, man. Those parts give for years—swap 'em out on a '98 or an '03, don't matter. Shit's interchangeable as a motherfuck. I'm in the parking lot, got me a black hoodie and these jeans, ain't no one seeing me. She come out, go to the Accord. I run up, let her see my black face and my black nine? Should be enough. But she talks shit at me and she won't let go them keys. She just keeps holding on, and then her hand slips and hits my arm? And, like I said, *pop*. She drops. I'm all, 'Ho, *shit*!' But I need my clear, so I grab the keys. I get in the car and punch it out of there but all these shields start blowing into the lot, cherry bars flashing. I didn't even get a mile before they box my ass up." He shrugged. "That's it. Cold? I know it. If she'd just given up the keys, though . . ." He bit down on something and looked at the floor. When he looked back up, tears poured down his face.

I ignored them. "You said she talked shit. What'd she say?"

"Nothing, man."

I came to the bars. I looked through them into his face. "What did she say?"

"Said she needed the car." He looked down again and nodded several times to himself. "Said she needed that car. How's anyone need a car that much?"

"You know any bus lines run at three in the morning, Bigs?"

He shook his head.

"The woman you killed? She worked two jobs. One in Lewiston, one in Auburn. Her shift in Lewiston ended half an hour before her shift in Auburn began. You seeing it now?"

He nodded, the tears coming off him in strings, shoulders quaking.

"Peri Pyper," I said. "That was her name."

He kept his head down.

I turned to Coach Mayfield. "I'm done."

I stood by the door while Coach Mayfield conferred with

his client for a few minutes, their voices never rising above whispers, and then he picked his briefcase up off the bench and headed toward me and the guard.

As the door opened, Bigs yelled, "It was just a fucking *car*."

"Not to her."

"I'M NOT GOING TO GIVE YOU a bunch of bleeding-heart bullshit about Bigs being a great kid and all," Coach Mayfield said. "He was always high-strung, always shortsighted when it came to the big picture. Always had a hair-trigger temper and when he wanted something, he wanted it now. But he wasn't *this*." He waved out the window of his Chrysler 300 as we drove through the streets with their white-steeple churches, broad green commons, and quaint B&Bs. "You look behind the face this town puts up, you find a lot of cracks. Unemployment's double-digits and those who are hiring ain't paying shit. Benefits?" He laughed. "Not a chance. Insurance?" He shook his head. "All the stuff our fathers took for granted as long as you worked hard, the great safety net and the fair wage and the gold watch at the end of it all? That's all gone around here, my friend."

"Gone in Boston, too," I said.

"Gone all over, I bet."

We drove in silence for a bit. While we'd been inside the jail, the blue sky had turned gray. The temperature had dropped a good ten degrees. The air felt like it was made of wet tin foil. No question—snow was coming.

"Bigs had a shot at going to Colby. They told him if he spent a year at community college getting his grades up just north of acceptable, they'd hold him a place on next year's baseball team. So, he buckled down." He looked over at me with eyebrows raised in confirmation. "He did. Went to school days, worked nights."

"So what happened?"

"Company he worked for shitcanned everyone. Then after a month, they offered them their jobs back. It's that cannery right over there." As we rolled over a small bridge, he pointed to a beige brick building along the banks of the Androscoggin River. "Only the unskilled labor got the offer; the skilled labor just got dumped. But the company offered the unskilled their jobs back at half their previous hourly wage. No bennies, no insurance, no nothing. But plenty of overtime if they wanted it, long as they didn't expect time and a half or any of that commie bullshit. So he takes the job back, Bigs. To make his rent and pay for school? He's working seventy-hour weeks. And going to school full-time. So guess how he stays awake?"

"Crank."

He nodded as he turned into the parking lot of his law firm. "The shit that cannery pulled? Companies pulling that all over town, all over the state. And the meth business? Well, that's booming."

We got out of his car and stood in the cold parking lot. I thanked him and he shrugged it off, a guy far more comfortable with criticism than praise.

"He did a piece-of-shit thing, Bigs did, but until he started tweeking, he was not a piece of shit."

I nodded.

"Don't make it right what he did," he said, "but it didn't come from a vacuum."

I shook his hand. "I'm glad he's got you looking out for him."

He shrugged that compliment off, too. "Over a fucking car."

"Over a fucking car," I said and got into my own car and drove off.

AT A REST STOP JUST OVER the Massachusetts border, I stopped for something to eat and sat in my car with it and opened my laptop on the front seat. I tapped my keyboard to bring it out of sleep mode. A pleasant tingle coursed over my scalp. When I reached the home page for IntelSearchABS, I entered my user name and password and clicked my way to the Individual Search Records page. A little green box waited there for me. It asked for a name or alias. I clicked on NAME.

Angie would kill me. I was supposed to be done with this rogue shit. I'd gotten my laptop back. I'd gotten my laptop bag and my picture of Gabby. I'd gotten my answers about Peri Pyper. It was over and done with. I could walk away.

I remembered Peri and myself having drinks at the Chili's in Lewiston and the T.G.I. Friday's in Auburn. Less than a year ago. We'd traded childhood anecdotes, argued over sports teams, jabbed each other for our political differences, quoted movies we both loved. There was zero connection between her whistle-blowing and her getting shot by some dumb, fucked-up kid in a parking lot at three in the morning. No connection whatsoever.

But it's all connected.

This should not be about that, a voice said. *You're just pissed off. And when you're pissed off, you lash out.*

I leaned back in my seat, closed my eyes. I saw Beatrice McCready's face—pained and prematurely aged and possibly crazed.

Another voice said, *Don't do this.*

That voice sounded uncomfortably like my daughter's.

Leave it be.

I opened my eyes. The voices were right.

I saw Amanda from my morning dream, the envelopes she'd tossed in the bushes.

It's all connected.

No, it's not.

What had I said in the dream?

I'm just the mailman.

I leaned forward to shut down my computer. Instead, I typed in the box:

Kenneth Hendricks

I hit RETURN and sat back.

PART II
MORDOVIAN RHYTHM & BLUES

CHAPTER NINE

KENNETH JAMES HENDRICKS HAD SEVERAL aliases. He'd been known, at various times, as KJ, K Boy, Richard James Stark, Edward Toshen, and Kenny B. He was born in 1969 in Warrensburg, Missouri, the son of an aircraft mechanic stationed with the 340th Bombardment Wing at Whiteman Air Force Base. From there, he'd bounced all over the United States—Biloxi, Tampa, Montgomery, Great Falls. First juvenile arrest occurred in King Salmon, Alaska; the second in Lompoc, California. At eighteen, he was arrested in Lompoc on charges of assault and battery and charged as an adult. The victim was his father. Charges dropped by alleged victim. Second arrest as an adult, two days later. Assault and battery again, same victim. This time his father pressed charges, maybe because his son had tried to cut off his ear. Kenny had been halfway through the job when his father's shrieks alerted a neighbor. Hendricks did eighteen months for the assault, plus three years' probation. His father died while he was in prison. Next arrested in Sacramento for loitering in an area known to be popular among male prostitutes. Six weeks later, still in Sacramento, his third assault arrest. This one for pummeling a man at the Come On Inn along I-80. The victim, a Pentecostal deacon and prominent political fund-raiser, had a hard time explaining how he'd come to be naked in a motel room with a male prostitute, so he refused to press charges. The State of California revoked Kenny's parole anyway, for being under the influence of alcohol and cocaine during his arrest.

When he got out of prison in 1994, he'd picked up a Waffen SS tattoo at the base of his neck, courtesy of his new best buddies in the Aryan Brotherhood. He'd also picked up a dedicated criminal trade—all his arrests for the next several years were for suspicion of identity theft. The more sophisticated personal computers grew, the more sophisticated Kenny grew with them. Couldn't quite tame the old ways, though, and in '99 he was picked up for rape and battery of a minor in Peabody, Massachusetts. She was seventeen or sixteen, depending on which time of night the rape actually occurred. Kenny's lawyer fought hard on the issue. The DA realized that if he put the victim on the stand, what was left of her would just get chewed to the marrow. Kenny ended up pleading to the reduced charge of sexual battery on an adult. Because the state took rape so seriously, he was given two years, less time than he'd done in '91 for snorting a couple of lines of Sacramento blow and chugging a six of Bud. Final arrest was in 2007. He was caught receiving fifty grand worth of TVs he'd purchased with a stolen identity. The plan had been to sell them out the back door for five hundred dollars less than he'd paid using the corporate credit card of one Oliver Orin, owner of the Ollie O's chain of sports bars, several of which had just finished structural renovations. I had to hand it to him—if anyone could order fifty K worth of plasma TVs without raising an eyebrow it would be a guy like Oliver Orin. Because of his priors, Kenny was convicted and sentenced to five years. He served just short of three. Since then, no convictions.

"But a nice man, all the same," Angie said.

"A charmer, no doubt."

"Just needs snuggle-time, a good hug."

"And free weights."

"Well, of course," Angie said. "We're not barbarians."

We were in the spare bedroom/closet where we keep the home office desk. It was a little past nine and Gabby had dropped off around eight. Since then, we'd been digging deeper into Kenny Hendricks's history.

"So this is Helene's boyfriend."

" 'Tis."

"Oh, well, it's all fine, then."

She sat back and blew air up at her eyebrows, a sure sign she was about to pop.

"God knows I never expected Helene to be a good parent," she said, "but I didn't expect even that crack whore to be this retarded with her child."

"There, there," I said, "she strikes me more as a tweeker than a crackhead. Technically that would make her a meth whore."

Angie shot me the darkest look she'd shot me in months. Playtime was over. The elephant in the middle of our relationship that neither of us talked about was the actions we'd taken back when Amanda McCready disappeared the first time. When Angie was faced with choosing between the law and a four-year-old's well-being, her reaction at the time could be summed up thusly: Fuck the law.

I, on the other hand, had taken the high road and helped the state return a neglected child to her neglectful parent. We broke up over it. Went nearly a year without speaking. Some years are longer than others; that year was about a decade and a half. Since we'd reconciled, we hadn't said the names *Amanda* or *Helene McCready* in our home until three days ago. In those three days, every time one of us mentioned one of those names, it felt like someone had pulled the pin from a grenade.

Twelve years ago, I'd been wrong. Every day that had passed since, roughly 4,400 of them, I was sure of that.

But twelve years ago, I'd been right. Leaving Amanda with kidnappers, no matter how vested they were in her welfare, was leaving her with kidnappers. In the 4,400 days since I'd taken her back, I was sure this was true. So where did that leave me?

With a wife who was still certain I'd fucked up.

"This Kenny," she said, tapping my laptop, "do we know where he lives?"

"We know his last known address."

She ran her hands through her long, dark hair. "I'm going to step out on the porch."

"Sure."

We put our coats on. Out on our back porch, we carefully closed the door and Angie opened the top of the barbecue grill where she kept a pack of cigarettes and a lighter. She swore she only smoked a couple a day, but there were days I'd noticed the pack was a lot lighter than it should have been. So far she'd kept evidence of the vice from Gabby, but the clock was ticking and we both knew it. Yet as much as I'd love my wife to be vice-free, I normally can't stand vice-free people. They conflate a narcissistic instinct for self-preservation with moral superiority. Plus, they suck the life right out of a party. Angie knows I'd love it if she didn't smoke, and Angie would love it if she didn't smoke. But, for now, she smokes. I, for my part, deal with it and stay off her ass.

"If Beatrice isn't crazy," she said, "and Amanda really is missing again, we've got a second chance."

"No," I said, "we do not."

"You don't even know what I was going to say."

"Yes, I do. You were going to suggest that if we somehow manage to locate Amanda McCready, then *this time* we can make up for the sins of the past."

She gave me a rueful smile as she blew smoke out over the railing. "So you did know what I was going to say."

I took a vicarious whiff of secondhand smoke and planted a kiss on my wife's collarbone. "I don't believe in redemption."

"I thought you didn't believe in closure."

"That either."

"So what do you believe in again?"

"You. Her. This."

"Babe, you've got to find more balance."

"What're you, my sensei?"

"*Hai.*" She gave me a small bow. "I'm serious. You can either sit around the house brooding on what happened to Peri Pyper and how you helped a classic d-bag like Brandon Trescott avoid any responsibility for his actions, or you can do some good."

"And this is good, uh?"

"You're damn right it is. Do you believe a guy like Kenny Hendricks should be around Amanda McCready?"

"No, but that's not enough to go mucking around in people's lives."

"What is?"

I chuckled.

She didn't. "She's missing."

"You want me to go after Kenny and Helene."

She shook her head. "I want *us* to go after Kenny and Helene. And I want *us* to find Amanda again. I might not have much free time."

"You don't have any."

"Okay, any," she admitted, "but I still have mad computer skills, m' man."

"Did you say *mad* computer skills?"

"I'm reliving the early aughts."

"I remember the early aughts—we made money then."

"And we were prettier and your hair was a lot thicker." She put both palms on my chest and stood on tiptoe to kiss me. "No offense, babe, but what else are you doing these days?"

"You're a cold bitch. I love you. But you're a cold bitch."

She gave me that throaty laugh of hers, the one that slides through my blood.

"You *love* it."

HALF AN HOUR LATER BEATRICE MCCREADY sat at our dining-room table. She drank a cup of coffee. She didn't look quite as broken as she had the other day, quite as lost, but that didn't mean she wasn't.

"I shouldn't have lied about Matt," she said. "I'm sorry."

I held up a hand. "Beatrice, Jesus. No apology necessary."

"He just . . . It's one of those things you know you probably won't get over but you still got to function, go about your day. Right?"

"My first husband was murdered," Angie said. "That doesn't mean I know about your grief, Bea, but I did learn that having one moment in a given day, just one second, when you're not grieving? That's never a sin."

Beatrice gave that a soft nod. "I . . . Thank you." She looked around our small dining room. "You have a girl now, uh?"

"Yes. Gabriella."

"Oh, that's a pretty name. Does she look like you?"

Angie looked at me for confirmation, and I nodded.

"More me than him, yeah," she said. She pointed to a picture of Gabby that sat atop the credenza. "That's Gabby."

Beatrice took the photo in and eventually smiled. "She looks feisty."

"She's that," Angie said. "They say the terrible twos?"

Beatrice leaned forward. "Oh, I know, I know. It starts at eighteen months and it goes until they're three and a half."

Angie nodded vigorously. "She was a monster. I mean, God, it was—"

"Awful, right?" Beatrice said. She looked as if she were about to tell us an anecdote about her son but caught herself. She looked down at the table with a strange smile on her face and rocked a bit in her chair. "But they grow out of it."

Angie looked at me. I looked back at her, clueless about what to say next.

"Bea," she said, "the police said they investigated your claim and found Amanda in the house."

Beatrice shook her head. "Since they moved, Amanda calls me every day. Never missed until two weeks ago. Right after Thanksgiving. I haven't heard from her since."

"They moved? Out of the neighborhood?"

Bea nodded. "About four months ago. Helene owns a house in Foxboro. A three-bedroom."

Foxboro was a suburb, about twenty miles south. It wasn't Belmont Hills or anything, but it was a tall step up from St. Bart's Parish in Dorchester.

"What's Helene do for work these days?"

Beatrice laughed. "Work? I mean, last I heard, she was working the Lotto machine at New Store on the Block, but that was a while ago. I'm pretty sure she managed to get fired from there just like every other place. This is a woman who managed to get fired from Boston Gas back in the day. Who gets fired from a utility?"

"So, if she's not working much . . ."

"How's she afford a house?" She shrugged. "Who knows?"

"She didn't get anything from the city in those lawsuits, did she?"

She shook her head. "It all went into a trust for Amanda. Helene can't touch it."

"Okay," Angie said. "I'll pull the tax assessment on the property."

"What about the restraining orders against you?" I asked as softly as I could.

Beatrice looked over at me. "Helene works the system. She's been doing it since she was a teenager. Amanda was sick a couple years ago. The flu. Helene had some new guy, a bartender who fed her free drinks, so she kept forgetting to check on Amanda. This is when they were in the old place by Columbia Road. I still had a key and I started letting myself in to care for Amanda. It was either that or let her catch pneumonia."

Angie glanced at the photo of Gabby and then back at Bea. "So Helene found you there and filed the restraining order."

"Yeah." Bea fingered the edge of her coffee cup. "I drink more than I used to. Sometimes I get stupid and drunk-dial." She looked up at me. "Like I did with you the other night. I've done it with Helene a few times. After the last time, she filed for another restraining order. That was three weeks ago."

"What made you, I don't want to say 'harass' her, but . . . ?"

" 'Harass' is okay. Sometimes I like harassing Helene." She smiled. "I had talked to Amanda. She's a good kid. Hard, you know? Way older than her years, but good."

I thought of the four-year-old I'd returned to that house. Now she was "hard." Now she was "way older than her years."

"Amanda asked me to check the mail at the old place, just some stuff that the PO forgot to forward. They do that all the time. So I went by there and it was mostly junk mail." She reached into her purse. "Except for this."

She handed me a piece of ivory paper: a Commonwealth of Massachusetts Birth Certificate, Suffolk County, for Christina Andrea English, DOB 08/04/93.

I handed it to Angie.

"Similar age," she said.

I nodded. "Christina English would be a year older."

We were thinking the same thing. Angie laid the birth certificate beside her laptop and her fingers danced across the keyboard.

"How did Amanda react when you told her you'd found this?" I asked Bea.

"She stopped calling. Then she disappeared."

"So you started calling Helene."

"And demanding answers. You're fucking right I did."

"Good for you," Angie said. "I wish I'd been with you."

I said, "So you called Helene?"

She nodded. "A bunch. And left several angry messages."

"Which Helene saved," Angie said, "and brought before a judge."

Beatrice nodded. "Exactly."

"And you're sure Amanda is not at the Foxboro house."

"Positive."

"Why?"

"Because I staked it out for three days."

"Staked it out." I grinned. "With a restraining order on you. Damn. You're hardcore, Bea."

She shrugged. "Whoever the police talked to, it wasn't Amanda."

Angie looked up from the computer for a second, her fingers still hitting the keys. "No local grammar school records on Christina English. No social. No hospital records."

"What's this mean?" Bea asked.

"It means Christina English could have moved out of state. Or—"

"I got it," Angie said. "DOD 9/16/93."

"—she's dead," I finished.

"Car crash," Angie said. "Wallingford, Connecticut. Both parents deceased same date."

Bea looked at us, confused.

Angie said, "Amanda was trying to assume Christina English's identity, Bea. You interrupted. There's no Massachusetts death certificate on file. There might be a Connecticut death certificate—I'd have to dig deeper—but there's a solid chance someone could pretend to be Christina English and the state would never be the wiser. You could get a social security card, forge an employment history, and someday, if you felt like it, fake an injury at your nonexistent job and collect state disability."

"Or," I said, "she could wrack up six figures on multiple credit cards in a thirty-day period and never pay them off because, well, she doesn't exist."

"So either Amanda's working for Helene and Kenny in a fraud operation . . ." Angie said.

"Or she's trying to become someone else."

"But then she'd never get the two million the city owes her next year."

"Good point," I said.

"Though," Angie said, "just because she assumes a new identity doesn't mean she forfeits her authentic one."

"But I intercepted the birth certificate," Bea said, "so she can't be anyone but herself anymore. Right?"

"Well, the Christina English identity is probably done for," I said.

"But?"

"But," Angie said, "it's like avatars in computer games. She could have several if she's really smart. Is Amanda really smart?"

"Off the charts," Bea said.

We sat in silence for a minute. I caught Bea staring at the photo of Gabriella. We'd taken it last autumn. Gabby sat in a pile of leaves, arms stretched wide as if posing for the top of a trophy, her megawatt smile as big as the leaf pile. A million pictures just like it adorned mantels and credenzas and buffet tables and the tops of TVs across the globe. Bea kept staring at it, falling into it.

"Such a great age," she said. "Four, five. Everything's wonder and change."

I couldn't meet my wife's eyes.

"I'll take a look," I said.

Angie gave me a smile bigger than Suffolk County.

Bea reached her hands across the table. I took them. They were warm from the coffee cup.

"You'll find her again."

"I said I'll take a look, Bea."

The gaze she fixed on me was evangelical. "You'll find her again."

I didn't say anything. But Angie did.

"We will, Bea. No matter what."

AFTER SHE LEFT, WE SAT in the living room and I looked at the photo of Bea and Amanda in my lap. It had been taken a year ago at a K of C function hall. They stood in front of a wood-paneled wall. Bea looked at Amanda and love poured out of her like a flashlight beam. Amanda looked right at the camera. Her smile was hard, her gaze was hard, her jaw slightly skewed to the right. Her once-blond hair was a cherry brown. She wore it long and straight. She was small and slim and wore a gray Newbury Comics T-shirt, a navy blue Red Sox warm-up jacket, and a pair of dark blue jeans. Her slightly crooked nose was sprayed with a light dusting of freckles, and her green eyes were very small. She had thin lips, sharp cheekbones, a squared-off chin. There was so much going on in her eyes that I knew the picture could not do her justice. Her face probably changed thirty times in fifteen minutes. Never quite beautiful but never less than arresting.

"Whew," Angie said. "That kid is no kid anymore."

"I know." I closed my eyes for a second.

"What'd you expect?" she said. "Helene for a mother? If Amanda avoids rehab until her twentieth birthday, she's a raging success."

"Why am I doing this again?" I asked.

"Because you're good."

"I'm not this good," I said.

She kissed my earlobe. "When your daughter asks what you stand for, don't you want to be able to answer her?"

"That'd be nice," I said. "It would. But this recession, this depression, this whatever the fuck—it's real, honey. And it's not going away."

"Yes, it is," she said. "It is. Someday. But where you stand, right here, right now? That's forever." She turned on the couch, brought her legs up and held them by the ankles. "I'll join you for a couple-three days. That'd be fun."

"Fun. How you going to—?"

"PR owes me for last summer when I watched the Beast. She'll watch Gabby while I gallivant with you for a couple days."

The Beast was the son of Angie's friend Peggy Rose—or PR. Gavin Rose was five years old and, to the best of my knowledge, never slept and never stopped breaking shit. He also enjoyed screaming for no good reason. His parents thought it was cute. When PR's second child was born last year, the birth coincided with the death of her mother-in-law, which is how

Angie and I ended up with the Beast for five of the longest days known to man.

"She does owe us," I said.

"Yes, she does." She looked at her watch. "Too late to call now, but I'll try her in the morning. You can check back in during the afternoon, see if you got a partner."

"It's sweet of you," I said, "but it's not going to bring in any more money. And that's what we need. I could find day labor. There's always ways to scoop up, I dunno, something. The docks? I could unload cars from the ships over in Southie. I could . . ." I stopped talking, hating the desperation I heard in my own voice. I leaned back on the couch and watched wet snow spit against the window. It eddied under the street lamps and swirled along the telephone lines. I looked over at my wife. "We could go broke."

"It'll take you a couple days, a week tops. And if, in that time, Duhamel-Standiford calls and offers you another case, you walk away. But for now, you try to find Amanda."

"Soup-kitchen broke."

"Then we eat soup," Angie said.

CHAPTER TEN

UNTIL THREE WEEKS AGO, AMANDA McCREADY had attended the Caroline Howard Gilman School for Girls. The Gilman was tucked on a side street just off Memorial Drive in Cambridgeport, a few oar pulls up the Charles River from MIT. It had started out as a high school for daughters of the upper crust. Its 1843 mission statement proclaimed, "A necessity in confounding times, the Caroline Howard Gilman School for Girls will turn your daughter into a young lady of impeccable manners. When her husband takes her hand in marriage, he will shake yours in thanks for providing him with a wife of unparalleled breeding and substance."

The Gilman had changed a bit since 1843. It still catered to the wealthy, but its student body had become known less for their manners than for their lack of them. Now, if you had the money and connections to send a child to the Winsor or St. Paul's but the child had a history of either significant underachievement or, worse, behavioral problems—you sent her to the Gilman.

"We don't like being characterized, however charitably, as a 'therapeutic' school," the principal, Mai Nghiem, told me as she led me to her office. "We'd prefer to think we're the last outpost before that option. A good number of our young women will go on to Ivies or the Seven Sisters; their journeys are just a bit less traditional than those of some of their counterparts. And because we do get results, we get healthy funding, which allows us to enroll intelligent young women from less privileged backgrounds."

"Like Amanda McCready."

Mai Nghiem nodded and led me into her office. She was in her mid-thirties, a small woman with long, straight hair so black it was nearly blue. She moved as if the floor beneath her feet was softer and smoother than the floor beneath mine. She wore an ivory off-the-shoulder blouse over a black skirt and pointed me to a seat as she walked behind her desk. When Beatrice had called her at home last night to arrange this appointment, she'd been reluctant, but as I knew from personal experience, Beatrice could wear reluctance down pretty quick.

"Beatrice is the mother Amanda should have had," Mai Nghiem said. "Woman's a saint."

"Preaching to the choir."

"I don't mean to be impolite, but I'm going to have to multitask during this conversation." Mai Nghiem scowled at her computer screen and tapped a couple of keys.

"Not a problem," I said.

"Amanda's mother called us and said Amanda'd be out of school a couple of weeks because she'd gone to visit her father."

"I wasn't aware she knew her father."

Mai's dark eyes left the screen for a moment, a grim smile on her face. "She doesn't. Helene's story was BS, but unless a parent has shown violent proclivities toward a child—*and* we've documented those proclivities—there's not a lot we can do but take them at their word."

"Do you think Amanda could have run away?"

She gave it some thought and shook her head. "This is not a kid who runs away," she said. "This is a kid who wins awards and more awards and gets a scholarship to a great school. And flourishes."

"So she flourished here."

"On an academic level, absolutely."

"On a nonacademic level?"

Her eyes went back to the screen and she blasted out a few sentences on the keyboard using only one hand. "What do you need to know?"

"Everything. Anything."

"I don't follow."

"Sounds like she was a practical kid."

"Very."

"Rational?"

"Exceptionally."

"Hobbies?"

"I'm sorry?"

"Hobbies. Things she liked to do besides be rational all the time."

She hit RETURN and sat back for a moment. She tapped a pen on her desk and looked up at the ceiling. "She liked dogs."

"Dogs."

"Any kind, any shape. She volunteered at Animal Rescue in East Cambridge. An act of community service is a prerequisite for graduation."

"What about the pressure to fit in? She's a kid from the wrong side of the tracks. The girls here drive Daddy's Lex. She doesn't even get Daddy's bus pass."

She nodded. "Her freshman year, I seem to remember, some of the girls got a little cruel. They taunted her about her lack of jewelry, her clothes."

"Her clothes."

"They were perfectly acceptable, don't get me wrong. But they were from Gap or Aéropostale, not Nordstrom or Barneys. Her sunglasses were Polaroids you'd buy at CVS. Her classmates wore Maui Jim and D&G. Amanda's bag was Old Navy . . ."

"The other girls had Gucci."

She smiled and shook her head. "More like Fendi or Marc Jacobs, maybe Juicy Couture. Gucci skews a bit older."

"How tragically unhip of me."

Another smile. "That's the thing—*we* can joke about it. To us, it's silly. To fifteen- and sixteen-year-old girls, though?"

"Life and death."

"Pretty much."

I thought of Gabby. Was this the world I was raising her for?

She said, "But then the harassment just stopped."

"Just stopped."

Another nod. "Amanda's one of those rare kids who truly doesn't seem to care what you think. Compliment her or criticize her, you get the same even gaze coming back at you. I wonder if the other girls got tired of throwing paint at her when none of it would stick." A bell rang and she looked out her window for a moment as a dozen teenage girls flowed past. "You know, I misspoke at the outset."

"How so?"

"I said Amanda wouldn't run away and I believe that she wouldn't *physically* run away. But . . . well, she was, in another sense, running away all the time. That's what brought her here. That's what got her straight A's. She was putting more distance between herself and her mother every day of her life. Are you aware that Amanda orchestrated her own admission to this school?"

I shook my head.

"She applied, she filled out the financial aid forms, even applied for some rare and rather obscure federal grants. She started doing all her prep work in the seventh grade. Her mother never had a clue."

"That could be Helene's epitaph."

She gave Helene's name a soft roll of her eyes. "When I met with Amanda and her mother for the first time, Helene was actually annoyed. Here was her daughter, set to attend a reasonably prestigious prep school on full financial aid, and Helene looked around this office and said, 'Public school was good enough for me.'"

"Sure, she's a poster child for Boston public schools, ol' Helene is."

Mai Nghiem smiled. "Financial aid, scholarships—they cover just about everything if you know how to look for the applicable ones, and Amanda did. Tuition, books, covered. But never fees. And fees add up. Amanda paid hers every term in cash. I remember one year, forty dollars of it was paid in coins she'd earned from a tip jar at a doughnut shop. I've met few students in my career who were given less by their parents yet worked so hard you knew nothing would stop them."

"But something has derailed her. At least recently."

"That's what troubles me. She was going to Harvard. On a full ride. Or Yale. Brown. Take your pick. Now, unless she comes back real quick, and erases three weeks of missed exams, missed papers, gets her GPA all the way back up to above-flawless, where's she going to go?" Another shake of her head. "She didn't run."

"Well, that's unfortunate."

She nodded. "Because now you have to assume she was taken. Again."

"Yeah, I do," I said. "Again."

An incoming mail message dinged on her computer and she glanced at the screen, gave whatever she saw there an almost imperceptible head shake. She looked back at me. "I grew up in Dorchester, you know. Just off the Ave. In between Savin Hill and Fields Corner."

"Not far from where I grew up."

"I know." She tapped the keyboard a couple of times and sat back. "I was a junior at Mount Holyoke when you found her the first time. I was obsessed with the case. I used to hurry back to my dorm to see the six o'clock news every night. We all thought she was dead, that whole long winter and into the spring."

"I remember," I said, wishing I didn't.

"And then—wow—you found her. All those months later. And you brought her home."

"And what'd you think?"

"About what you did?"

"Yeah," I said.

"You did the right thing," she said.

"Oh." I almost smiled in gratitude.

She met my eyes. "But you were still wrong."

AT AMANDA'S LOCKER, I STARED at textbooks that were stacked tallest to shortest, the edges of their spines precisely aligned to the edge of the shelf. A Red Sox jersey hung from a hook on the door, dark blue with red piping, a red 19 on the back. Otherwise, nothing. No pictures taped to the door, no decals on the wall, no array of lip gloss or bracelets.

"So she likes dogs and the Red Sox," I said.

"Why do you say the Red Sox?" Mai asked.

"She's wearing a Sox warm-up jacket in a photo I have."

"I've seen her wear this jersey a lot. Sometimes a T-shirt. And I've seen the warm-up jacket. But *I'm* a fan, you know? I can talk till I'm blue about the farm system and the logic—or lack thereof—behind Theo's latest trade, et cetera."

I smiled. "Me, too."

"Amanda, though? Couldn't. I tried to engage her half a dozen times until I realized, looking in her eyes one day, that she couldn't name the starting rotation. She couldn't tell you how many seasons Wakefield was with the team or even how many games out of first they were this week."

"So a fair-weather fan?"

"Worse," she said, "a fashion fan. She liked wearing the colors. That's all."

"The heathen," I said.

"SHE WAS THE PERFECT STUDENT," Stephanie Tyler said. "I mean, per-fect." Miss Tyler taught AP European History. She was about twenty-eight. She had ash-blond hair cut in a bob and not a strand of it out of place. She had the look of someone used to being tended to. "She never spoke out of turn and always came to class prepared. You never caught her tweeting or texting in class, playing video games on her BlackBerry or what-have-you."

"She had a BlackBerry?"

She gave it some thought. "Amanda, no, come to think of it. She had a regular old cell. But you'd be amazed how many of these girls have BlackBerrys. Freshmen, too. Some have cell phones *and* BlackBerrys. The juniors and seniors drive BMW 5 series and *Jaguars*." The outrage made her lean forward, as if we were conspiring. "High school's a whole new world, don't you find?"

I kept my face noncommittal. I wasn't sure if high school was much different than it had ever been; only the accessories were.

"So Amanda . . ."

"Per-fect," Miss Tyler said again. "Showed up every day, answered when called upon, usually correctly, went home at day's end, and prepared for tomorrow. You can't ask for more."

"Any friends?"

"Just Sophie."

"Sophie?" I said.

"Sophie Corliss. Her father's the local fitness guy? Brian Corliss. He gives advice on the Channel 5 news sometimes."

I shook my head. "I only watch *The Daily Show*."

"So how do you get your news?"

"I read it."

"Right," she said with a sudden glazing of the eyes. "Anyway, a lot of people know who he is."

"Uh, okay," I said. "And his daughter?"

"Sophie. She and Amanda were like twins."

"They looked alike?"

Stephanie Tyler cocked her head slightly. "No, but I had to remind myself who was who. Isn't that strange? Amanda was shorter and fairer-skinned, Sophie was darker and much taller, but I had to keep remembering those differences."

"So they were tight."

"Since first period, first day, freshman year."

"What did they bond over?"

"They were both iconoclasts, though with Sophie, I think it was more a matter of fashion than nature. It was like . . . Amanda's an outsider because she doesn't know any other way to be, which makes other kids respect her. Sophie, though, she chose to define herself as an outsider, which makes her . . ."

"A poseur," I said.

"A bit, yeah."

"So other kids respected Amanda."

Miss Tyler nodded.

"Did they like her?"

"No one *disliked* her."

"But."

"But no one really knew her either. I mean, other than Sophie. At least, no one I can think of. That kid's an island."

"GREAT STUDENT," TOM DANNAL SAID. Dannal taught AP Macroeconomics but looked like the football coach. "One in a million, really. Everything we say we want our kids to be, you know? Polite, focused, smart as a whip. Never acted up or gave anyone a minute's trouble."

"I keep hearing this," I said. "The perfect kid."

"Right," he said. "And who the fuck wants that?"

"Tommy," Mai Nghiem said to him.

"No, no, really." He held up a hand. "I mean, Amanda, okay, she was nice. She could be pleasant and personable. But, you know that saying about there being no *there* there? That's her. I had her in microec last year and macroec now, and she was my best student in both. And yet? Couldn't tell you thing-one about her outside of her work. Not one. You ask her a personal question, she turns it back on you. Ask her how things are going, you get, 'Fine. You?' And she always seemed fine. She did. Always seemed content. But you'd look in her eyes and you'd get the impression she was approximating human behavior. She'd studied people, learned how to walk and talk like one, but she was still outside looking in."

"You're saying she was an alien."

"I'm saying she was one of the loneliest people I've ever known."

"What about her friend?"

"Sophie?" A cold chuckle. " 'Friend' is a generous word."

I looked over at Principal Nghiem. She gave me a small shrug.

"I heard from another faculty member that Amanda and Sophie were pretty much joined at the hip."

"I'm not saying they weren't. I just said 'friends' wasn't how I'd describe the relationship. It was a bit more *Single White Female* than that."

"On whose end?"

"Sophie's," Mai Nghiem said, nodding to herself. "Yeah, now that Tom mentions it. Amanda was oblivious, I think, but Sophie clearly idolized her."

"And the more Amanda didn't notice," Tom Dannal said, "the higher Sophie pushed her up the pedestal."

I said, "So, I guess I got a new million-dollar question."

Tom nodded. "Where's Sophie? Right?"

I looked over at Principal Nghiem.

"She dropped out."

My eyes widened. "When?"

"Beginning of the school year."

"And you don't think there could be a connection?"

"Between Sophie Corliss deciding not to come back for senior year and Amanda McCready not showing up for classes after Thanksgiving?"

I looked around the empty classroom and tried not to let my frustration show. "Anyone else I can talk to?"

IN THE STUDENT LOUNGE, I MET with seven homeroom classmates of Amanda and Sophie. Principal Nghiem and I sat in the center of the room with the girls arrayed before us in a half-circle.

"Amanda was just, ya know," Reilly Moore said.

"I don't," I said.

Giggles.

"Like, ya know."

Eye rolls. More giggles.

"Oh," I said, "she was *like* ya know. Now I get it."

Blank stares, no giggles.

"It's, like, if you were talking to her," Brooklyn Doone said, "she, like, listened? But if you waited for her to tell you stuff, like, who she dug or what apps were on her iPad or like that? You'd, like, wait a long time."

The girl beside her, Coral or Crystal, rolled her eyes. "For, like, ever."

"Like, ev-er," another girl said, and they all nodded in agreement.

"What about her friend, Sophie?" I asked.

"Ewww!"

"That daggy bee-atch?"

"That chick was wannabe-dot-com."

"Dot-*org*."

"I'm sayin'."

"I heard she, like, tried to list you as her friend on her Facebook page."

"Ewww!"

"I'm sayin'."

After my daughter was born, I'd considered buying a shotgun to ward off potential suitors fourteen or so years up the road. Now, as I listened to these girls babble and imagined Gabby one day talking with the same banality and ignorance of the English language, I thought of buying the same shotgun to blow my own fucking head off.

Five thousand years of civilization, more or less, twenty-three hundred years since the libraries of Alexandria, over a hundred years since the invention of flight, wafer-thin computers at our fingertips, which can access the intellectual riches of the globe, and judging by the girls in that room, the only advance we'd made since the invention of fire was turning *like* into an omni-word, useful as a verb, a noun, an article, the whole sentence if need be.

"So none of you knew either of them well?" I tried.

Seven blank stares.

"I'll take that as a no."

The world's longest silence broken only by some fidgeting.

"'Member that guy?" Brooklyn said eventually. "He looked kinda like Joe Jonas."

"Like, he's so, like, hot."

"The guy?"

"Joe Jonas. Duh."

"I think he looks, like, so queer."

"Uh-ah."

"Uh-huh."

I focused on the one who'd brought it up. "This guy—he was Amanda's boyfriend?"

Brooklyn shrugged. "I dunno."

"What *do* you know?"

This annoyed her. Sunshine probably annoyed her. "I dunno. I just saw her with some guy once at South Shore."

"South Shore Plaza? The mall?"

"Uh," she pulsed her eyes at my cluelessness, "yeah."

"So you were at the mall and—"

"Yeah, like, me and Tisha and Reilly." She indicated two of the other girls. "And we ran into them coming out of Diesel. They didn't buy anything, though."

"They didn't buy anything," I said.

She looked down at her nails and crossed her legs and let out a sigh.

"Anything else?" I asked the room.

Nothing. Not even blank stares. They'd all decided to investigate their nails or their shoes or their reflections in the windows.

"Well, thank you," I said. "You've all been very helpful."

"Whatever," two of them said.

———

On the front steps, I exchanged business cards with Principal Nghiem and shook her small, smooth hand.

"Thank you," I said. "You've been a huge help."

"I hope so. Good luck."

I started down the stairs.

"Mr. Kenzie."

I looked back up at her. The sun had popped out, hard and strong. It turned last night's snow into a brook that gurgled as it rushed along the gutters toward the sewer grate.

Mai shaded her eyes. "Those exams she missed? Those overdue papers? If you get her back here soon, we'll find a way to make up all that work. Without damage to her academic file. She'll get that scholarship to a great school, I promise."

"I just have to find her soon."

She nodded.

"So," I said, "I'll find her soon."

"I know you will."

We acknowledged the gravity of the situation with the briefest of nods, and I felt something else in the exchange, too, something a little warm and a little wistful and better left unacknowledged and unexamined.

She turned back and entered the school, and the heavy green door closed behind her. I walked up the street to my Jeep. As I clicked the remote to unlock the door, a girl came out from behind it.

She was one of the seven I'd just interviewed. She had dark eyes pooled in shadow and lank dark hair and skin as white as Styrofoam. Of the seven girls in the room, she was the only one who'd said nothing.

"What're you going to do if you find her?"

"Bring her home."

"What home?"

"She can't stay out there by herself."

"Maybe she's not by herself. Maybe 'out there' ain't so bad."

"It's pretty bad sometimes."

"Have you seen where she lives?" She lit a cigarette.

I shook my head.

"Well, break in sometime, m' man. Check out the microwave for starters."

"The microwave."

She repeated it as she blew a series of smoke O's out of her mouth. "The mi-cro-wave. Yes."

I looked in her dark eyes, which were fringed by even darker eye shadow. "Amanda doesn't strike me as the kind of girl who takes friends by her house."

"I never said it was Amanda who brought me into her house."

It took me a few seconds. "You went there with Sophie?"

The girl said nothing, just chewed the left corner of her upper lip.

"Okay. So is Sophie still there?"

"Might be," the girl said.

"And Amanda—where's she?"

"I honestly don't know. Swear."

"Why are you talking to me if you don't want me to find her?"

She crossed her arms so that her right elbow was cupped in her left palm as she took another drag. A smattering of pink scars rose up her inner arms like railroad ties. "I heard a story going around about Amanda and Sophie. I heard five people went into a room over Thanksgiving. You with me so far?"

"Yeah, I think I can follow."

"Two people in that room died. But four people walked back out."

I chuckled. "What are you smoking besides that cigarette?"

"Just remember what I said."

"Could you *be* more cryptic?"

She shrugged and bit a nail. "Gotta go."

As she walked past me, I said, "Why talk to me?"

"Because Zippo was a friend of mine. Last year? He was more than a friend. First more-than-a-friend I ever had."

"Who's Zippo?"

Her façade of apathetic cool collapsed and she looked about nine years old. Nine years old and abandoned by her parents at the mall. "You're serious?"

"I am."

"Christ," she said, and her voice cracked. "You don't know anything."

"Who's Zippo?" I said again.

"Buzzer's buzzed, man." She flicked her cigarette to the street. "Gots to get my education on. You drive safe."

She walked up the street as the melted snow continued to rush along the gutters and the sky turned to slate. As she vanished through the same door Principal Nghiem had gone through, I realized I'd never gotten her name. The door closed, and I climbed in my Jeep and drove back across the river.

CHAPTER ELEVEN

WHILE I'D SPENT THE MORNING interviewing annoying prep-school girls, Angie's friend, PR, had agreed to watch Gabby for a few afternoons. So it was that my wife joined me on casework for the first time in almost five years, and we drove north of the city to meet Sophie Corliss's father.

Brian Corliss lived in Reading on a maple-lined street with wide white sidewalks and lawns that looked like they shaved twice a day. It was a solidly middle-class section of town, leaning toward upper maybe, but not to an elitist degree. The garages were two-car, not four, and the cars were Audis and 4Runner Limiteds, not Lexuses and BMW 740s. All the houses looked well cared for, and all were adorned with Christmas lights and decorations. None more so than the Corliss house, a white Colonial with black shutters and window trim, a black front door. White icicle lights dripped from the gutters, porch posts, and railings. A wreath as big as the sun hung above the garage door. In front of the bushes on the front lawn stood a manger replica and figures of the three kings, Mary, Joseph, and a menagerie of animals arrayed around an empty cradle. To their right stood a somewhat incongruous menagerie of snowmen, elves, reindeer, Santa and Mrs. Claus, and a leering Grinch. On the roof, a sled sat by the chimney and more lights spelled out MERRY CHRISTMAS. The mailbox post was a candy cane.

When we pulled up the driveway, Brian was in his garage, unloading groceries from the back of an Infiniti SUV. He greeted us with a wave and a smile as open as a heartland prairie. He was a trim man who wore a denim Oxford unbuttoned over a white T tucked into a pair of sharply pressed khakis. His canvas safari jacket was maroon with a black leather collar. He was in his mid-forties and looked to be in exceptional shape. This made sense, because he'd made his living the last ten years first as a fitness trainer and then as a fitness guru. He traveled New England speaking to small companies about how they could raise their productivity by getting their employees into better shape. He'd even written a book, *Lose the Fat and All That,* which had become a local bestseller for a few weeks, and a cursory study of his Web sites (he had three) and his autobiography suggested he hadn't neared his career ceiling yet. He shook our hands, not overdoing the grip the way a lot of workout fiends do, and thanked us for coming and apologized for not being able to meet us halfway.

"It's just the city traffic, you know? After two, forget about it. But I mentioned it to Donna and she said, 'But won't the detectives have to drive back in that same traffic?'"

"Donna's your wife?"

He nodded. "She had a point. So I feel guilty."

"But we're imposing on you," I said.

He waved that off. "You're not imposing at all. If you can help bring my daughter back to me, you're most definitely not imposing."

He lifted a grocery bag off the floor of the garage. There were six of them, and I reached for two. Angie took two more.

"Oh, no," he said. "I can get them."

"Don't be ridiculous," Angie said. "It's the least we can do."

"Jeesh," he said. "You're very kind. Thank you."

He closed the hatch of the Infiniti and I was mildly surprised to see one of those moronic 9/11 Terrorist Hunting Permit decals on the rear window. I suppose I should have felt safer knowing that if Bin Laden dropped by to borrow a cup of sugar, Brian Corliss was ready to put out his lights for America, but mostly I just felt annoyed that the thousands who had died on September 11 were being exploited for a dumb fucking decal. Before my mouth could get me into trouble, though, we were following Brian Corliss up the path to the black front door and entering his two-hundred-year-old house.

We stood by the granite kitchen counter as he unloaded the groceries into the fridge and cabinets. The first floor had been gut-remodeled so recently you could smell the sawdust. Two hundred years ago, I doubt the builder had seen the need to go with the sunken living room or the pressed copper ceiling in the dining room or the Sub-Zero in the kitchen. All the window frames were new and uniform eggshell. Even so, the house had a mismatched feel. The living room was white on white—white couch, white throw rugs, off-white fireplace mantel, ash-white logs in the ivory metal log basket, a huge white Christmas tree towering over it all from a corner. The kitchen was dark—cherrywood cabinets and dark granite counters and black granite backsplash. Even the Sub-Zero and the chimney hood above the stove were black. The dining room was Danish Modern, a clean, blond hard-edged table surrounded by hard-edged high-backed chairs. The ultimate effect was of a house that had been furnished from too many catalogs.

Framed pictures of Brian Corliss and a blond woman and a blond boy sat on the mantel, on the shelves of a credenza, on top of the fridge. Collages of them hung on the walls. You could follow the boy's growth from birth to what looked like four. The blond woman was Donna, I assumed. She was attractive the way sports bar hostesses and pharmaceutical reps are— hair the color of rum and lots of it, teeth as bright as Bermuda. She had the look of a woman who kept her plastic surgeon on speed dial. Her breasts were prominently displayed in most of the photos and looked like perfect softballs made of flesh. Her forehead was unlined in the way of the recently embalmed and her smile resembled that of someone undergoing electroshock. In a couple of the photos—just a couple—stood a dark-haired girl with anxious eyes and an unsure, fleshy chin: Sophie.

"When was the last time you saw her?" I asked.

"It's been a few months."

Angie and I looked across the counter at him.

He held up both palms. "I know, I know. But there were extenuating . . ." He grimaced and then smiled. "Let's just say parenting is not easy. You have any kids?"

"One," I said. "Daughter."

"How old?"

"Four."

"Little child," he said, "little problems. Big child, big

problems." He looked across the counter at Angie. "And you, miss?"

"We're married." Angie tilted her head toward me. "Same four-year-old."

That seemed to please him. He smiled to himself and hummed under his breath as he put a dozen eggs and a half-gallon of skim milk into the fridge.

"She was such a happy child." He finished emptying the bag and folded it neatly before putting it under the counter. "A joy every day. I fully admit I was unprepared for the day she turned into such a Sullen Sally."

"And what turned her into . . . that?" Angie asked.

He peered at the eggplant he pulled from the next bag, frozen for a moment. "Her mom," he said. "God rest her. But, yes, she . . ." He looked up from the eggplant as if surprised to find us there. "She left."

"How old was Sophie when she left?"

"Well, she left with Sophie."

"So, she left you. She didn't leave Sophie." Angie glanced at me. "I'm a little lost, Brian."

Brian put the eggplant into the crisper drawer. "I regained custody when Sophie was ten. She—this is hard—Sophie's mother? She developed a chemical dependency. First on Vicodin, then on OxyContin. She stopped acting like a responsible adult. Then she left me and went to live with someone else. And they created a wholly unfit environment for a child to grow up in, believe me." He looked at both of us, waiting, it appeared, for an indication of agreement.

I gave him my best empathetic nod and commiserating gaze.

"So I sued for custody," he said, "and eventually I won."

"How many years was Sophie with her mother before that?" Angie asked.

"Three."

"Three . . ."

"Sophie's mother was addicted to painkillers throughout that time?" I asked.

"Eventually. I mean, she stopped, or claimed she did. For the full three years."

"So what created the unsafe environment?"

He gave us a warm smile. "Nothing I feel comfortable discussing right now."

"Okay," I said.

Angie said, "So you brought Sophie back here when she was ten?"

He nodded. "And at first it was a little awkward, because I hadn't been a permanent fixture in her life for six years, but then, I'll tell you something, we figured it out. We found our rhythm. We did."

"Six years," Angie said. "I thought you said three."

"No, no. Her mother and I separated when Sophie was just turning seven and then I had to fight three years for custody, but the six years I'm talking about were the first six years of her life. I was overseas during most of that. And Sophie and her mother were here."

"So really," Angie said with an edge in her voice I wasn't real keen on, "you missed her whole life."

"Huh?" His open face closed and darkened.

"Overseas, Brian?" I said. "As in military?"

"Affirmative."

"Doing what?"

"Protecting this country."

"No doubt," I said. "And thank you. Sincerely. Thank you. I'm just wondering where you served."

He closed the fridge door and folded and stowed the last of the paper bags. He gave me that warm, warm smile of his. "So you can second-guess the gravity of my contribution?"

"Definitely not," I said. "It's just a question."

After an awkward few seconds, he held up a hand and smiled wider. "Of course, of course. I apologize. I was a civil engineer with Bechtel in Dubai."

Angie kept her voice light. "I thought you said you were in the military."

"No," he said, his eyes fixed on nothing. "I agreed to your partner's description when he said *as in* the military. When you're in the Emirates, working for a government friendly to ours, you may as well be in the military. You are most certainly a target of any jihadist who decides to blow you into meat scraps because you symbolize his cockeyed idea of Western corruption and influence. I didn't want my daughter growing up in that."

"So why take the job in the first place?"

"I'll tell you, Angela, I've asked myself that a thousand times, and the answer's not one I'm proud of." He gave us the hapless shrug of a charming child. "The money was too good to pass up. There. I admit it. The tax break, too. I knew if I worked my tail off for five years, I'd come home with a king's ransom I could put toward my family and toward building my personal-training enterprise."

"Which you obviously did," I said. "And quite well." I was good cop, today. Maybe even kiss-ass cop. Whatever works, says I.

He looked from his kitchen bar at his living room like a modern-day Alexander with no worlds left to conquer. "So, yes, it was not the greatest idea to think I could hold a family together while I was six thousand miles away. And I own that failure. I do. But when I returned, I came home to a wife with substance abuse issues and a value system I found"—he shrug-winced—"distasteful. We fought a lot. I couldn't get Cheryl to see how destructive she was being to Sophie. And the more I tried to get her to see the truth, the more she retreated into denial. One day, I came home to an empty house." Another wince, another shrug. "I spent the next three years fighting for my rights as a father and, eventually, I won. I won."

"You got sole custody?"

He led us into the sunken living room. Brian and I took seats on the sofa, while Angie sat on the love seat across from us. On the coffee table between us was a white copper bucket filled with bottled water. Brian offered us the bottles and we each took one. The labels advertised Brian's weight-loss book.

"Once Cheryl died, I did, yes."

"Oh," Angie said, her eyes wider than usual, her jaw working to mask her frustration, "your wife died. And *then* you, uh, won custody?"

"Exactly. She contracted stomach cancer. I'll go to my grave knowing it was the drugs that did it to her. You can't abuse your body that way and expect it to continually repair itself."

I noticed that the skin closest to his eyes, where the crow's feet should have been, was whiter and tighter than the rest of his face. Circles the size of sand dollars indented the flesh. Like his wife, he'd had work done. Apparently his body didn't repair itself continually.

"So you received sole custody," Angie said.

He nodded. "Thank God they were living in New Hampshire. If it had been Vermont or here? I'd probably have had to fight another three years."

Angie looked over at me. I gave her my flattest gaze, the one I reserve for situations that make the hairs on the back of my neck stand up.

"Brian, excuse me for jumping to conclusions," she said, "but are we talking about a same-sex-marriage issue?"

"Not marriage." He placed the tip of one index finger on the coffee table and bent it until the flesh turned a pink-lemonade shade. "Not marriage. Not in New Hampshire. But, yes, a domestic partnership of that nature was being enacted in full view of my daughter. If they'd been allowed to marry, who knows how long the custody fight could have worn on?"

"Why?" I asked.

"Excuse me?"

Angie said, "Did your ex-wife's partner—?"

"Elaine. Elaine Murrow."

"Elaine, thank you. Did Elaine legally adopt Sophie?"

"No."

"She ever begin proceedings in pursuit of that?"

"No. But if they had found the right activist judge? And that's not hard around here. Who's to say they couldn't have turned my attempt to regain custody into a test-case to overturn the entire idea of biological parental rights?"

Angie gave me another careful look. "That seems a bit of a stretch, Brian."

"Does it?" He twisted the cap off his water. He took a long swig. "Well, not to me. And I lived it."

"Fair enough," I said. "So once Sophie came to live with you and you two ironed out the bumps, things were good?"

"Yeah." He placed the water bottle on the coffee table and for a moment his face glowed with some distant memory. "Yeah. For about three years, things were very good. Sure, she had some issues over the passing of her mother and the move from New Hampshire, but generally? Things were very fine between us. She was respectful, she made her bed every morning, she seemed to take to Donna, she performed well in school."

I smiled, feeling the warmth of his memories. "What'd you guys talk about?"

"Talk about?"

"Yeah," I said. "My daughter and I, we both like cameras, you know? I got this black SLR and she's got this pink baby-digital and we—"

"I mean"—he shifted a bit on the couch—"we were more about *doing* things together. Like, well, I got her jogging and doing a yoga-Pilates fusion with Donna that really helped them bond. And she used to come to the fitness center I run in Woburn. The one that started my company? That's where we broadcast our Sunday-morning show and do the mail order. She was great helping out. Just great."

"And then?"

"War," he said. "One day, no rhyme or reason to it. I'd say black, she'd say white. I'd serve chicken for dinner, she'd tell us she'd become a vegan. She started doing her chores sloppily or not at all. Once BJ was born, it got out of control."

"BJ?"

He indicated the small boy in the photos. "Brian Junior."

"Ah," I said. "BJ."

He turned to face me, his hands clasped at his knees. "I'm not a taskmaster. I only have a few rules in this house, but they're firm rules. You understand?"

"Of course," I said. "With a kid, you've got to have rules."

"So, okay." He began ticking them off on his fingers. "No profanity, no smoking, no boys over when I'm not home, no drugs or alcohol, and I'd like to know what you're doing on the Internet."

"Perfectly reasonable," I said.

"Plus, no dark lipstick, no fishnet stockings, no friends with tattoos or nose rings, no junk food, processed food, or sodas."

"Oh," I said.

"Right," he said, as if I'd said "Atta boy." He leaned forward a bit more. "The junk food contributed to her acne. I told her that, but she didn't listen. And all the sugar contributed to her hyperactivity and inability to concentrate in school. So her grades went down and her weight went up. It was a terrible example for BJ."

"Isn't he, like, three?" Angie asked.

Wide eyes and rapid nodding. "A very impressionable three. You don't think this starts early, the national obesity crisis? And then let's consider the national learning crisis we have. Angela, it's all connected. Sophie, with her self-indulgence and her constant fits of *drama,* was setting a terrible example for our son."

"She'd entered puberty, though," Angie said. "And she was in high school. Everything that does a number on a girl's head."

"Which I appreciated." He nodded. "But plenty of recent studies have shown that it's our coddling of pubescent children in this country that contributes to an extended adolescence and arrested development."

"I still can't believe they canceled that show," I said. "It was genius."

"What?"

"My bad," I said. "I was thinking of something else."

Angie would have shot me if she could have cleared the room of witnesses.

"Go on," I said.

"So, yes, Sophie was going through puberty. I get that. I get it. I do. But there are still rules to adhere to. Yes? She refused. I finally drew a line in the sand—lose ten pounds within forty days or leave the house."

Something groaned below us, something mechanical, and then we heard the heat begin venting from the baseboards.

"I'm sorry," Angie said. "I missed something. You made your daughter's food and shelter conditional on her going on a diet?"

"It's hardly that simple."

"Then I'm missing a complicated wrinkle?" Angie nodded. "So, okay, what is that wrinkle, Brian?"

"The issue was not whether I would withhold certain things if—"

"Food and shelter," I said.

"Yes," he agreed. "It was not about withholding those things if she refused to diet. It was about *threatening* to withhold those things if she didn't regain her self-respect and live up to our expectations. It was about turning her into a strong, proud, American woman with worthwhile values and authentic self-esteem."

"How much self-esteem do you gain living on the streets?" Angie asked.

"Well, I didn't think it would come to that. Obviously, I was wrong."

Angie looked off at the kitchen, then to the foyer. She blinked several times. She slipped her bag strap back over her shoulder and came off the couch. She gave me a helpless smile, her lips tight against her teeth. "Yeah, I just can't. I can't sit here anymore. I'm going to go out front and wait for you. Okay?"

"Okay," I said.

She offered her hand to a baffled Brian Corliss. "A pleasure meeting you, Brian. If you see smoke floating past your window, don't call the fire department. It's just me having a cigarette in your driveway."

She left. Brian and I sat in her wake, the heat hissing its way into the house.

"She smokes?" he said.

I nodded. "Loves cheeseburgers and Cokes, too."

"And she looks like that?"

"Like what, dude?"

"That good? She's, what, mid-thirties?"

"She's forty-*two*." I won't deny I enjoyed the look of shock on his face.

"She's had some work done?"

"God, no," I said. "It's just genes and a shitload of nervous energy. She bikes a lot, too, but she's no fanatic."

"You're saying I'm a fanatic."

"Not at all," I said. "It's your job and it's your life choice. Good for you. I hope you live to a hundred and fifty. I just notice people sometimes mistake their life choices for their moral ones."

We said nothing for a moment. We each took a drink of water.

"I kept thinking she'd come back." His voice was soft.

"Sophie."

He stared at his hands. "After a few years of her acting up while we tried to raise a *toddler*? I just thought, you know, I'd get back to old-school logic. In the old days, kids didn't have eating disorders and they didn't have ADHD and they didn't talk back or listen to music that glorified sex."

I gave that a bit of involuntary frown. "I don't think the old days were all that, man. Go listen to *Wake Up, Little Susie* or *Hound Dog* and tell me again what they were singing about. ADHD, eating disorders? Do you *remember* eighth grade? Come on, Brian. Just because it wasn't treated doesn't mean it wasn't there."

"Okay," he said. "What about the culture? You didn't have all these magazines and reality TV shows that *glorify* the stupid and the craven. You didn't have 'Net porn and instant, viral communication—without any context whatsoever—of the most insipid ideas. You weren't sold the concept that not only could you become a superstar of something, but you were *entitled* to. Forget the fact that you have no idea what that *something* is, and shelve the uncomfortable fact that you possess no talent. So what? You *deserve* everything." He looked at me, suddenly forlorn. "You have a daughter? Well, let me tell you something, we can't compete with *that*."

"That?"

"That." He pointed at his windows. "The world out there."

I followed his gaze. I considered mentioning that the World Out There didn't kick her out of her own home, the World In Here did. But I said nothing instead.

"We just can't." He let loose another gargantuan sigh and arched his back against the couch cushion to reach for his wallet. He rummaged around in it and came out with a business card. He handed it to me.

```
ANDRE STILES
Caseworker
Department of
Children & Families
```

"Sophie's DCF worker. He worked with her up until recently, I think, when she turned seventeen. I'm not sure if she still sees him, but it's worth a shot."

"Where do you think she is?"

"I don't know."

"If you absolutely, positively had to guess."

He gave it some thought as he returned the wallet to his back pocket. "Where she always is. With that friend of hers, the one you're looking for."

"Amanda."

He nodded. "I thought, at first, she was a stabilizing influence on Sophie, but then I discovered more about her background. It was pretty sordid."

"Yeah," I said, "it was."

"I don't like sordid. There's no place for it in a respectable life."

I looked at his white-on-white living room and his white Christmas tree. "You know anyone named Zippo?"

He blinked a few times. "Is Sophie still seeing him?"

"I don't know. I'm just compiling data until it makes sense."

"That's part of your job, eh?"

"That *is* my job."

"Zippo's name is James Lighter." He turned his palm up toward me. "Hence the nickname. I don't know anything else about him except that the one time I met him he smelled of pot and looked like a punk. Exactly the type of boy I would have hoped would never enter my daughter's life—tattoos everywhere, droopy pants with the boxers exposed, rings in his eyebrows, one of those tufts of hair between his bottom lip and his chin." His face had torqued into a fist. "Not a suitable human being at all."

"Do you know of any places your daughter and Amanda, and maybe even Zippo, any places they hang out that I might not know about?"

He thought about it long enough for us both to drain our water bottles.

Eventually, he said, "No. Not really."

I flipped open my notepad, found the page from earlier in the day. "One of Amanda's and Sophie's schoolmates told me Sophie and four other people went into a room. Two people in the room died, but—"

"Oh, dear God."

"—four people walked back out. Does this make any sense to you?"

"What? No. It's gibberish." He came off the couch, one hand jiggling the keys in his pocket as he rocked back and forth against his heels. "Is my daughter dead?"

I held his desperate gaze for a moment.

"I have no idea."

He looked away and then back again. "Well, that's the problem when it comes to kids, isn't it? We have no idea. Not one of us."

CHAPTER TWELVE

WHILE SHE'D BEEN SMOKING HER CIGARETTE, Angie had called 411 for the phone number of Elaine Murrow of Exeter, New Hampshire. She'd then called Elaine, who agreed to see us.

We spent the early portion of our thirty-minute drive to the Granite State in silence. Angie looked out the window at the bare brown trees along the highway, the cake frosting of last night's snow hugging the ground in quickly balding patches.

"I just wanted to go over that coffee table," she said eventually, "and gouge his fucking eyes out of his head."

"Amazing you never got invited to the debutantes ball," I said.

"Seriously." She turned from the window. "He's sitting there talking about 'values' as he sends his daughter to sleep on some bench in some bus station. And calling me 'Angela' like he fucking knows me. I hate, hate, fucking *hate* when people do that. And, Jesus, did you hear him ranting on about the dead mother's 'wholly unfit environment'? Because, what, she liked granola and watching *The L Word*?"

"You done?"

"Am I what?" she said.

"Done," I said. "Because I was there to get information on a missing girl who can lead me to another missing girl. I was doing, ya know, my job."

"Oh, I thought you were shining his shoes with your tongue."

"My other option was what? To get all self-righteous and blow up at him?"

"I didn't blow up at him."

"You were unprofessional. He could feel you judging him."

"Isn't that what they say about you at Duhamel?"

Damn. Not bad.

"But I was never a tenth as bad as you were in there."

"A tenth, huh?"

"A tenth."

"So, I'm just supposed to sit back and let an emotionally abusive parent swim in his own self-righteousness?"

"Yes."

"I can't."

"I noticed."

"I mean, is this it?" she said. "Is this the job? Did I forget it's just talking to people who make you want to scour your skin with a Brillo pad?"

"Sometimes." I looked over at her. "All right—most times."

Traffic thinned as we neared the New Hampshire border.

I picked up enough speed so that the trees along the highway turned into a brown blur.

"Trying to close out the year with one final speeding ticket?" Angie asked.

As long as my daughter wasn't in the car, I always drove fast. And Angie had long ago accepted it the way I accepted her smoking. Or so I'd thought.

"What," I said, "the fuck crawled up your ass this morning, babe?"

The silence that followed got thick enough to make me consider rolling down the windows, but then Angie slammed the back of her head against the headrest and slapped the soles of her shoes against the glove compartment, and let loose a long "Arrgggghhh." She followed it with, "I'm sorry. Okay? I truly am. You were right. I was unprofessional."

"Could you repeat that into my tape recorder, please?"

"Seriously."

"I am serious."

She rolled her eyes.

"Okay, okay," I said. "Apology accepted. And greatly appreciated."

"I really did blow it back there."

"No, you didn't. You *almost* did. But I smoothed it over. It's all cool."

"It wasn't, though."

"You haven't done this in a while. There's bound to be rust."

"Yeah." She ran her hands back through her hair. "And I'm covered in it."

"You still got those, uh, mad computer skills, though."

She smiled. "Yeah?"

"Yeah. Think you could hop on your BlackBerry and Google James Lighter?"

"Who's . . . ?"

"Zippo. Let's see if he shows up anywhere."

"Ah." She tapped the keys for a bit and then said, "Oh, he shows up all right. Shows up very dead."

"No shit?"

"No shit. He's positively ID'd as a corpse found in Allston about three weeks ago." She read it aloud to me. The body of James Lighter, 18, had been found in a field behind a liquor store in Allston the weekend after Thanksgiving. He'd been shot twice in the chest. Police had no suspects and no witnesses.

Midway through the article, his predictably shitty back story appeared: when he was six years old, his single mother gave him to a friend to babysit and never came home again. To this day, the whereabouts of Heather Lighter were unknown. Her son, James, grew up in a series of foster homes. His last foster parent, Carol "Weezy" Louise, was quoted as saying she'd always known he'd end up this way, ever since he'd stolen her car when he was fourteen.

"Steal Weezy's car," I said, "and you apparently deserve two in the chest."

"What a waste," Angie said. "A whole life adds up to . . ." She searched for the word.

"Zip," I said.

"I'M NOT GOING TO CLAIM SOPHIE was some perfect kid until her father came along and destroyed everything." Elaine

Murrow sat on a red metal couch without cushions in the center of the converted barn she used as a studio for her sculpture. We sat on red stools across from her. They were metal, too, and cushionless and about as comfortable as sitting on the mouth of a wine bottle. The barn was warm, but the sculptures kept it from being cozy; they were all metal or chrome and I wasn't sure I could recognize what they were supposed to represent. If I had to guess, I'd say most were supposed to be oversize fuzzy dice. Without the fuzz. And there was a coffee table (I think it was a coffee table) in the shape of a chain saw. Which is to say, I don't understand modern art and I'm fairly certain it doesn't understand me, so we leave it at that and try not to bother each other.

"She was an only child," Elaine said, "so she was a bit bratty and self-centered. Her mother had a flair for the dramatic, so Sophie did, too. But Brian, believe me, never gave a shit about his daughter until her mother left him. And even then, what he cared about most was getting Cheryl to return to him so he wouldn't have to live with what her rejection said about him."

"When did he begin showing serious interest in gaining custody?" I asked.

She chuckled. "When he found out *who* Cheryl left him for. He was clueless for a good six months. He thought she was living with a girl friend, not a *girlfriend*. I mean, look at me—do I look like I ever lived a straight day in my life?"

She had heavily gelled spiked hair the white of Liquid Paper. She wore a sleeveless plaid work shirt over dark jeans and brown Doc Martens. When it came to Elaine Murrow, if we were operating under the policy of Don't Ask, Don't Tell, no one would need to ask.

"Not to me," I said, "no."

"Thank you. But dipshit Brian? He didn't pick up on it at first."

"And once he finally clued in?" Angie asked.

"He'd show up here in a rage and scream at her, 'You can't be a lesbian, Cheryl. I won't accept it.' "

"*He* wouldn't accept it," Angie said, "so it must not be true."

"Exactly. Once it finally got through to him that not only was Cheryl not going back to him but that she was, in fact, very much in love with me and this wasn't some identity-crisis fling? Well . . ." She blew air out of her mouth, her cheeks puffing and unpuffing. "All Brian's rage, all his feelings of inadequacy and self-loathing, which had probably been eating at him since, I dunno, birth—guess what form they took? A moral crusade to rescue the daughter he'd never known from the clutches of an immoral lifestyle. From there on, when he'd come to pick up Sophie, he'd wear T-shirts that said charming things like GOD MADE ADAM & EVE, NOT ADAM & STEVE, or the word DE-EVOLUTION over a drawing of a man lying with a woman, followed by a man lying with a man, followed by a man lying with—wanna guess?"

"I'm betting some type of livestock."

She nodded. "A sheep." She wiped the corner of one eye. "He wore that around a child, and then he preached to us about sin."

A large dog—part collie, part who-knew—wandered into the converted barn from a dog door in the back. It ambled between the sculptures and put its chin on Elaine's thigh. She scratched the side of its face and ear.

"In the end," she said, "Brian threw everything at us. Every day was a pitched battle. Every morning, we opened our eyes and our hearts filled with dread. Just . . . dread. Would he show up at one of our jobs with a picket sign filled with biblical verse and calling us child abusers? Would he file some ridiculous order with the court based on alleged conversations he'd had with Sophie about our drinking or pot smoking or having sex openly in front of her? All it takes to turn a custody battle into—I dunno, carnage?—is someone with no love for the actual child involved. Brian would make any claim, no matter how outlandish, invent ridiculous lies and put them in Sophie's mouth. She was seven when this started. Seven. The court costs drained us financially, his ridiculous lawsuit, which he'd been told from the start didn't have a chance. I—" She realized she'd been scratching the dog's ear a little too hard. She took her hand back and it was shaking.

"Take your time," Angie said. "It's okay."

Elaine nodded her thanks and closed her eyes for a moment. "When Cheryl first complained about acid reflux, we thought, 'It figures,' given all the stress we'd been under. When she was diagnosed with stomach cancer, I remember standing in that doctor's office and picturing Brian's smug, dumb fucking face and thinking, 'Wow. The bad guys really do win.' They do."

"Not always," I said, though I wondered if I believed it.

"The night Cheryl died, Sophie and I were with her until the last breath left her body. We finally leave the hospital, and it's three in the morning, it's damp and raw out, and guess who's waiting in the parking lot?"

"Brian."

She nodded. "He had this look on his face—I'll never forget it—his mouth was turned down, his forehead furrowed so he *looked* contrite. But his eyes? Man."

"They were lit up, huh?"

"Like he'd just won the fucking Powerball. Two days after the funeral, he showed up here with two state policemen and he took Sophie away."

"Did you stay in contact?"

"Not at first. I'd lost my wife and then I lost the child I'd come to think of as my daughter. Brian forbade her to call me. I had no legal rights with regard to her, so after the second time I drove to Boston to visit her at her school during recess, he filed a restraining order."

"I changed my mind," Angie said. "I wish I'd been more judgmental on this asshole. I wish I'd kicked in his larynx."

Elaine's face cracked around a smile. "You can always make a second trip."

Angie reached out and patted her hand and Elaine squeezed my wife's fingers and nodded several times as tears fell to her jeans.

"Sophie began contacting me again when she was fourteen or so. By that point she was so confused and filled with rage and loss, it was like talking to somebody else. She lived with an asshole faux father, a trophy wife faux mother, and a spoiled prick of a half brother who hates her. So, in the logic of human nature, *I* was one of her favorite targets—Why'd I let her go? Why hadn't I done enough to save her mother? Why hadn't we moved to a state where Cheryl and I could have legally married, so I could have adopted her? Why were we fucking dykes in the first place?" She sucked a clogged breath in and let a clogged breath out. "It was brutal. All the scabs got torn off. After a while, I stopped answering her calls because I couldn't stomach the rage and recrimination for crimes I hadn't even committed."

"Don't blame yourself on that one," I said.

"Easy to say," she said. "Hard to live."

"So you haven't heard from her in a while?" Angie asked.

Elaine patted Angie's hand one last time before letting it go. "A couple times in the last year. She was always high."

"High?"

She looked at me. "High. I've been in recovery ten years. I know when I'm talking to somebody who's fucked up."

"On what?"

She shrugged. "I'd guess a hard upper. She'd get that edgy motormouth vibe cokeheads get. I'm not saying it was coke, but it was something that jacks you up."

"She ever mention Zippo?"

"Boyfriend, yeah. Sounded like a beaut. She was very proud of his connections to some Russians."

"As in the Russian mob?" Angie asked.

"That was my inference."

"Joy," I said. "How about Amanda McCready? She ever mention her?"

Elaine whistled. "The goddess? The idol? Everything Sophie wanted to be? Never met her, but she sounds . . . formidable for a sixteen-year-old."

"That's the impression we get. Sophie the type of girl who looks for a leader?"

"Most people do," Elaine said. "They wait their entire lives for someone to tell them what to do and who to be. It's all they want. Whether it's a politician they're waiting for or a spouse or a religious leader, all they really want in life is an alpha."

"And Sophie," Angie said, "found her alpha?"

"Yup." She stood from her chair. "She sure did. She hasn't called me in . . . Since July, maybe? I hope I was some help."

We assured her she was.

"Thanks for coming."

"Thanks for talking to us."

We shook her hand and followed her and the dog out of the barn and down the dirt path to our car. Dusk was settling into the bare treetops and the air smelled of pine and damp, decaying leaves.

"When you find Sophie, what will you do?"

I said, "I was hired to find Amanda."

"So you won't feel obligated to bring Sophie home."

I shook my head. "She's seventeen now. I couldn't do anything if I wanted to."

"But you don't want to."

Angie and I spoke at the same time. "No."

"Would you do me a favor *if* you do find her?"

"You bet."

"Tell her she has a place to stay. Any hour of the day. High or not. Angry or not. I don't care about my feelings anymore. I only want to know she's safe."

She and Angie hugged then in that unforced way women can pull off that eludes even those men in the world who are at ease with the bro clench. Sometimes, I give Angie shit about it. I call it the Lifetime Hug or the Oprah, but there was no easy sentiment powering this one, just a recognition, I guess, or an affirmation.

"She deserved you," Angie said.

Elaine wept silently into her shoulder and Angie held the back of her head and rocked her a bit the way she so often does with our daughter.

"She deserved you."

CHAPTER THIRTEEN

WE MET ANDRE STILES OUT FRONT of the DCF offices on Farnsworth Street and the three of us walked down along the Seaport in a light flurry to a tavern on Sleeper Street.

Once we were settled in our seats and the waitress had taken our orders, I said, "Thanks again for seeing us on such short notice, Mr. Stiles."

"Please," he said, "don't call me 'Mister.' Just call me Dre."

"Dre it is."

He was about thirty-seven or thirty-eight, brown hair cut short, the gray just finding its way along the temples and along the edges of his goatee. Well-dressed for a social worker— black cotton crewneck and dark blue jeans far nicer than anything you'd find at The Gap, black cashmere overcoat with red lining.

"So," he said, "Sophie."

"Sophie."

"You met her father."

"Yup," Angie said.

"What'd you think?"

The waitress brought our drinks. He plucked the lemon wedge out of his vodka tonic, stirred the drink, and then placed the stirrer beside the lemon wedge. His fingers moved with the confident delicacy of a pianist.

"The father," I said. "Piece of work, isn't he?"

"If by piece of work you mean douche bag, yeah, he's that."

Angie laughed and drank some wine.

"Don't sugarcoat it, Dre."

"Please, don't," Angie said.

He took a sip of his drink, chewed a chip of ice. "So many of the kids I deal with, the problem's not the kid. It's that the kid drew an asshole in the parental lottery. Or two assholes. I could sit here and be all PC about it, but I do that enough at work all day."

"Last thing we want is PC," I said. "Anything you can tell us would be greatly appreciated."

"How long you two been private investigators?"

"I've been on a five-year sabbatical," Angie said.

"Until when?"

"This morning," she said.

"You missed it?"

"I thought I did," she said. "Not so sure anymore, though."

"You?" he asked me. "How long have you been at it?"

"Too long." It unsettled me how true those words felt. "Since I was twenty-three."

"You ever think of doing anything else?"

"More and more every day. You?"

He shook his head. "This *is* my second career."

"What was your first?"

He finished his drink and caught the waitress's eye. I still had half my scotch and Angie still had two-thirds of her wine, so he pointed at his own drink and showed her one finger.

"My first career," he said. "I was a doctor, believe it or not."

Suddenly the delicate grace of his fingers made sense.

"You think it's going to be about saving lives but you find out quick it's about turnover, just like any other business. How many services can you deliver at a premium price with the lowest expenditure on supplies and labor? Treat 'em, street 'em, and upsell 'em when the opportunity presents itself."

Angie said, "And you weren't any more PC then, I take it?"

He chuckled as the waitress brought his drink. "I was fired from four hospitals in a five-square-mile area for insubordination. It's a record of some kind, I'm pretty sure. I suddenly found myself unhireable in the city. I mean, I could have moved to, I don't know, New Bedford or something. But I like the city. And I woke up one day and realized I hated my life. I hated what I was doing with it. I'd lost my faith." He shrugged. "A couple days later I saw an ad for a human services position with the DCF, and here I am."

"You miss it?"

"Sometimes. More often than not, though? Not so much. It's like any dysfunctional relationship—sure there were good things about it or else how would you get into it in the first place? But for the most part, it was killing me. Now I have regular hours, I do work I'm proud of, and I sleep like a baby at night."

"And the work you did with Sophie Corliss?"

"Confidential mostly. She came to me for help, and I tried to help. She's a pretty lost kid."

"And the reason she dropped out of school?"

He gave me an apologetic grimace. "Confidential, I'm afraid."

"I can't really get a clear picture of her," I said.

"That's because there isn't one. Sophie's one of those people—she entered adolescence with no real skills, no ambition, and zero sense of self. She's smart enough to know she has deficiencies but not smart enough to know what they are. And even if she did, what could she do about them? You can't *decide* to be passionate about something. You can't manufacture a vocation. Sophie's what I call a floater. She bobs along waiting for someone to come along and tell her where to go."

"You ever meet a friend of hers named Amanda?" Angie asked.

"Ah," he said, "Amanda."

"You've met her?"

"If you meet Sophie, you meet Amanda."

"So I've heard," I said.

"You met Amanda?"

"I knew her a long time ago when she was—"

"Ho," he said, pushing his chair back a bit. "You're the guy who found her back in the '90s. Right? Jesus. I knew the name sounded familiar."

"There you go then."

"And now you're looking a second time? A bit ironic." He shook his head at that irony. "Well, I don't know what she was like then, but now? Amanda's a real cool kid. Maybe too cool, you know? I never met anyone of any age so self-possessed. I mean, to be comfortable in your own skin is a rare quality in a sixty-year-old, never mind a sixteen-year-old. Amanda knows exactly who she is."

"And who is that?"

"I don't follow."

"We've heard about Amanda's cool from a lot of people, and you describe her as knowing exactly who she is. My question is—who is she?"

"She's whoever she needs to be. She's adaptability personified."

"And Sophie?"

"Sophie is . . . pliable. She'll follow any philosophy if it brings her closer to the group-think of the room. Amanda *adapts* to whatever the group *thinks* it wants. And she sheds it as soon as she leaves that room."

"You admire her."

"'Admire' is a little strong, but I'll admit she's an impressive kid. Nothing affects her. Nothing can change her will. And she's sixteen years old."

"That's impressive," I said. "I wish, though, that just one person I talked to mentioned something about her that was goofy or warm or, I don't know, messy."

"That's not Amanda."

"Apparently not."

"What about a kid named Zippo? You ever hear of him?"

"Sophie's boyfriend. I think his real name is, like, David Lighter. Or Daniel. I can't be positive on that one."

"When's the last time you saw Sophie?"

"Two weeks ago, maybe three."

"Amanda?"

"Around the same time."

"Zippo?"

He drained his drink. "Christ."

"What?"

"It's been three weeks on him, too. They all . . ." He looked at us.

"Vanished," Angie said.

OUR DAUGHTER CLIMBED THE JUNGLE GYM in the center of the Ryan Playground. It had been snowing since sundown. There was a foot of sand below the jungle gym but I kept my hand nearby anyway.

"So, Detective," Angie said.

"Yes, Junior Detective."

"Oh, I'm Junior Detective, huh? Wow, there really is a glass ceiling."

"You're Junior Detective for one week. After that I'll give you a promotion."

"Based on what?"

"Solid casework and a certain nocturnal inventiveness after lights-out."

"That's harassment, you cad."

"Last week that harassment made you forget your name."

"Mommy, why would you forget your name? Did you hit your head?"

"Nice," Angie said to me. "No, Mommy didn't hit her head. But you're going to fall if you don't pay attention. Watch that bar. There's ice there."

My daughter rolled her eyes at me.

"Listen to the boss," I said.

"So what'd we learn today?" Angie asked me as Gabby went back to climbing.

"We learned that Sophie is probably the girl who talked to the police and said she was Amanda. We learned Amanda is very cool and collected. We learned Sophie is not. We learned five people walked into some room, two died, but four walked out. Whatever that means. We learned that there's a kid in this world named Zippo. We learned it's possible Amanda was abducted, because no one thinks she'd run away with so much to stay in school for." I looked over at Angie. "I'm out. You cold?"

Her teeth chattered. "I never wanted to leave the house. How'd we get Edna the Eskimo for a kid?"

"Irish genes."

"Daddy," Gabby said, "catch me."

Two seconds after she said it, she pitched herself off the bar and I caught her in my arms. She wore earmuffs and a hooded pink down coat and about four layers of underclothing, including thermal leggings—so much clothing the little body wrapped inside felt like a snap pea in its pod.

"Your cheeks are cold," I said.

"No they're not."

"Uh, okay." I hoisted her up onto my shoulders and gripped her ankles. "Mommy's cold."

"Mommy's always cold."

"That's because Mommy's Italian," Angie said as we walked out of the playground.

"*Ciao*," Gabby chirped. "*Ciao, ciao, ciao.*"

"PR can't take her tomorrow—dentist—but she can take her the next couple days."

"Cool."

"So what're you going to do tomorrow?" Angie asked me.
"Watch that ice."

I stepped over the ice patch as we reached the crosswalk.
"You don't want to know."

CHAPTER FOURTEEN

ELENE McCready's current abode was, on the surface, a hell of a step up from the Dorchester three-decker apartment where, until recently, she'd seen fit to poorly raise her daughter. She and Kenny Hendricks lived at 133 Sherwood Forest Drive in Nottingham Hill, a gated community two miles off Route 1, in Foxboro. All I knew about Foxboro was that the Patriots played there eight times a year and it wasn't too far from the outlet mall in Wrentham. After I accessed those two factoids, I was out. End of list.

It turned out Foxboro was also home to half a dozen adorably named gated condo communities. En route to Nottingham Hill, I also passed Bedford Falls, Juniper Springs, Wuthering Heights, and Fragrant Meadows. All, as mentioned, gated. I couldn't understand what the gates were for, though; Foxboro had an extremely low crime rate. Other than a parking space on game day, I had no idea what they'd want to steal out here, unless there was a sudden shortage of barbecue utensils or power mowers.

The gate at Nottingham Hill wasn't hard to circumvent, since there was no gatekeeper. A sign on the kiosk read DURING DAYLIGHT HOURS, PRESS *958 FOR SECURITY. A couple of car lengths past the kiosk, the main road, Robin Hood Boulevard, forked. Four arrow signs at the left fork directed me to Loxley Lane, Tuck Terrace, Scarlett Street, and Sherwood Forest Drive. The road was straight, and what lay ahead appeared to be the kind of middle-class cookie-cutter subdivision I'd expected.

To the right, however, the arrows promised to lead me to Archer Avenue, Little John Lane, Yorkshire Road, and Maid Marian's Meeting House, but the road led only to a collection of sand mounds with a lone yellow backhoe sitting atop one. Somewhere during the Nottingham Hill development boom, the boom had lowered.

I took the left fork and found 133 Sherwood Forest Drive at the end of a cul-de-sac. The backyards around here were the same tan sand as the mounds where Maid Marian's Meeting House was supposed to stand, and both 131 and 129 were vacant, the building permits still hanging in windows speckled with sawdust. The front lawns were green, however, even in front of the vacant houses, so someone at the holding company still believed in proper upkeep. I circled the cul-de-sac, slowly enough to note that the curtains were drawn across Helene and Kenny's windows, those facing north, south, and west. The east windows faced the tan mounds of sand in the rear, so I couldn't see them. But I was willing to bet their curtains were drawn, too. On my way back up the street, I counted two more FOR SALE signs, one with a smaller sign dangling underneath that read SHORT SALE. MAKE AN OFFER. PLEASE.

I cut over to Tuck Terrace and parked by a half-finished ranch at the end of another cul-de-sac. Houses to the right and the left had been completed. They stood empty, though, the lawns and shrubs recently planted and green as shamrocks, even in December, but the driveways awaiting a paving crew. I went through the skeleton of the half-finished ranch at 133 Tuck Terrace and crossed an acre of tan sand with wooden stakes and blue yarn carving out the backyards-to-be. Soon enough I stood behind Helene and Kenny's house. It was the two-story Italianate model, a McMansion-wannabe so predictable I could smell the granite kitchen countertops and the hot tub in the master bath from the almost-backyard.

There were about forty different ways I hadn't cased the place properly. I'd driven around the front so slowly a three-legged basset hound with hip dysplasia could have lapped me. I'd parked my car in the vicinity—a block over, but still. I'd approached across open ground. I hadn't come at night. Short of standing out front with a sandwich board that read BROTHER, CAN YOU SPARE A FRONT DOOR KEY? I couldn't have made myself more conspicuous.

So the smart move would have been to walk straight past the house, hope anyone inside took me for a land surveyor or a finish carpenter, and hightail it back home. Instead, I decided the odds had been working in my favor so far—it was two in the afternoon and I hadn't seen a soul since I'd pulled into the development. It's stupid to believe in luck, but we do it every time we cross a busy street.

And mine kept holding. The sliding glass doors around back couldn't keep out Gabby. Or even me with my rusty B&E skills. I picked the lock with a keychain bottle-opener and a credit card. I entered the kitchen and waited by the door in case an alarm sounded. When none did, I jogged up the carpeted stairs to the second floor. I passed through all the bedrooms only long enough to confirm no one was in them and then worked my way back downstairs.

I counted nine computers in the living room. The closest one had a pink stickie attached that read BCBS, HPIL. The next one had a yellow stickie: BOA, CIT. I tapped the keyboard of the first computer and the screen pulsed softly. For a moment, I saw a screen saver of the Pacific, and then the screen turned lime green and a quartet of animated figures with the heads of the cast of *Diff'rent Strokes* danced across the screen. A speech bubble appeared by Willis's head and a cursor blinked. Arnold said, "Whachoo talkin' 'bout, Willis?" Kimberly was sparking a blunt when she rolled her eyes and said, "Password, dickhead." A stopwatch appeared in the thought bubble above Mr. Drummond's head. It ticked down from ten as Kimberly did a striptease and Arnold changed into a security guard's uniform and Willis hopped into a convertible and immediately crashed it. As it burst into flames, the clock above Mr. Drummond's head exploded and the screen went black.

I called Angie.

"The entire cast of *Diff'rent Strokes*?"

"Now that you mention it, Mrs. Garrett wasn't there."

"Must have been the *Facts of Life* years," she said. "Whatta you got?"

"Computers with password protections. Nine of them."

"Nine passwords?"

"Nine computers."

"That's a lot of computers for a living room with no furniture. Did you find Amanda's room yet?"

"No."

"See if there's a computer there. Kids are less likely to password-protect."

"Okay."

"If you can get on, just get me an IP address, and the incoming and outgoing servers. Most people, no matter how many computers they've got, use just one server. If I can't hack it, I know someone who can."

"Who *do* you meet online?"

We hung up and I went upstairs to the bedrooms. Helene and Kenny's was as expected—Bob's Furniture dresser and chest covered in wrinkled clothes, box spring on the floor, no nightstands, several empty beer cans on one side of the bed, several empty glasses sporting some sort of sticky residue on the other side. Ashtrays on the floor, wall-to-wall carpeting already soiled.

I passed through the master bathroom, gave the hot tub a smile, and entered the next bedroom. It was tidy and empty. The faux-walnut dresser, chest, matching bed and nightstand all looked cheap but respectable. The drawers were empty, the bed was made. The closet was two dozen empty hangers, evenly spaced.

Amanda's room. She'd left nothing behind but hangers and the sheets on the bed. On the wall, she'd left a framed Red Sox jersey, signed by Josh Beckett, and a Just Puppies calendar. It was the first hint of sentiment I could attach to her. Otherwise, all I got was the same impression of precision I'd been getting off her trail from the beginning.

The bedroom across the hall was another story. It looked like someone had tossed it in a blender, pressed STIR, and then removed the cap. The bed hid under a patchwork of comforter, blanket, jeans, sweater, sweatshirt, denim jacket, capri cargo pants. The dresser sported open drawers and a vanity mirror. Sophie had tucked photographs into the left and right sides of the mirror, between the glass and the frame. Several were of a boy in his late teens. Zippo, I assumed. He usually wore a Sox cap turned sideways. A stripe of hair extended from ear to ear like a chin strap and a matching tuft of hair sprouted from the space between his lower lip and chin. Tats on the side of his neck and silver rings protruding from his eyebrows. In most of the photos, he had his arm around Sophie. In all of them, he was brandishing a beer bottle or a red plastic cup. Sophie wore big smiles but she seemed to be trying them out, looking for one that fit what she thought people were looking for. Her eyes seemed sensitive to light—in every photo she looked one step from squinting. Her tiny teeth peeked out uncertainly from her smile. It was hard to imagine her happy. Tucked above and below the photos were club postcards for dates long past—last spring and early summer, mostly. All the venues were over-21 clubs.

Sophie definitely cultivated an over-21 look. But you couldn't overlook the baby fat that hung, pupa-like, from the underside of her chin or covered her cheekbones. Any club let her in knowing she was underage. Most of the photos were of her and Zippo; two were of her and other girlfriends, none of whom I recognized and none of whom was Amanda, though both photos had been cropped on the left-hand side, amputating Sophie's shoulder at the point where it had presumably touched someone else's.

I tossed the rest of the room and found some pills I didn't recognize, with a holistic-medicine vibe to the labels. I snapped photos of them with my Droid and moved on. I found several wristbands, enough to suggest a fetish for wristbands or a purpose. I took a closer look at them. Most of them were stacked in a pile on the upper shelf of the closet, but a few were strewn in with the general mess.

I pulled all the covers off the bed and pushed the clothes out of the way and found the laptop waiting for me, the power light blinking. I flipped it open and was greeted by a screen saver of Sophie and Zippo, flashing the universal two-fingered "gangsta" sign, which immediately defined them as white non–gang members. I double-clicked on the Apple icon in the top left corner of the screen and worked my way into the main control panel without a single password prompt. There I discovered the IP server info Angie required. I copied it all onto my Droid and texted it to her.

I clicked back to the main screen and then clicked on the mail icon.

Sophie wasn't a big deleter. Her inbox had 2,871 messages dating back over a year. Her SENT folder contained 1,673 messages, also dating back over a year. I called Angie and told her what I'd found. "With the IP info, you can hack this?"

"Candy from a baby," she said. "How long have you been in there?"

"I don't know. Twenty minutes."

"That's a lotta time to be in the house of people who don't have predictable work schedules."

"Yes, Mom."

She hung up.

I put everything back the way I'd found it and worked my way downstairs. In the dining room, I found a cardboard box filled with mail on the card table in the center of the room. Nothing out of the ordinary about the mail—utility bills mostly, some credit-card bills and bank statements—until I looked at the names and addresses of the recipients. None of them lived here. There was mail for Daryl Bousquet in Westwood, Georgette Bing in Franklin, Mica Griekspoor in Sharon, Virgil Cridlin in Dedham. I thumbed through the stack and counted nine more names, all living in nearby towns—Walpole, Norwood, Mansfield, and Plainville. I looked through the portico into the living room at the bank of computers. A barely furnished house, what furniture there was from a discount wholesaler, and no sense that anyone intended to make this a ten-year abode. Nine computers. Stolen mail. If I had another hour, somewhere I'd find birth certificates for babies who'd died decades ago. I'd bet every dime I had on it.

I looked at the mail again. Why so stupid, though? Why password-protect the computers but forget to turn on the house alarm? Why pick a perfect spot to do this kinda shit—in a house at the end of a cul-de-sac in a stalled development—and leave stacks of stolen mail in a box?

I looked around the kitchen, found nothing but empty cabinets and a fridge filled with Styrofoam take-out containers, beer, and a twelve-pack of Coke. I closed a cabinet and remembered what Amanda's classmate had said about the microwave.

I opened it and stared inside. It was a microwave. White walls, yellow light, circular heating tray. I was about to close it when I got a strong whiff of something acrid and I took another look at the walls. They were white, yes, but there was an extra layer of white. When I tilted my head and adjusted my eyes, I saw the same film on the yellow bulb. I found a butter knife and scraped one of the walls very lightly, and what came off was a fine powder, as white and light as talc.

I closed the microwave door, returned the knife to its drawer, and went back into the living room. That's when I heard the front door knob turn.

I hadn't been face-to-face with her in eleven years. I'd kind of liked it that way. But here she was, four steps into her living room when her eyes locked on mine. She'd gained weight, mostly in the hips and the face, the sides of her neck. Her skin was splotchier. Her cornflower eyes, always her most attractive feature, remained so. They widened under her feather-cut ginger hair, the roots showing gray by the crown, and her mouth opened into a tight, wrinkled oval, then formed a hesitant P.

It wasn't like I could claim I was here to fix the garbage disposal. I gave her what I'm sure was a hapless smile, held out my arms, and shrugged.

She said, "Patrick?"

"How you doing, Helene?"

CHAPTER FIFTEEN

KENNY CAME IN BEHIND HER. He looked confused for about half a second before he reached behind his back. I reached behind mine.

He said, "Ho."

I said, "Hey."

A young girl came in behind him. She opened her mouth wide but no sound came out. She wrung her hands by her side as if she'd stepped on the third rail. I got a good look as she stepped hard to her left to get out of our line of fire. Sophie Corliss. She'd lost the weight her father had demanded of her. And then some. She was gaunt and sweaty and stopped acting electrified long enough to sink her hands into the back of her head and pull at her own hair.

I held out one hand. "This does not have to go this way."

"What way?" Kenny said.

"The way where we both pull our guns."

"You tell me, sport, which other way this can go."

"Well," I said, "I could remove my hand from my gun."

"But I might just shoot you for your trouble."

"There's that," I agreed.

"And if I remove my hand?" He frowned. "It's the same result, different victim."

"If we did it at the same time?" I offered.

"You'd cheat," he said.

As I nodded, he cleared his gun and pointed it at me.

"Sneaky," I said.

"Let me see the hand."

I removed my hand from behind my back and held up my cell phone.

"It's nice," Kenny said, "but I think mine has more bullets."

"True, but did your gun call anyone?"

He took a step forward and then another. My screen read HOME. CONNECTED: 39 SECONDS.

"Oh," he said.

"Yeah."

Helene said, "Fuck," very softly.

"You put the gun down or my wife calls the police and gives up our location."

"Let's—"

"Tick, tock," I said. "It's fairly obvious you're ripping identities and committing a few thousand levels of consumer fraud here. Plus you're making crank somewhere nearby and then you're baking the used coffee filters in the microwave just to squeeze out that little extra. You want the police en route within, oh, thirty more seconds, keep holding the gun on me, Kenny."

Angie's voice came through the cell phone. "Hi, Kenny. Hi, Helene."

Helene said, "Is that Angie?"

"It is," Angie said. "How you doing?"

"Oh," Helene said, "you know."

Kenny frowned and looked terribly tired all of a sudden. He thumbed the safety forward and handed me the gun. "You're one frustrating motherfucker."

I put the gun, an S&W Sigma 9mm, in the pocket of my jacket. "Thank you." I turned my lips toward the phone. "Catch you later, honey."

"Grab some bottled water on the way home, would you? Oh, and some half-and-half for the morning."

"Sure. Anything else?"

Kenny rolled his eyes.

"Yeah, but I can't remember what it is."

"Well, call me when you think of it."

"Cool. Love you."

"Love you, too."

I hung up.

"Sophie?" I said.

She looked over at me, surprised I knew her name.

"You carrying?"

"Huh?"

"A gun, Sophie. Are you carrying a gun?"

"No. I hate guns."

"Me, too," I said.

"But you've got one in your pocket."

"That's called irony. How strung out are you right now?"

"Oh, I'm not bad," Sophie said.

"You look bad."

"Who *are* you?"

"That's Patrick Kenzie." Helene lit a cigarette. "He found Amanda that time?"

Sophie hugged herself and fresh beads of sweat popped on her forehead.

"Helene?" I said.

"What?"

"I'd feel a lot better if you put that bag you're carrying on that couch and step away from it."

She placed the bag on the couch and came back over to Kenny's side.

"Let's all go in the dining room."

We sat at the card table and Kenny fired up a cigarette while I got a closer look at Sophie. She kept running her tongue behind her upper lip, back and forth, back and forth. Her eyes rolled right to left, left to right, right to left like they were on ball bearings. It was forty-two degrees outside and she was sweating.

"I thought you were going to let this go," Kenny said.

"You thought incorrectly."

"She won't pay you."

"Who?"

"Bea."

"Or Amanda," Helene said. "She doesn't come into her money for, like, another year."

"Well, then, it's settled," I said. "I quit. But since we're on the subject, where's Amanda?"

"She went to visit her father in California," Helene said.

"She has a father in California?" I said.

"She didn't come out of a cereal box," Helene said. "She had a mother and a father."

"What's her father's name?"

"Like you don't remember."

"From a case I worked twelve years ago, Helene? No, I don't remember."

"Bruce Combs."

"But his friends call him B Diddy?"

"What?"

"Never mind. Where's Bruce live?"

"Salinas."

"And that's where Amanda flew into?"

"Yeah."

"Which airport?"

"Salinas Airport."

"Salinas doesn't have a commercial airport. You mean she flew into either Santa Cruz or Monterey."

"Yeah."

"Which one?"

"Santa Cruz."

"Yeah, they don't have a commercial airport, either. So there goes your dumbass Salinas story, Helene."

Kenny exhaled a chuck of cigarette smoke and looked at his watch.

"You got someplace to be?"

He shook his head.

Behind him, Sophie fidgeted and kept looking at a spot over my head. I turned, saw the clock on the wall. I caught Helene looking at it too.

"You don't have someplace to be," I said to Kenny.

"No."

"You're supposed to be here," I said.

"Now you're getting it."

"Someone's coming a-calling."

A tight nod followed by a rapping on the sliding glass door behind us.

I turned in my chair as Kenny said, "Punctual fuckers, I'll give 'em that."

The two guys on the other side of the glass weren't particularly tall but they were poster boys for stocky. They both wore black leather car coats. The one on the left had belted his at the waist, the other left his open. They both wore turtlenecks—the one on the left wore a white one. His partner's was baby blue. The one on the left had a black beard, the one on the right had a blond one. They both had full heads of hair and bushy eyebrows and mustaches thick enough to misplace a purse in. The one on the left knocked again and gave a little wave and smiled a big, toothy smile. Then he tried the door. He cocked his head when he couldn't open it and looked back through the glass at us, his smile beginning to fade.

Helene shot from her chair and unlocked the door. The darkhaired guy pulled it back. He entered in a rush and took her face in his hands and said, "Miss Helene, how are you today?" and gave her a kiss on the forehead. He released her face as if he were shot-putting it, and Helene stumbled backward a step. He clapped together a pair of massive hands as he entered the dining room and gave us all another big smile. His companion shut the door behind him and strolled into the room lighting a cigarette. Both of them had long hair, parted down the middle, à la Stallone circa 1981, and even before the dark-haired one had spoken, I'd pegged them for Eastern Europeans—whether they were Czechs, Russians, Georgians, Ukrainians, or, hell, Slovenians was beyond my ear at the moment, but their accents were as thick as their beards.

"How are you, my friend?" the dark-haired one asked me.

"Not bad."

"Not bad!" He seemed to love that. "Then that is good, yes?"

"You?" I said.

He gave my question a happy jerk of his eyebrows. "I am great, my main man. I am super-duper."

He sat in the chair Helene had vacated and slapped my shoulder. "You do business with this man?" He jerked his thumb at Kenny.

"Occasionally," I said.

"You should stay away from him. He big trouble, this one. He bad guy."

Kenny said, "No."

The dark-haired guy nodded earnestly at me. "You can trust me. You see what he do to this poor girl?" He pointed at Sophie, who stood against the fridge, shaking and sweating all the more. "Little girl, and he give her a big drug habit. He a real piece of shit."

"I believe you," I said.

He widened his eyes at that. "You should believe me, guy. He's crazy cowboy, this one. He doesn't listen. He breaks deals."

Kenny said, "If you just tell Kirill we're looking. We're *looking*. It's all we do."

The guy hit my chest lightly with the back of his hand, wildly amused. "'Tell Kirill.' You ever hear a thing so dumb? Hey? *Tell* Kirill. Like a man tell Kirill anything. A man ask Kirill. A man beg Kirill. A man go to his knees before Kirill. But tell Kirill?" He turned away from me and bore in on

Kenny. "Tell him what, piece of shit? Tell Kirill you *looking*? You searching? You out there, guy, beating the hedges to find his property?" He reached out and took a cigarette from the pack Kenny had left on the table. He lit it with Kenny's lighter and then threw the lighter in his lap. "Kirill says to me this morning, he says, 'Yefim, wrap this up. No more waiting. No more junkie bullshit.'"

Kenny said, "We are *this* close. We know almost where she is."

Yefim knocked over the table. I barely saw his arm move but the table was suddenly not in front of us anymore or, more important, not between Yefim and Kenny. "I fucking tell you, guy, not to fuck this up. You make us money, yeah yeah yeah. You always deliver, yeah yeah yeah. Well, you didn't fucking deliver this for Kirill, my man. And more, you didn't deliver this for Kirill's wife and she have her heart set on this. She's . . ." He snapped his fingers a couple times and then looked back over his shoulder at me. "What you say, my friend, when someone finds no happiness in life anymore and no one can change that?"

"I'd say they're inconsolable."

The smile that blew across his face was the kind movie stars give on red carpets—that much wattage, that much charm.

"Inconsolable!" He gave me a thumbs-up. "You right on that, my good friend, thank you." He turned back to Kenny, then changed his mind and looked back at me. He spoke very softly. "No, really. Thank you."

"You're welcome."

"You a good fucker, man." He patted my knee and then turned away. "Violeta, Kenny? She's inconsolable, guy. That's what she is. She's inconsolable, and Kirill, he love her so crazy, man, now *he's* inconsolable. And you, you're supposed to fix that. But you don't."

"I'm trying."

Yefim leaned forward, his voice soft, almost gentle. "But you don't."

"Look, ask anyone."

"Who I ask?"

"Anyone. I'm out there looking. It's *all* I do."

"But you don't," he said again, even softer this time.

Kenny said, "Just give me a couple more days."

Yefim shook his bison head. "A couple more days. Pavel, you hear him?"

The blond guy who stood behind Kenny said, "I hear him."

Yefim pulled his chair closer to Kenny. "You teach Amanda what she know. So, how she get the drop on you?"

"I taught her what she knows," Kenny agreed. "But I didn't teach her *all* she knows."

"She smarter than you, I think."

"Oh, she's smart," Helene said from the doorway. "She's all A's in school. Last year, she even got—"

"Shut up, Helene," Kenny said.

"Why you talk to her like that?" Yefim said. "She's your lady. You should show more respect." He turned to Helene. "You tell me—what did Amanda get? She get some award?"

"Yeah," Helene said, drawing the word out into three syllables. "She got gold ribbons in trig, English, and computer science."

Yefim slapped Kenny's knee with the back of his hand. "She got gold ribbons, man. What you get?"

Yefim stood and dropped his cigarette on the rug and

ground it out with the toe of his work boot. He lifted the table off the floor and righted it. He and Pavel looked at each other for a solid minute, neither of them blinking, just breathing through their noses.

"You have two days," Yefim said to Kenny. "After that, you were your mother's dream, guy. You understand?"

Kenny said, "Yeah, yeah. Absolutely. Yeah."

Yefim nodded. He turned and held out his hand to me and I shook it. He looked in my eyes. His were a liquid sapphire and reminded me of a candle flame slipping under the surface of melting wax. "What's your name, my friend?"

"Patrick."

"Patrick"—he placed a hand to his chest—"I am Yefim Molkevski. This is Pavel Reshnev. Do you know who Kirill is?"

I wished I didn't.

"I assume you mean Kirill Borzakov."

He nodded. "Very good, my friend. And who is Kirill Borzakov?"

"He's a businessman from Chechnya."

Another nod. "A businessman, yes. Very good. Though he's not from Chechnya. You're a Slavic businessman in this country, everybody thinks you Chechen or"—he spit on the carpet—"Georgian. But Kirill, like me and Pavel, is Mordovian. We take the girl."

"What?" I said.

Pavel crossed the dining room and grabbed Sophie off the wall. She didn't scream, but she wept a fair amount, shaking hands held up by her ears like she was trying to ward off wasps. Pavel's free hand remained in the pocket of his car coat.

Yefim snapped his fingers and extended his palm in my direction. "Give to me."

" 'Scuse me?"

All the light drained from his eyes. "Patrick. Dude. You so smart up to now. Stay smart, guy." He wiggled his fingers. "Come. Give me the gun in your left pocket."

Sophie said, "Let me go," but there was no heat in it, only resignation and more tears.

Pavel was turned all the way toward me, hand in his pocket, awaiting instruction. If Yefim sneezed, Pavel would put a bullet in my brain before anyone could say, "Gesundheit."

Yefim wiggled his fingers again.

Holding the grip by two fingers, I removed the handgun from my jacket pocket and handed it to Yefim. He placed it in his coat pocket and gave me a small bow. "Thank you, dude." He turned to Kenny. "We take her. Maybe we have her make us another one. Maybe we test Pavel's new gun on her, yes? Shoot her many times."

Sophie shrieked through her tears and it came out strangled and wet. Pavel hugged her tighter to him but seemed otherwise unconcerned.

"Either way," Yefim said to Kenny and Helene, "she is ours now. She is not yours ever again. You find the other girl. You find Kirill's property. You return it to us by Friday. Do not screw the poop on this one, piece of shit."

He snapped his fingers and Pavel dragged Sophie past me and past Helene and over to the sliding glass doors.

Yefim gave my shoulder a fist chuck. "Be well, my good friend." On his way out of the dining room, he grasped Helene's face in his hands and gave her another hard kiss on the forehead and another push backward. This time she fell on her ass.

His back to us, he held up a finger. "Don't make a asshole of me, Kenny. Or I make a big asshole of you."

And then they were gone. Within a few seconds, a truck engine came to life and I got to the kitchen window in time to see a Dodge Ram bump out into the untilled mounds behind the house.

"Do you have another gun?" I said.

"What?"

I looked at Kenny. "Another gun."

"No, man. Why?"

He was lying, of course, but I didn't have time to argue. "You're some kind of douche, Kenny."

He shrugged and lit a cigarette and then yelled, "Hey," when I swiped his car keys off the granite countertop in the kitchen and ran out the front door.

A yellow Hummer sat in the circular drive. The poster child for How Detroit Got It Wrong. An utterly useless behemoth that got such piss-poor mileage the Sultan of Brunei might be embarrassed to drive it. And we were shocked when GM came asking for a bailout.

I had the Dodge Ram in sight for half a minute as I climbed into the Hummer. It bounced across the field, up one furrow, down another, Pavel's blond hair distinct behind the wheel. When they bounced out of the field, they went east toward the entrance gate, and I lost sight of them, but I figured I had at least a fifty percent shot of them heading for Route 1. When I barreled out of Sherwood Forest Drive and back up Robin Hood Boulevard, I saw their tire tracks had turned right out of the entrance toward Route 1. I goosed the gas as much as I could, but I didn't want to overdo it and ride up their ass.

I almost did anyway. I came over a rise on the country road I'd been zipping along, and there they were at the bottom, sitting at a red light in front of a combination grocery store/post office. I tried to bring my speed down as casually as possible, while keeping my head down like I was consulting a map on my seat, but trying to look inconspicuous in a yellow Hummer is like trying to look inconspicuous walking naked into a church. When I looked up again, the light had turned green and they punched the gas and took off at a good speed, though not tires a-screaming.

In another mile, they reached Route 1 and headed north. I gave it thirty seconds and pulled on. Traffic wasn't thick, but it wasn't thin, either, and I easily dropped back several car lengths and over two lanes. When you're trying to stay undercover in a yellow Hummer, every little bit helps.

Only a suicide takes on Russian guns. And I liked life. A lot. So I had no intention of doing anything but keeping a soft tail on them until I saw where they took Sophie. Soon as I had an address, I'd make a 911 call and be done with this.

And that's what I told my wife.

"Get off their tail," she said. "Now."

"I'm not on their tail. I'm five cars back, two lanes over. And you know how good I am on a tail."

"I do. But they could be better. And you're fucking driving a yellow fucking *Hummer*. Just get their license plate, call it in, and drive away."

"You think they're driving a car registered with the RMV? Come on."

"You come on," she said. "These guys are a whole different level of dangerous. *Bubba* thinks the Russian mob is too crazy to deal with."

"As do I," I said. "I'm just going to observe and report. They kidnapped a teenage girl, Ange."

At that moment, my daughter called, "Hi, Daddy," from somewhere in the background.

"You want to talk to her?" Angie asked.

"That's low," I said.

"I never said I fight fair."

I passed Gillette Stadium on my right. Without a game being played inside, it looked large and alone. There was a mall beside it, a few cars in the parking lot. Up ahead, Pavel turned on his right blinker and drifted over into the far right lane.

"I'll be home soon. Love you," I said and hung up.

I moved over one lane, then another. There was only a red PT Cruiser between the Hummer and their Ram, so I kept the distance to a hundred yards.

At the next intersection, the truck turned right on North Street and then took an immediate right into a lot filled with tractor trailers backed up to a long, white distribution terminal. From the road, I could see the Ram drive down a dirt path alongside a row of tractor trailers and then take a left toward the back of the terminal.

I pulled into the lot and followed. To my right stood a retaining wall by the Route 1 overpass. Beneath the overpass, freight train lines and commuter rails fed north into the city or south toward Providence. To my left were the tractor trailers backed into their receiving bays. In one receiving bay, a few beefy guys pushed through thick strips of plastic to load boxes onto a trailer with Connecticut plates.

At the end of the path, the rail lines stretched off to my right while the brown dirt road curved to the left. I curved left around the terminal. The pickup truck sat in the middle of the path about fifteen yards away. Its parking lights were on. The engine idled. The passenger door was wide-open.

Yefim hopped off the passenger seat, screwing a suppressor onto the end of a semiautomatic handgun. In the time it took me to compute this, he walked five paces and extended his arm. The first shot punched a puckered hole in my windshield. The next four shots took out my front tires. The tires were just starting to hiss when the sixth shot added another puckered hole to the windshield. The hole sprouted veins. The veins widened, and the windshield crackled like popcorn in a microwave. Then it collapsed. Two more shots ripped up the hood, though I couldn't be positive of either the number or their locations, because I was curled on the front seat, covered in windshield.

"Hey, guy," Yefim said. "Hey, guy."

I shook some glass out of my hair and off my cheeks.

Yefim leaned into the Hummer, his elbows on the window frame, the pistol and silencer dangling from his right hand. "License and registration."

"Good one." I eyed that pistol.

"No good one," he said. "Serious request. License and registration." He tapped the silencer against the side of the window frame. "Right fucking now, guy."

I sat up and searched for the registration. Eventually, I found it tucked into the visor. I handed it to him, along with my driver's license. He took a long look at them and handed the registration back.

"It's registered to piece-of-shit Kenny. Piece-of-shit Kenny drives piece-of-shit fag-yellow Hum-vee. I knew it wasn't yours. You too classy, man."

I brushed some windshield pebbles off my coat. "Thank you."

He fanned the air with my driver's license and then put it in his pocket. "I keep this. I keep it, Patrick Kenzie of Taft Street, so you remember. So you know that I know who you are and where you live with your family. You have family, yes?"

I nodded.

"Go to your family, then," he said. "Give them big hugs."

He rapped the door with the gun one last time and walked back to the pickup truck. He climbed in, shut the door, and they drove away.

CHAPTER SIXTEEN

ONE POSITIVE THING I LEARNED about a Hummer—bitch didn't drive too bad with its front tires blown out. As a few brave truckers and freight loaders worked their way out of the nearest loading bays, I backed the Hummer up twenty yards, pinned the wheel, and then popped it into drive and headed for the train tracks. Those front tires were slap-slap-slapping away as the men shouted at me but nobody gave chase; an SUV sporting eight fresh bullet holes tends to diminish the desire to confront its owner.

Or, in this case, its driver. Kenny was its owner, and Kenny was fucked when the police found the car and saw who it was registered to. Not my problem, though. I drove it down the freight train tracks a couple hundred yards to a depot that led to the parking lot of Gillette Stadium. The only cars nearby were parked by the executive offices of One Patriot Place. The fan parking areas were barren for a couple hundred yards until you reached the shopping center next door. That's where I drove the yellow Hummer. As I drove, I wiped. I used a handkerchief on the seat, the steering wheel, and the dashboard. I'm quite sure I didn't get every fingerprint I'd left, but I didn't have to. No one was going to get all *CSI* on the interior when it was registered to an ex-con who lived within two miles of the stadium.

I parked on the outer fringe of the mall lot and took the escalator into the movie theater. It was Cinema De Lux, so I could have enjoyed table service from the balcony and paid $20 to watch a movie that would be on DVD for a buck in three months, but my mind was elsewhere. I found a bathroom with a handicapped stall and its own sink. I closed the door and removed my jacket and shook all the glass from it. I did the same with my shirt and then I used a wad of paper towels to push all the glass into one corner of the stall. I put my shirt back on, doing my best to ignore the tremors in my hands, but it was hard to do so when my fingers shook so much I couldn't get the buttons into their holes. I gripped the sink and bent at the waist and took a dozen long, slow breaths. Every time I closed my eyes, I saw Yefim walking toward me, casually extending his arm, casually firing into the windshield, casually ending my life if the situation had called for it. I opened my eyes. I stared at my reflection in the mirror and splashed some water on my face and stared at myself a little longer until my reflection looked a bit more in command of itself. I splashed some water on the back of my neck and tried to button my shirt again. My hands still shook but not as violently, and eventually I made do. Five minutes later, I left the bathroom looking a little bit better than when I'd entered.

I went back down the escalator. A dark green cab sat out front of the theater. I hopped in and gave the driver the address of the house two doors over from where I'd left my car. A security guard was parked behind the Hummer, roof lights flashing. As we exited the parking lot, a Foxboro Police cruiser passed us. Kenny was almost out of time.

The cab dropped me in front of the house on Tuck Terrace. I left the driver a solid tip but not so solid he'd be able to pick me out of a lineup. I walked to the house as he backed onto the road. I pretended to put a key in the front door as he pulled forward and then rode up the street. I walked over to the house where I'd left my Jeep. Back through the half-finished ranch, back across the field of sand, and I was once more at Kenny and Helene's sliding glass door. It was unlocked, and I let myself in and stood watching as Kenny added the laptops to a duffel bag on the floor and Helene packed up the cable modems.

Kenny noticed me. "You got my keys?"

I patted my pockets and was surprised to find them. "Here you go." I tossed him the keys.

He zipped the duffel bag and lifted it off the floor. "Where's it parked?"

"Yeah," I said slowly, "about that."

"I CAN'T BELIEVE YOU KILLED my ride," Kenny said as we drove past the empty Nottingham Hill security kiosk in my Jeep.

"I didn't kill it. Yefim did."

"I can't believe you just fucking left it."

"Kenny, your Hummer looks like the bus at the end of *The Gauntlet*. The only way it was reaching your house was by U.N. airlift."

We came to the same stoplight where I'd almost run into Yefim and Pavel's truck. A small armada of Foxboro Police cruisers came tear-assing down the road from the other direction. Kenny and Helene dropped in their seats as the cruisers blew through the red light, sirens a-rage. In another fifteen seconds, all four cruisers had disappeared over the rise behind us as if they'd never existed at all. I looked at Kenny, crammed under my glove compartment.

"Subtle," I said.

"We don't like calling attention to ourselves," Helene said from the backseat.

"Which is why you drive a yellow Hummer," I said as the light turned green.

On Route 1, we passed the stadium again. The Hummer was surrounded by local and state police, a black-panel crime scene truck, and two news vans. Kenny looked at the state of it—the blown tires, the shattered windshield, the shot-up hood. Another news van pulled into the lot. A helicopter flew overhead.

"Shit, Kenny," I said, "you're big-time."

"Please," he said, "can't you let a man grieve in peace?"

WE STOPPED IN DEDHAM, BACK BEHIND the Holiday Inn at the intersection of Route 1 and Route 1A.

"Okay," I said. "In case you haven't figured it out, you two are screwed. I saw you grab the computers, but I'm sure you left something behind in the house that'll tie you to all the wonderful fraud and identity theft you've been up to. Not to mention the meth dust in the microwave. I'm only half as smart as most cops at this, so let's assume they'll have you two charged

by midday and will be out on the prowl with no-knock war-
rants by dinnertime."

"You're such a bad bluffer." Helene lit a cigarette.

"You think?" I reached over the backrest, took the cigarette
out of her mouth and flicked it out the window past Kenny's
face. "I got a four-year-old, you moron. She rides in this car."

"So?"

"So, I don't want her going to the playground smelling like
a Newport."

"Touchy, touchy."

I held out my hand to her.

"What?"

"Gimme the pack."

"Nigger, please."

"Gimme the pack," I repeated.

Kenny sounded weary. "Give it to him, Helene."

She handed over the pack. I slid it into my pocket.

"So," Kenny said, "you got a solution for us?"

"I dunno. Tell me what Kirill Borzakov wants with
Amanda."

"Who said he wants Amanda?"

"Yefim did."

"Oh, right."

"So what's Amanda got that they could want?"

"She ripped a load, took it on the run with her."

I made the sound of an NBA buzzer when the shot clock
runs out. "Bullshit."

"No, he's serious." Helene, all wide-eyed.

"Get out of my car."

"No, listen."

I reached across Kenny and pushed his door open. "See ya."

"No, really."

"Really. We've got less than two days to trade whatever Amanda's got for Sophie. Now I know you don't give a shit about the life of a teenage girl, but I'm kind of a dinosaur that way, and I do."

"So go to the police."

I nodded as if that made perfect sense. "Testify in open court against the Russian mob." I scratched my chin. "By the time it's safe for my daughter to leave Witness Protection, she'll be fifty-fucking-five." I looked at Kenny. "No one's going to the cops."

"Can I have my cigarettes back?" Helene said. "Please."

"You going to smoke in my ride?"

"I'll open the door."

I tossed them back over the seat to her.

"So where's this leave us?" Kenny said.

"What I said—we need to make a trade. The more you two dick me around on what exactly it is they want from Amanda, the less chance Sophie will be in anything less than three or four pieces by the time Friday rolls around."

"And we told you," Kenny said, "Amanda ripped off their—"

"It's a piece of fucking jewelry," Helene said. She opened the back door wide and placed one foot on the ground as she lit her cigarette. She blew the smoke out past the door and gave me a look like *Satisfied?*

"Jewelry."

She nodded as Kenny closed his eyes and rested his head against the seat. "Yeah. Don't ask me what it looks like or how she got it, but she stole this, what, crucifix?"

"Well, it's not a crucifix," Kenny said. " 'Least I don't think so. They keep calling it a 'cross.'" He shrugged. "That's all we know."

"And you don't know how this cross got into her possession?"

Another head shake. "Nope."

"So you have no idea how Amanda might have had the opportunity to put her hands on this cross, or why she was hanging out with the Russian mob. Is that what you're selling?"

"We don't smother her," Helene said.

"What?"

"Amanda," Helene said. "We let her make her own decisions. We're not up her ass all the time. We show her respect as a person."

I looked out the car window for a bit.

After the silence went on a bit too long, Helene said, "What're you thinking?"

I looked over the seat at her. "I'm thinking how I've never had the impulse to hit a woman in my life, but you get me in an Ike Turner frame of mind."

She flicked her cigarette into the parking lot. "Like I haven't heard that before."

"Where. Is. She."

"We. Don't. Know." Helene bulged her eyes at me like a pissy twelve-year-old, which, in terms of emotional development, wasn't far off the mark.

"Bullshit."

Kenny said, "Man, I taught that girl how to create new identities so tight she could join the CIA. Obviously, she created a few I didn't know about and now she's running around with one of those identities. And she's got a flawless fucking social security card and birth certificate, I assure you. And once you got those, you can create a ten-year credit history in about four hours. And once you've done *that*? Shit. The country's one big ATM."

"You told Yefim you were close."

"I woulda told that ice-blood motherfucker anything he needed to hear, long as it got him to leave my kitchen."

"So you're not close."

He shook his head.

I looked at Helene in the rearview. She shook her head.

We sat in silence again for a bit.

"Then what good are you?" I said eventually and started the Jeep. "Get out of my car."

I WAS SCHEDULED TO HAVE a beer with Mike Colette, my friend who owned the distribution warehouses. He'd hired me to discover which of his employees was embezzling, and I'd found an answer he wasn't going to like. I thought of canceling the meeting, because I was still a hair shaky from the eight bullets that had been fired in my direction, but we'd agreed to meet in West Roxbury and I was already over on that side of town, so I called his cell and told him I was on my way.

He sat at one of the bar tops by the window at West on Centre and gave me a wave as I came through the door, even though he was the only guy at the tables. He'd been like that since we'd met at UMass, an earnest, solid guy of entrenched decency. I never met a soul who didn't like him. The logic among our friends was if you didn't like Mike, it said nothing about him but everything about you.

He was a small guy with close-shorn curly black hair and the kind of handshake that you could feel in every bone of your body. He gave it to me when I reached the table and I was so distracted I hadn't prepared for it. I damn near ended up on my knees and I was pretty sure carpal tunnel set in immediately.

He pointed at the beer in front of my chair. "Just ordered it for you."

"Thanks, man."

"Get you anything? Appetizer or something?"

"Oh, no, I'm fine."

"Sure? You look a little off, man."

I took a sip of beer. "I had a run-in with some Russians."

He drank from his own frosted mug, his eyes wide. "They're a fucking menace in the trucking business, man. I mean, not all Russians, but Kirill Borzakov's crew? Whew. Stay away from those guys."

"Too late."

"No shit?" He put his beer on the coaster. "You had a run-in with Borzakov's guys?"

"Yup."

"Kirill's not just a thug, man, he's an out-of-his-fucking-mind thug. You heard he got another DUI?"

"Yeah, last week."

"Last *night*." Mike pushed a folded *Herald* across the table at me. "And this one beats all."

I found it on page 6: "'Butcher' Borzakov's Bezerko Blowup." He'd taken his Targa into a Danvers car wash. Half-way through the service, he'd apparently become impatient. This was bad news for the car that sat ahead of his in the wash. Kirill rammed it. The car was propelled out of the wash, but the engine of Borzakov's Targa seized up. Police found him in the parking lot, covered in suds as he tried to attack one of the

Panamanians who worked the gas pumps with a wiper blade he'd snapped off his own car. He was Tasered and taken to the ground by four staties. He posted first-quarter NBA numbers on the Breathalyzer and the staties also found a half-gram of cocaine in his seat console. It took him all the way to dinnertime to make his bail. In the sidebar, they ran the names of the four men whose deaths he was suspected of ordering this past year.

I folded the paper. "So it's not the fact that he's a killer that should bother me, it's that he's a killer having some kind of psychological meltdown?"

"For starters." He placed an index finger to his nose. "I hear he's dipping into his own supply."

I shrugged. Man, was I sick of this shit.

"Patrick, no offense, but you ever think of doing something else?"

"You're the second person to ask me that today."

"Well, I could be in the market for a new manager after this lunch, and you did work in trucking all through college, if I remember."

I shook it off. "I'm good. Thanks, Mike."

"Never say never," he said. "All I'm saying."

"I appreciate that. Let's talk about your case."

He folded his hands together and leaned into the table.

"Who do you think is embezzling from you?"

"My night manager, Skip Feeney."

"It's not him."

His eyebrows went up.

"I thought it was him, too. And I'm not saying he's a hundred percent trustworthy. My guess is he takes a box off a

truck every now and then. If you went to his house you'd probably find stereo equipment that matched missing shipments,
that kind of thing. But he's only able to fuck with the shipping manifests. He's not able to get to invoices. And, Mike, the
invoices are the key. In some cases, you're being double- and
triple-billed for shipments that don't originate with you and
don't arrive at their destinations because they don't exist."

"Okay," he said slowly.

"Someone ordering five pallets of Flowmaster mufflers.
That sound right to you?"

"Yeah, that's about right. We'll sell them all by July, but
if we waited until April to order them, the price would be another six, seven percent higher. It's a smart risk, even if it eats
a little space."

"But you've only got four pallets in the warehouse. And
the invoice reads 'four.' But the payment was for five. And I
checked—they shipped five." I pulled a notepad from my laptop
bag and flipped it open. "What can you tell me about Michelle
McCabe?"

He sat back in his chair, his face drawn.

"She's my accounts-receivable manager. She's the wife of a
buddy of mine. A good buddy."

"I'm sorry, man. I am."

"You're sure?"

I reached back into the laptop bag, came out with my case
file. I slid it across the table to him. "Go through the top twenty
invoices. Those are the dirty ones. I attached the invoices the
companies received so you can compare."

"Twenty?"

"Could be more," I said, "but those are the ones would
hold up in any court if she ever sued you. Or if she files a griev-

ance with the Labor Board, throws any sort of wrongful termi-
nation shit at you. If you want to have her arrested—"

"Oh, no."

Of course that would be his reaction.

"I know, I know. But *if* you did, all the proof you need is
right there. At the very least, Mike, you should consider making
her pay restitution."

"How much?"

"This past fiscal year alone? She took you for twenty thousand minimum."

"Jesus."

"And that's just the stuff I found. A true auditor, knowing
where to look, who knows what he'd find?"

"This economy, and you're telling me I got to shitcan my
accounts-receivable manager *and* my floor manager?"

"For different reasons, but yeah."

"Christ."

We ordered two more beers. The place began to fill up; the
traffic outside thickened on Centre Street. Across the street,
people pulled up in front of the Continental Shoppe to pick
up their dogs from a day's grooming. While we sat there, I
counted two poodles, one beagle, one collie, and three mutts.
I thought of Amanda and her thing for dogs, the only trait I'd
heard ascribed to her that sounded soft, humanizing.

"Twenty thousand." Mike looked like someone had swung
a bat into his stomach, then slapped him in the face while he
was doubled over. "I ate dinner at their house last week. We
went to the Sox a couple times last summer. Christ, two years
ago, she'd just started for me? I gave her an extra thousand as
a Christmas bonus because I knew they were about to get their
car repo'd. I just . . ." He raised his hands above his head and

brought them back down helplessly behind his skull. "I'm forty-four years old and I don't understand anything about people. I just don't get them." He brought his hands back to the table. "I don't understand," he whispered.

I hated my job.

CHAPTER SEVENTEEN

I T HAD BEEN A FEW HOURS since my encounter with Yefim and I still couldn't shake it. Back in the day, I would have manned up with a drink or six, maybe called Oscar and Devin so we could meet at some dive to out-understate one another when it came to violent encounters.

Oscar and Devin had retired from the BPD several years ago, though, and bought a failing bar together in Greenwood, Mississippi, where Oscar's people hailed from. The bar was just up the street from Robert Johnson's purported grave site, so they'd turned it into a blues club. Last I heard, it was still failing, but Oscar and Devin were too drunk to care, and the Friday-afternoon barbecues they threw in their parking lot were already the stuff of local legend. They were never coming back.

So there went that outlet for me. Not that it was much of an outlet. What I really wanted was just to get back home. Hold my daughter, hold my wife. Shower off the smell of my fear. I was planning to do just that, taking the Arborway over toward Franklin Park so I could cut through to my side of town, when my cell rang and I saw Jeremy Dent's name on the caller ID.

"Fuck me," I said aloud. I had *Sticky Fingers* in my CD player, turned up loud, the way *Sticky Fingers* should always be played, and I was right at the point in "Dead Flowers" where I always sang along to Jagger getting goofy with the words "Kentucky Derby Day."

I turned down the music and answered my phone.

"Merry Almost Christmas," Jeremy Dent said.

"Merry Almost Festivus," I said back.

"You got a minute to drop by the office?"

"Now?"

"Now. I got a yuletide present for you."

"Really."

"Yeah," he said, "it's called a permanent job. Like to discuss?"

Health insurance, I thought. Day care, I thought. Kindergarten. College fund. A new muffler.

"On my way."

"See you soon." He hung up.

I was halfway through Franklin Park. If I hit the lights on Columbia Road just right, I would reach home in about ten minutes. Instead, I banged a left onto Blue Hill Avenue and headed back downtown.

"RITA BERNARDO TOOK A JOB in Jakarta, of all places." Jeremy Dent leaned back in his chair. "Booming security business there these days, all those wonderful jihadists—bad for the world but great for our bottom line." He shrugged. "So, anyway, she's off to keep Indonesian discos from blowing up and that opens up a slot we'd like to offer you."

"What's the catch?"

He poured himself a second scotch and tilted the bottle toward my glass. I waved it off. "No catch. Upon further evaluation, we came to the conclusion that your investigatory skills, not to mention your experience in the field, are assets too valuable to pass up. You can start right now."

He pushed a folder across his desk and it cleared the edge and landed on my lap. I opened it. Clipped to the inside cover was a photo of a young guy, maybe thirty years old. He looked vaguely familiar. A slim guy with dark, tightly coiled hair, a nose that fell just a half-inch short of beakish, and a café-au-lait complexion. He wore a white shirt and a thin red tie and held a microphone.

"Ashraf Bitar," Jeremy said. "Some call him Baby Barack."

"Community organizer in Mattapan," I said, recognizing him now. "Fought that stadium plan."

"He's fought a lot of things."

"Loves the camera," I said.

"He's a politician," Jeremy said. "By definition that makes him an Olympic-level narcissist. And don't let the Mattapan roots and the Mattapan address fool you. He shops at Louis."

"On what? Sixty K a year?"

Jeremy shrugged.

"So what do you need?"

"A microscope on his whole fucking life."

"Who's the client?"

He sipped his scotch. "Immaterial to your efforts."

"Okay. When do you need me to start?"

"Now. Yesterday. But I told the client tomorrow."

I took a sip from my own glass of scotch. "Can't do it."

"I just offered you a permanent position with this firm, and you're already being difficult?"

"I had no idea this was in the wind. I had to take a case to put food on the table. I can't walk away in the middle of it."

He gave a slow, that-doesn't-concern-me blink. "How long before you can divest yourself?"

"Couple more days."

"That puts us at Christmas."

"Yeah, it does."

"So let's say you free up by Christmas, can I tell our client you'll close his case"—he pointed at the folder—"by New Year's?"

"*If* I'm done with my current case by Christmas, sure."

He sighed. "How much they paying you, your current client?"

I lied. "A fair wage."

I CAME HOME WITH FLOWERS I couldn't afford and Chinese takeout I couldn't afford, either. I took the shower I'd been fantasizing about all afternoon and changed into a pair of jeans and a T-shirt from Pela's one and only concert tour, then joined my family for dinner.

After we ate, we played with Gabby. Then I read to her and put her to bed. I came back into the living room and told my wife about my day.

Once I'd finished, Angie went straight to the porch for an

American Spirit Light. "So the Russian mob has your driver's license."

"Yes."

"Which means they know our home address."

"Said information usually appears on a driver's license, yes."

"And if we tell the police they kidnapped a young girl . . ."

"They would be perturbed with me," I agreed. "Did I mention the part where Duhamel offered me a permanent position?"

"A thousand times," she said. "So you're going to walk away. As in, right now."

"No."

"Uh, yes."

"No. They kidnapped a seventeen—"

"—year-old girl. Yes. I heard you. I also heard the part where they shot the shit out of a car you were driving and took your license so they could come here if they felt like it and kidnap *our* child. So, I'm sorry about the seventeen-year-old girl, but I've got a four-year-old girl right here who I'm going to protect."

"Even at the cost of another life."

"You're damn right."

"This is bullshit."

"This is not."

"Yes, it is. *You* asked me to take this case."

"Lower your voice. Okay, yes, I asked you to—"

"Knowing what it did to me the last time I searched for Amanda. What it did to us. But you were all about the greater good. And now that the greater good is biting us in the ass and another kid is in danger, you want me to pack it in."

"We're talking about our daughter's safety."

"But that's not *all* we're talking about. We're in this now. You want to take Gabby and go see your mom, I think that's a great idea. They're dying to see each other. But I'm going to find Amanda and I'm going to get Sophie back, too."

"You'd choose this case over—"

"No. Don't try that shit on me. Do not."

"Volume control, please."

"You know who I am. You knew the minute you convinced me to do what Beatrice asked that I would never stop until I found Amanda again. And now you want to tell me it's over? Well, it's not. Not until I find her."

"Find who? Amanda? Or Sophie? You can't even differentiate anymore."

Both of us had reached one step below atomic and we knew it. And we knew how bad it would get if we took the next step. Marry an Irish temper to an Italian temper and you often get broken dishes. We'd done a little counseling just before our daughter was born, to help us keep our hands off the nuke button when the air in the silo got too tight, and most times, it helped.

I took a breath. My wife took a breath and then a drag off her cigarette. The air on the porch was cold, bracing even, but we were dressed for it and it felt good in my lungs. I let out a long breath. A twenty-year breath.

Angie stepped in close to my chest. I wrapped my arms around her and she placed her head under my chin and kissed the hollow below my throat.

"I hate fighting with you," she said.

"I hate fighting with you."

"Yet we manage to disagree fairly often."

"That's because we like making up so much."

"I *love* making up," she said.

"You and me both, sister."

"YOU THINK WE WOKE HER?"

I went to the door that separated our bedrooms and opened it, watched my daughter sleep. She didn't sleep on her stomach so much as on her upper chest, head turned to the right, butt sticking up in the air. If I looked in two hours from now, she'd be on her side, but pre-midnight, she slept like a penitent.

I shut the door and came back to bed. "She's out."

"I'm going to send her."

"What? Where?"

"To see my mom. If Bubba will take her."

"Call him. You know exactly what he'll say."

She nodded. It was barely a question, really. Angie could tell Bubba she needed him yesterday in Katmandu and he'd remind her that he was already there. "How's he going to get weapons on a plane?"

"It's Savannah. I'm quite sure he has connections there."

"Gabby'll love to see her nonnie, that's for sure. She's been talking about it nonstop since the summer. Well, that and trees." She looked over at me. "You good with that?"

I looked at her. "These are bad fucking people I'm going to take on. And, like you said, they know where we live. I'd put her on a plane tonight, if I could. But what about you? You're going to put the spurs on again, join me on the wagon trail?"

"Yeah. Might speed the process up."

"Sure. But what's the longest you've been away from Gabby since we had her?"

"Three days."

"Right. When we went to Maine and you whined about missing her the whole friggin' time."

"I didn't *whine*. I stated the obvious a few times."

"And then restated it. That's called whining."

She slapped my head with a pillow. "Whatever. Anyway, that was last year. I've matured. And she's going to love this— going on an adventure to see her nonnie with Uncle Bubba? If we told her tonight, she'd never have fallen asleep." She rolled on top of me. "So what's your immediate plan?"

"Find Amanda."

"Again."

"Again. Trade the cross she stole for Sophie. Everyone goes home."

"Who says Amanda's going to give it up?"

"Sophie's her friend."

"The way I've heard it, Sophie's her Robert Ford."

"I don't know if it's that bad." I scratched my head. "I don't know a lot, though. Which is why I've gotta find her."

"How, though?"

"Question of the month."

She reached across my body and grabbed my laptop bag off the floor. She opened it, pulled out the file marked A. Mc-CREADY and opened it on the pillow to the right of my head. "These are the shots you took of her room?"

"Yeah. No, not those—those are of Sophie's room. Keep going. Those there."

"Looks like a hotel room."

"Pretty impersonal, yeah."

"Except for the Sox jersey."

I nodded. "Know what's weird? She isn't a fan. She never

talked about the team or went to Fenway or wondered aloud what Theo was thinking when he made the Julio Lugo deal or traded Kason Gabbard for Going Going Gagne."

"Maybe it's just Beckett."

"Huh?"

"Maybe she's just got a crush on Josh Beckett."

"Why do you say that?"

"Well, that's his jersey, right? Number 19. Why are you whiter than usual suddenly?"

"Ange."

"What?"

"It's not the Red Sox she's obsessed with."

"No?"

"And she doesn't have a crush on Josh Beckett."

"Yeah, he's not my type either. So why the jersey?"

"Twelve years ago, where'd we find her?"

"At Jack Doyle's house."

"And where was that?"

"Some little Podunk town in the Berkshires. What was it, like, fifteen miles from the New York border? Twenty? They didn't even have a coffee shop."

"What was the name?"

"Of the town?"

I nodded.

She shrugged. "You tell me."

"Becket."

"GIVE DADDY A HUG."

"No."

"Sweetie, please."

"No, I said."

We were in tantrum mode. Standing in the C Terminal of Logan, Bubba and Gabby with their tickets in hand, a surprisingly light security check-in line awaiting them, and Gabby pissed off at me like only a four-year-old can get pissed off. The arm-folding, the foot-stomping, the whole deal.

I knelt by her and she turned her head. "Sweetie, we talked about this. Throwing a tantrum in the house is what?"

"Our problem," she said eventually.

"And what's throwing a tantrum outside our house?"

She shook her head.

"Gabriella," I said.

"Our embarrassment," she said.

"Exactly. So give your old man a hug. You can be mad at me, but you still have to give me a hug. That's our rule. Right?"

She dropped Mr. Lubble and jumped on me. She held on so tight her thumb knuckles dug into my spine and her chin dug into the side of my neck.

"We'll see you real soon," I said.

"Tonight?"

I looked at Angie. Christ.

"Not tonight. But real soon."

"You're always going away."

"No suh."

"Yes suh. You go away at night and you're gone when I get up in the morning times, too. And you're taking Mommy away, too."

"Daddy works."

"Too *much*." She had a catch in her voice that suggested another meltdown was imminent.

I propped her in front of me. She looked in my eyes, a tiny-doll version of her mother. "This is the last time, honey. Okay? Last time I go away. Last time I send you away."

She stared at me, eyes and lips bubbling. "Swear."

I held up my right hand. "I swear."

Angie knelt beside us and kissed our daughter. I stepped back and let them have their own moment, which was even more emotionally fraught than mine.

Bubba stepped in close. "She going to cry on the plane, make a scene, shit like that?"

"I doubt it," I said. "But if she does and anyone gives you a dirty look, you have my permission to bite them. Or at least growl at them. And if you see any Russians giving her funny looks—"

"Man," he said, "anyone gives that kid a funny look? Their eyes will end up on the ground looking back up at their head as I cut it off their fucking neck."

ON THE OTHER SIDE OF SECURITY, they looked back at us, Bubba holding Gabby up by his shoulder as he lifted their bags off the conveyor belt. They waved.

We waved back, and then they were gone.

PART III
THE BELARUS CROSS

CHAPTER EIGHTEEN

THE CLOUDS HUNG LOW UNDER a pale sky as we exited the Mass Pike and followed the line on the map toward Becket. The town lay twenty-five miles south of the New York border in the heart of the Berkshires. This time of year, the hills were sprinkled with snow and the damp roads were black and slick. Becket had a main road but no Main Street. It had no town center we could find, no one-block strip containing a general store, a hairdresser, a Laundromat, and the local Realtor. Neither, as Angie had noted, did it have a coffee shop. For any of that, you had to go to Stockbridge or Lenox. Becket had houses and hills and trees and more trees. An amoeba-shaped pond the color of cream soda. More trees, the tops of some half-hidden in the low clouds.

We drove around Becket and West Becket all morning—up, down, all four points of the compass, and back again. Most of the roads in the hills dead-ended, so we got several curious or hostile looks as we pulled up to someone's property and then had to back out the way we'd come, wheels crunching gravel. But none of those curious or hostile faces belonged to Amanda.

After three hours of this, we broke for lunch. We found a diner a few miles away in Chester. I ordered a turkey club, no mayo. Angie ordered a cheeseburger and a Coke. I sipped my bottled water and pretended I didn't really want her meal. Angie rarely watches what she eats and has the cholesterol issues of a newborn. I eat fish and chicken ninety percent of the time and have the high LDL levels of a retired sumo wrestler. Life, it's so fair that way. There were eight other patrons in the place. We were the only people not wearing boots. Or plaid. The men all wore ball caps and jeans. A couple of the women wore the kind of sweaters you get at Christmas from elderly aunts. Parka vests were popular.

"How else to get the lay of the land?" I asked Angie.

"Local newspaper."

I looked around for a newspaper but didn't spy one, so I did my best to catch the counter girl's attention.

She was about nineteen. A pretty face had been damaged by acne scars and she wore an extra forty pounds on her frame like a threat. Her eyes were dull with anger disguised as apathy. If she kept on her current path, she'd grow into the type of person who fed her kids Doritos for breakfast and purchased angry bumper stickers with lots of exclamation points. But right now, she was just another in a long line of pissed-off small-town girls with a shitty outlook. When I finally flagged her down and asked if there was a newspaper behind the counter, she said, "A what?"

"A newspaper."

Blank stare.

"A newspaper," I said. "It's like a home page without a scroll button?"

Stone face.

"The front page usually has pictures on it and, you know, words below those pictures. And sometimes? Pie charts in the lower left corner."

"We're a restaurant," she said, as if that explained everything. Then she went over and leaned against the counter by the coffeemaker and began texting on her cell.

I looked over at the guy nearest to me, but he was engrossed in his meat loaf. I looked at Angie. She shrugged. I swiveled my stool and spotted a wire rack by the door that held some kind of printed matter. I crossed to it and discovered the top rack offered a real estate monthly while the lower rack held brochures of the region. Nothing fancy on the outside—local ads mostly. When I opened it, though, we were greeted with a color map. The gas stations were labeled, as were the summer stock theaters and antique shops, the outlet mall in Lee and the glassworks in Lenox, places that sold Adirondack chairs and others that sold quilts and spools of yarn.

We found Becket and West Becket on the map easily enough. A school we'd passed on a hill this morning was, I learned, the Jacob's Pillow Dance School, the pond we'd passed a few dozen times was apparently unnamed. Otherwise, the only attractions labeled in Becket were the Middlefield State Forest and McMillan Park, which contained, within its environs, Paw Prints Pet Park.

"Dog park," Angie said just as I was noticing it. "Worth a stab in the dark."

The counter girl plopped Angie's cheeseburger on the coun-

ter and then placed the turkey club in front of me with a weary
drop of her hand and disappeared into the back before I could
mention that I'd asked for no mayo. While we'd been looking at the map, most of the patrons had cleared out. We were
alone except for a middle-aged couple who sat by the window
and stared out at the road rather than at each other. I walked
two stools over and found myself a knife and fork wrapped
in a paper napkin and I used the knife to scrape most of the
mayo off my bread. Angie watched me, bemused, and then
went back to her cheeseburger. As I bit into my sandwich, the
short-order cook disappeared from behind the kitchen cut-in.
A door opened somewhere out back and shortly thereafter I
could smell cigarette smoke and hear him talking in low tones
to the counter girl.

My sandwich sucked. Turkey so dry it was chalky. Rubbery
bacon. Lettuce that browned as I watched. I dropped it on my
plate.

"How's your burger?"

Angie said, "Awful."

"Why you still eating it?"

"Boredom."

I looked at the check left behind by Miss Charm School
Graduate—sixteen bucks for two crap lunches delivered by a
crappier personality. I left a twenty under the plate.

"You are *not* tipping her," Angie said.

"Of course I am."

"But she doesn't deserve it."

"No, she doesn't."

"So . . . ?"

"All the years I waited tables before becoming a PI?" I said.
"I'd tip Stalin."

"Or his granddaughter, apparently."

We left the money, took the map, and walked out.

McMILLAN PARK CONTAINED A BASEBALL field, three tennis courts, a large playground for school-age kids and a smaller, more brightly painted one for toddlers. Just past that were the two dog parks—the one for small dogs formed a fenced-in oval within the park for larger dogs. Someone had put a lot of thought into the park—it was strewn with tennis balls and had four water fountains that also fed large metal dog bowls at their bases. Several lengths of thick rope, the kind you'd use to tie off a boat, lay on the ground. It was good to be a dog in Becket.

It was the middle of the afternoon, so it wasn't terribly populous. Two guys, one middle-aged woman, and an elderly couple tended to two Weimaraners, a Labradoodle, and a pretty yippy corgi who bossed the other three dogs around.

No one recognized Amanda from the photo we passed around. Or maybe no one wanted to recognize her in front of us. Private investigators don't get much benefit of the doubt anymore. People often consider us just one more symbol of the End of All Privacy Age. And it's hard to argue the point.

The two guys with the Weimaraners did note that Amanda looked a little like the girl in the *Twilight* movies, if not in the hair and the cheekbones, then in the nose and the forehead and the close-set eyes, but then they got into an argument over whether said actress was a Kristen or a Kirsten, and I wandered over to the middle-aged woman before it devolved into a Team Edward vs. Team Jacob imbroglio.

The middle-aged woman was smartly dressed but you could

have stored loose change in the pockets under her eyes. The top third of the index and middle fingers of her right hand were yellowed by nicotine and she was the only one in the park who kept her dog, the Labradoodle, on a leash. Her teeth gritted every time he jerked against her hold, and the other three dogs taunted him.

"Even if I knew her," the woman said, "why would I tell you? I don't know you."

"But if you did," I assured her, "you'd think I was the cat's pajamas."

She gave me an unblinking stare that felt twice as hostile if only because there was nothing overtly hostile about it. "What'd this girl do?"

"Nothing," Angie said. "She's just missing from home. And she's only sixteen."

"I ran away at sixteen," the woman said. "I came back after a month. To this day, I don't know why I did. I could've stayed out there."

When she said "out there," she chin-gestured past the area where a group of mothers and toddlers gathered around the smaller playground, past the parking lot, and past the hills that rose and were subsumed into the great blue mass of the Berkshires. On the other side of that mountain range, the gesture seemed to say, a better life had waited.

Angie said, "This girl could very much regret running away. Harvard was waiting for her. Yale. Wherever she wanted to go."

The woman yanked on her dog's leash. "So she could, what, enter some cubicle at a slightly higher rate of pay? Hang her fucking Harvard diploma on the partition wall? She spends the next thirty-forty years learning how to short stock and steal people's jobs and houses, their 401(k)s? But that's okay because *she went to Harvard*. Sleeps like a baby at night, tells herself she's not to blame, it's the system. Then one day she finds a lump in her breast. And it's not okay anymore, but nobody gives a shit, honey, because you made your fucking bed. So do us all a favor and fucking die."

The woman's eyes were red by the time she finished and her free hand shook as she reached into her purse and came back with a cigarette. The air in the park felt raw. Angie looked like she was in minor shock. I'd taken one step back from the woman and both the gay couple and the elderly couple were staring at us. The woman had never raised her voice, but the rage she'd expelled into the atmosphere had been so torn and pitiable it rattled us all. And it wasn't rare. Quite the contrary. You asked a simple question lately or made an innocuous aside and suddenly you were the recipient of a howl of loss and fury. We no longer understood how we'd gotten here. We couldn't grasp what had happened to us. We woke up one day and all the street signs had been stolen, all the navigation systems had shorted out. The car had no gas, the living room had no furniture, the imprint in the bed beside us had been smoothed over.

"I'm sorry" was all I could think of to say.

She put the shaky cigarette to her lips and lit it with a shaky Bic. "Don't know what you're sorry for."

"I just am," I said.

She nodded and gave me and then Angie a soft, helpless look. "It just sucks. You know? This whole raw deal they sell us."

She bit her lower lip and dropped her eyes. Then she and her Labradoodle walked off toward the gate that led out the back of the park.

Angie lit her own cigarette as I approached the elderly couple with the photo of Amanda. The man gave it a glance, but the woman wouldn't even meet my eyes.

I asked her husband if he recognized Amanda.

He gave the photograph another glance and then shook his head.

"Her name's Amanda," I said.

"We're not much on names here," he said. "It's a dog park. That woman who just left? She's Lucky's Owner. We don't know her name beyond that, but we know she had a husband once, a family, but she doesn't have them anymore. Couldn't tell you why exactly. Just that it's sad. My wife and me? We're Dahlia's Owners. Those two gentlemen? They're Linus's and Schroeder's Owners. You, though? You're just the Two Assholes Who Made Lucky's Owner Sadder. Good day to you."

They all left. They walked out the side entrance to the park and congregated on the sidewalk. They opened their car doors and their dogs hopped in. We stood in the dog park without a dog, feeling ever the fools. There was nothing to say, so we just stood there as Angie smoked her cigarette.

"I guess we should go," I said.

Angie nodded. "Let's use that gate, though."

She indicated the gate on the other side of the dog park and we turned toward it, because we didn't want to exit past this group who suddenly despised us. The far gate led into the children's area and then the sidewalk beyond, where we'd parked our car.

A different group congregated here—mothers and their

children and their baby carriages and sippy cups and formula
bottles and diaper bags. There were half a dozen women and
one guy. The guy wore jogging clothes and stood by a jogging
stroller slightly away from the group as he drank continuously
from a water bottle the length of my leg. He seemed to be mod-
eling for the women and they seemed to be enjoying it.

Except for one. She stood a few feet away, closest to the
short fence that separated the children's park from the dog park.
She'd strapped her infant to her chest in a Björn, the baby's back
to her chest so the baby could look out at the world. The baby
wasn't interested in the world, though, she was interested in
squalling. She calmed down for a second when the mother put
a thumb in her mouth, but then, when she realized it wasn't the
nipple or the pacifier or the bottle she'd been looking for, the
howling started again and her body shook like she was being
electrocuted. I remembered when Gabby had behaved exactly
the same way, how helpless I'd felt, how utterly useless.

The woman kept looking over her shoulder. I assumed she'd
sent someone for the bottle or the pacifier and was wondering
where the hell they were. She bounced on her feet and the baby
bounced with her but not enough to stop screaming.

The mother's eyes met mine and I was about to tell her it
gets better, a lot better, but then her small eyes narrowed and
mine did, too, both of our mouths opening. The hair on top of
my head grew damp.

We hadn't seen each other in twelve years, but there she
stood.

Amanda.

And her baby.

CHAPTER NINETEEN

S HE COULDN'T RUN. Not with a baby strapped to her chest. Not with a stroller and a diaper bag to retrieve. Even if she had track-star speed and Angie and I had blown ACLs, she'd still have to get in the car, turn over the engine, and strap the baby in all at once.

"Hey, Amanda."

She watched me come. She didn't wear that hunted look worn by a lot of people who don't want to be found. Her gaze was level and open. The baby sucked her thumb into her mouth, having decided, I guess, that it was better than nothing, and Amanda used her other hand to stroke the top of the baby's head where thin wisps of light brown hair formed swirls.

"Hi, Patrick. Hi, Angie."

Twelve years.

"How you doing?" We reached the fence between her and us.

"Oh, you know."

I nodded at the baby. "Pretty girl."

Amanda gave the baby a tender glance. "She is, right?"

Amanda was pretty herself, but not in the way of models or beauty pageant contestants—her face had too much character, her eyes too much knowledge. Her slightly crooked nose was in perfect symmetry with her slightly crooked mouth. She wore her long brown hair down and heat-straightened so that it framed her small face and made her seem even smaller than she was.

The baby squirmed a bit and groaned, but then she went back to sucking Amanda's thumb.

"How old is she?" Angie asked.

"Almost four weeks. This is the first time she's been outside for any real amount of time. She liked it up until she started screaming."

"Yeah, they do a lot of screaming at that age."

"You have one?" She kept her eyes on the baby, fed her a bit more of her thumb.

"A daughter, yeah. She's four."

"What's her name?"

"Gabriella. Yours?"

The baby closed her eyes—from Armageddon to serenity in under two minutes. "Claire."

"Nice," I said.

"Yeah?" She gave me a smile that was wide and shy at the same time, which made it twice as charming. "You like it?"

"I do. It's not trendy."

"I hate that, right? Kids named Perceval or Colleton."

"Or remember the Irish phase?" Angie asked.

A nod and a laugh. "All the kids named Deveraux and Fiona."

"I know a couple, lived up off the Ave.?" I said. "Named their kid Bono."

A great laugh, sharp enough to jostle the baby. "No, they didn't."

"No, they didn't," I admitted. "I keed."

We were quiet for a moment, the smiles gradually dying on our faces. The mothers and the jogger paid us no attention, but I noticed a man standing in the park halfway between the playground and the road. His head was down and he walked in a slow circle, trying really hard, it appeared, not to look our way.

"That would be the daddy?" I said.

She looked over her shoulder, then back at me. "That would."

Angie squinted. "Seems a bit old for you."

"I was never interested in boys."

"Ah," I said. "What do you tell people—he's your father?"

"Sometimes. Sometimes uncle. Sometimes older brother." She shrugged. "Most times people assume what suits them and I don't have to say anything."

"He's not missed back in the city?" Angie said.

"He had some vacation time coming." She waved at him, and he stuffed his hands in the pockets of his jacket and began trudging across the field toward us.

"What'll you do when vacation time runs out?"

Another shrug. "Fall off that bridge when we come to it."

"And this is what you want—to build a life up here in the Berkshires?"

She looked around. "It's as good a place as any and better than most."

"So you remember some of this place," I said, "from when you were four?"

Those clear eyes pulsed. "I remember all of it."

That would include the wailing, the crying, the arrest of two people who'd loved her deeply, the social worker who'd had to wrench Amanda from the arms of those people. Me standing there, the cause of it, watching.

All of it.

Her boyfriend reached us and handed her the pacifier.

"Thanks," she said.

"No problem." He turned to me. "Patrick. Angie."

"How you doing, Dre?"

THEY LIVED JUST A MILE from the dog park on the main road in a house we'd passed at least a dozen times that morning. It was a Craftsman Foursquare, the stucco painted a dark tan that contrasted nicely with the off-white trim and the copper-colored stone porch supports. It was set back off the road a few yards, a wide sidewalk bordering the houses along that stretch of road in such a way that it felt more small-town than country. Across the street was a strip of common grass and then a small access road and a white-steepled church with a brook running behind it.

"It's so quiet here," Amanda said as we exited our cars and met on the sidewalk, "that sometimes the gurgling of the brook keeps you up at night."

"Yikes," I said.

"Not a nature enthusiast, I take it," Dre said.

"I like nature," I said. "I just don't like to touch it."

Amanda lifted Claire out of her car seat and said, "Would you mind?" and handed her to me. She came back out with the diaper bag and Dre pulled the stroller out of the back of their Subaru and we headed up the walk to the house.

"I can take her," Amanda said.

"I got her for a sec," I said. "If that's okay."

"Sure."

I'd forgotten how small a newborn was. She weighed, at most, eight and a half pounds. When the sun broke between two clouds and hit us, she scrunched up her face until it looked like a head of cabbage, her tight fists covering her eyes. Then her fists fell away and her face unscrunched and her eyes opened. They were the color of good scotch and they looked up at me with startled wonder. They didn't just ask, Who are you? They asked, *What* are you? What is this? Where am I?

I remembered Gabby having that look. Everything was unknown and unnamed. There was no "normal," no frame of reference. No language, no self-awareness. Even the concept of a concept was unknown.

The startled wonder turned to confusion as we crossed the threshold into the house and the light changed again and her face darkened with it. She had a gorgeous face. Heart-shaped, chubby-cheeked, those butter-toffee eyes, her mouth a rosebud. She looked like she'd grow into a stunner. Spin heads, halt hearts.

But as she began to fuss and Amanda took her from my arms, it also occurred to me that however she looked, she didn't look anything like Amanda or Dre.

"So, Dre," I said when we were all sitting in the living room by a hearth of smooth gray stone.

"So, Patrick." He wore dark brown jeans, a pearl henley beneath a navy blue pullover with an upturned collar, and a dark gray fedora on his head. He fit in up in the Berkshires about as well as a fire. He pulled a pewter flask from the inside pocket of his jacket and took a small sip. Amanda watched him return the flask to his pocket with something that resembled disapproval. She sat on the other end of the couch and rocked the baby softly in her arms.

I said, "I'm just trying to imagine how you'll go back to work for the Department of, uh, Children and Families when your family unit here is a bit, how do you say, fucking illegal."

"Please don't swear in front of the baby," Amanda said.

"She's three weeks old," Dre said.

"I still don't want anyone swearing in front of her. Did you swear in front of your baby, Patrick?"

"When she was a baby, yeah. Not now."

"How'd Angie feel about it?"

I looked over at my wife and we exchanged a small smile. "It annoyed her actually. A bit."

"It annoyed her greatly," Angie said.

Amanda gave us a pulse of her eyes that said: Exactly.

"Fair enough," I said. "I apologize. Won't happen again."

"Thank you."

"So, Dre."

"Yeah, yeah," he said. "You're asking how I plan to go back to work at DCF when I'm shacked up with a teenager."

"Something like that, yeah."

He leaned forward and clasped his hands together. "Who says anyone has to know?"

I gave that a big smile. "Let me give you a picture of what

the inside of my head looks like right now, Dre. I've got a four-year-old daughter. I'm imagining her in twelve years, shacked up, as you say, with a scumbag DCF worker twice her age who has the moral compass of a reality TV producer and hits the flask before noon."

"It's past noon," he said.

"But that's not your yardstick, is it, Dre?"

Before he could answer, Amanda said, "The bottle should be warm by now. It's in the bowl in the sink."

Dre got off the couch and went into the kitchen.

Amanda said, "Moral outrage isn't going to play well here, Patrick. I think we're all a little past that right now."

"We're above morality, are we, Amanda? At the ripe old age of sixteen?"

"I didn't say I was above morality. I said I was above expressions of moral outrage that are a bit self-serving given the histories of the people in this room. In other words, if you think you get some sort of second chance to save my honor twelve years after you handed me back to a mother you knew was incompetent, you don't. You want absolution, find a priest. One with a clear conscience of his own, if there are any of those left."

Angie gave me a look that said: You walked into that one.

Dre returned with the bottle of formula and Amanda gave him a sweet, weary smile as she took it from him and slipped the nipple into Claire's mouth. Claire immediately started sucking, and Amanda gave her cheek a soft caress. I wondered who were the adults and who the children in the room.

"So when'd you find out you were pregnant?" Angie said.

"May," Amanda said as Dre took his seat on the couch, closer to her and the baby now.

"Three months along," Angie said.

"Uh-huh."

I said to Dre, "Must have been a shock for you."

"Just a bit," he said.

I turned my eyes to Amanda. "Thank God you've got a neglectful mother, right?"

"I don't follow."

"It must have been a lot of help hiding the pregnancy," I said.

"It's done all the time."

"Oh, I know," I said. "I knew *two* girls who pulled it off in high school. One was overweight in the first place, so, you know, but the other, she just bought larger-size clothes and kept eating junk food in front of everyone and nobody picked up on it. She gave birth in a bathroom stall during fifth period, junior year. School janitor walked in on it, ran back out screaming, fainted in the hallway. True story." I leaned forward. "So, I know it's done all the time."

"Okay, then."

"But, Amanda, you don't have an extra pound on you."

"I work out." She looked over at Angie. "How much did you gain?"

"Enough," Angie said.

"She loves Pilates," Dre said.

I nodded as if that made perfect sense. "And you don't want me swearing around the baby, but you feed her formula?"

"Sure. What's wrong with formula?"

"For a lot of women? Nothing. But you? You're a tiger. I can see it in your eyes—someone looks at that kid wrong, you'd slash their throat."

She nodded without hesitation.

"You're not the type of woman gives a baby formula when she knows how much healthier breast milk is."

She rolled her eyes. "Maybe—"

"And that baby—no offense?—looks nothing like you. Or him."

Dre came off the couch. "Time to go, dude."

"No." I shook my head. "It's not. Sit down." I looked at him. "Dude."

Amanda said, "Claire is mine."

"We don't doubt that," Angie said. "But she didn't start that way, did she?"

"Sit down, Dre." Amanda shifted the baby against her chest and adjusted the bottle. She looked at Angie and then me. "What do you think is going on here?"

Dre took his seat. He took another hit off his flask, got another contemptuous flick of the eyes from Amanda.

"Well, you've got a bunch of lunatic Russians on your tail for a reason," Angie said.

"Ah," Amanda said, "you've met them?"

Angie shook her head and pointed at me.

"I met two of them," I said.

"Let me guess—Yefim and Pavel."

I nodded and noted the muscles tightening in Dre's face. Amanda, on the other hand, looked as calm as ever.

"And you know who they work for."

"Kirill Borzakov."

"The Borscht Butcher," Amanda said, caressing Claire's face again. "That's one of his nicknames."

"How *old* are you?" I said.

"Kirill's wife, you know about her?"

"Violeta? I've heard stories."

"Her father heads a Mexican drug cartel. She believes in some arcane religion that practices animal sacrifice and, if you believe the rumors, worse. She was diagnosed with severe mental problems—in Mexico. Her family dealt with it by killing the doctor. And she's married to Kirill, not just because their marriage gives Kirill's gang an unbreakable drug supply but because the only person crazier than Violeta is Kirill and they love each other for it."

"And you stole their baby," Angie said, and the moment the words left her mouth we both knew she was right.

The bottle slipped from Claire's mouth.

"I . . . what?"

"You have the Russian mob after you and it isn't because you're so great at identity theft they can't afford to lose you. Yefim took Sophie."

"He what?"

"Took her," I said. "And when he did, he said, 'Maybe we have her make us another one.'" I cocked my head, got a good look at Claire. That's where I'd seen those lips before, that hair. "That's Sophie's baby, not yours."

"She's mine," Amanda said. "Sophie didn't want her. Sophie was giving her up."

I turned to Dre. "And who would've helped facilitate that process?"

"Better than aborting them."

"Oh, yeah, I'm sure they have a great life. Claire's is certainly starting off wonderfully—you two on the run, a bunch of scary gangsters breathing down your necks, a small matter of identity theft and crank production being your primary sources of income up to this point. Oh, and illegal baby-brokering, I

assume. Yeah, Dre? That's the confidential part of your job—
you specialize in unwed mothers, I'll bet. How warm am I?"

He gave me an embarrassed smirk. "Blazing."

"Sounds like you guys got this all figured out."

"How am I any different," Dre said, "from any legal adop-
tion agency? I find parents for women who don't want their
babies."

"With zero oversight," Angie said. "You telling us you're
able to investigate the people the Russian mob sells babies to?
Are you serious?"

"Well, not all the time, sure, but—"

"Amanda," Angie said, "of all the babies you could have
stolen, why steal the one who was supposed to go to two of the
craziest sociopaths in the city?"

"Your answer is the question." Claire was asleep against her
breast. She placed the bottle on the coffee table and stood. "I
can only assume most times where the babies Dre brokers end
up. And no"—another damaging glance at Dre—"I don't normally assume it's a great place they go to." She placed Claire in
a dark rattan bassinet by the hearth. "But in this case? I *knew*
she'd end up in a bad place. Sophie's a crank-head. She stopped
doing it while she was pregnant, mostly because I had her move
in with me and I stayed on her ass. But she went right back to
it when Claire was born."

"Well, she had a reason," Dre said.

"Shut up, Dre." She turned back to me. "Sophie wasn't
going to be raising Claire anyway—Kirill and his certifiably
insane wife were." She came over by me and sat on the edge of
the coffee table so that our knees were almost touching. "They
want that child. And, yeah, the easy thing would be to give
her back. I sure don't want to imagine what's going to happen

when Yefim and Pavel get me in a room alone. Yefim keeps an acetylene torch in the back of his truck. The kind they use on construction sites, with the hood and everything?" She nodded. "That's Yefim. And he's the sanest one of that pack. So am I scared? I am petrified. And was taking Claire away from them borderline suicidal? Probably. But you two have a daughter. Would you want her growing up with Kirill and Violeta Borzakov?"

"Of course not," Angie said.

"Well, then?"

"It's not simply a case of the baby grows up with the Borzakovs or you kidnap her. There were other options."

"No," she said, "there weren't."

"Why?"

"You had to be there."

"Where?"

She shook her head and walked back to the bassinet and stood looking down into it, her arms crossed. "Angie, would you look at something for me?"

"Sure." Angie joined her by the bassinet and they both looked in at Claire.

"See those red marks on her leg? Are those bites?"

Angie bent at the waist, peered in.

"I don't think so. I think it's just a rash. Why don't you ask Dre. He was a doctor."

"Not a very good one," Amanda said, and Dre closed his eyes and lowered his head. "A rash?"

"Yeah," Angie said, "babies get rashes. A lot."

"Well, what do you do?"

"It doesn't look really serious, but I understand how you feel. When are you seeing her pediatrician next?"

She looked almost vulnerable for a moment. "Her one-month checkup is tomorrow, so, I mean, do you think it can wait till then?"

Angie gave her a soft smile and touched her shoulder. "Definitely."

We heard a sharp noise behind us and we all jumped in place, but it was just the mail being pushed through the brass slot in the door. It fell to the floor—two circulars, a few envelopes.

Amanda and I moved toward it at the same time, but I was closer. I scooped up three envelopes, all addressed to Maureen Stanley. One was from National Grid, a second was from American Express, and the third was from the U.S. Social Security Administration.

"Miss Stanley, I presume." I handed the mail to Amanda and she snatched it from my fingers.

We walked back over to the baby as Dre slid his flask back into his jacket.

Angie stood over the bassinet, looking in at the baby, her features softening until she looked ten years younger. She turned from the bassinet and her face grew harder. She looked at Dre and Amanda. "On the top of the list of things that don't add up about all the BS and half-truths you guys have been selling us since we walked through this door is this—why are you still here?"

"Here, as in Planet Earth?" Amanda said.

"No, here as in New England."

"It's my home. It's where I'm from."

"Yeah, but you're an identity-theft master," I said.

"I'm adequate."

"You got Russians with blowtorches on your ass and you

decide to hide out ninety miles away? You could be in Belize by now. Kenya. But you stayed. I'm with my wife on this one—why is that?"

Claire fussed and suddenly let out a wail.

"Now look," Amanda said, "you woke the baby."

CHAPTER TWENTY

SHE TOOK THE BABY into a bedroom off the living room and for a minute we could hear them in there—Amanda cooing, the baby crying—and then Amanda closed the door.

"When do they stop crying?" Dre asked us.

Angie and I both laughed.

"You're a doctor."

"I just deliver them. Once they leave the womb, they leave my sight."

"You didn't study child development in med school?"

"Sure, but that was a few years ago. And it was academic then. Now it's a bit more immediate."

I shrugged. "Every kid's different. Some start sleeping regular by the fifth or sixth week."

"Yours?"

"She went four and a half months before her sleep got dependable."

"Four and a half months? Shit."

"Yeah," Angie said, "and then she started teething not long after that. You think you know what screaming sounds like now. But you don't. You don't have a clue. And don't even get me started on ear infections."

I said, " 'Member when she got infections in both ears *and* a tooth coming in?"

"Now you're just fucking with me," Dre said.

Angie and I looked over at him and shook our heads slowly.

"How come they're never like this in TV shows and movies?" he said.

"Right? They always conveniently go away when the main characters don't need them around."

"I was watching this one show the other night, right? The father's an FBI agent, mother's a surgeon, and they got, like, a six-year-old? One episode opens, they're on vacation together, no kid. I figure, okay, the kid's with the nanny, but the next scene they show the nanny moonlighting at the mother's hospital. The kid? Driving stick-shift to get groceries, I guess. Playing hopscotch on the interstate."

"It's that Hollywood logic," Angie said, "the same way in the movies there's always a parking space right outside hospitals and city halls."

"But what do you care?" I asked him. "She's not yours."

"Yeah, but . . ."

"But what? Let me ask you now that we've gotten past the kid-is-yours bullshit—you sleeping with Amanda?"

He leaned back, propped his right ankle up on his left knee. "If I was?"

"We already went down that road. I'm asking if you're not."

"Why would you—?"

"You don't seem her type, man."

"She's seventeen years ol—"

"Sixteen."

"She turns seventeen next week."

"Then next week I'll say she's seventeen."

"My point is, what *type* could she possibly have at this age?"

"And my point is, not you." I spread my hands. "Sorry, man, but I just don't see it. I see the way you look at her and, yeah, I see a guy waiting for that seventeenth birthday so his conscience can let him off the hook. But I don't see anything like that when she looks at you."

"People change."

"Sure," Angie said, "but attraction doesn't."

"Oh, man," he said, and he suddenly looked forlorn and cast-off. "Man, I dunno, I dunno."

"What don't you know?" Angie asked.

When he looked at her, his hair was damper, his eyes had picked up a milky film. "I don't know why I keep fucking myself *up*. I do something like this every few years just to make absolutely positive I'll never have a normal life. And my shrink would say, sure, I engage in compulsive behaviors and I'm trying to replay patterns that go all the way back to my parents' divorce and somehow get a different result. And I understand that, I do, but I just want someone to tell me how to stop fucking doing dumb fucking things. I mean, you know how I ended up losing my medical license and owing the Russians?"

We shook our heads. "Drugs?" I offered.

"Well, sort of. I wasn't addicted to them or anything. It wasn't that. I met a girl. Russian girl. Well, Georgian. Svetlana. She was, whew, she was everything. Crazy in bed, crazy out of it, too. So beautiful you wanted to eat your hand just looking at her. She . . ." He dropped his right foot back on the floor, sat there looking down at it. "One day she asks me to write her a scrip for Dilaudid. I say, Of course not. I quote the Hippocratic oath, the Massachusetts statutes prohibiting doctors from writing scrips for anything but diagnosed medical conditions, blah, blah, blah. Cut to the chase, she wears me down in less than a week. Why? I don't know. Because I've got no center. Whatever. But she wears me down. Three weeks after that, I'm writing her OxyCon scrips and scrips for fucking fentanyl, for Christ's sake, and pretty much anything else she wants. When that starts leaving too much of a paper trail, I start clipping the shit outright from the hospital pharmacy. I even took a moonlighting job at the Faulkner so I could do it there, too. I didn't know it, but they were already investigating me by that point. Svetlana, God love her, she'd noticed how much I liked playing blackjack at Foxwoods the couple times we went, so she hooked me into this game over in Allston. They played it out of the back of a Ukrainian bakery. First time I played, I cleaned up. Good, fun guys, great-looking women hanging around, all of them probably stoned on my shit. Next time I go, I win again. A lot less, but I win. By the time I start losing, they're all nice about it—they'll accept more OxyCon in lieu of actual money, which is good, because Svetlana's pretty much cleaned me out of money. They give me a grocery list—Vicodin HP, Palladone, Fentora, Actiq, boring old Percodan, you name it. By the time the state medical board has me arrested and files charges, I'm already in the hole twenty-six grand to Kirill's sharks. But twenty-six grand is like tip-jar money at a coffee shop compared to what's on the horizon. Because unless I want to do three-to-six at Cedar Junction, I got to come up with money for good lawyers. Another two hundred fifty grand in the hole to pay Dewey, Screwum and Howe, but at least I only get my license revoked, no jail time, no criminal finding. Kirill slides up to me at one of his restaurants a couple weeks later, tells me that the 'no criminal finding'? That was his doing. And that costs another quarter-million. I can't prove he *didn't* influence the judge, and even if I could, if Kirill Borzakov says you owe him five hundred and twenty-six thousand dollars, guess what you owe Kirill Borzakov?"

"Five hundred and twenty-six thousand dollars," I said.

"Exactly."

My cell phone vibrated and I took it out, looked at the screen, saw a number I didn't recognize. I put it back in my pocket.

"Pretty soon, one of Kirill's guys—Pavel; I think you two met—he comes to me and says I should apply for a job opening at the Department of Children and Families. Turns out they got a guy in HR working off his own debt. So I apply and he waives the CORI check, and I get the job that I'm eminently overqualified for. A few weeks later, after a particularly attractive fourteen-year-old pregnant girl leaves my office, my phone rings and they tell me I have to present her with an offer."

"What do you get per baby?" Angie's voice was weary with contempt.

"One thousand off my debt."

"So you've got to get them five hundred and twenty-six babies before you're off the hook?"

He gave that a resigned nod.

"How close are you?"

"Not close enough."

My phone vibrated again. I looked at it. Same number. I put it back in my pocket.

My wife said, "You know even if you got them five hundred and twenty-six babies to sell on the black market . . ."

He finished the sentence. "They'll never be done with me."

"No."

My cell vibrated a third time. I had a text message. I flipped the phone open.

> **Hey guy. Anser your**
> **fucking phone. Sincerely**
> **Yefim.**

Dre took another hit from his flask. "You're like a fifteen-year-old girl with that thing."

"Yeah, well, you'd know all about that."

My phone rang again. I got off the couch and walked out to the front porch. Amanda was right—from here, you could hear the brook gurgle.

"Hello."

"Hello, my good guy. What you do with the Hummer?"

"I drove it over to the stadium and left it there."

"Ha. That's a good one. Maybe I see Belichick driving it one day in his hoodie."

In spite of myself, I smiled.

"What's up, Yefim?"

"Where you at, my friend?"

"Around. Why?"

"I thought maybe we could talk. Maybe we could help each other out here."

"How'd you get my phone number?"

He laughed, a deep, long belly chuckle. "You know what day it is?"

"It's Thursday."

"It is Thursday, yes, my friend. And Friday is a big day."

"Because you wanted Kenny and Helene to find you something by Friday."

I could hear the snort through the phone. "Kenny and Helene couldn't find a chicken in the chicken soup, my man. But you? I look in your eyes after I shoot that faggot car and I see you're afraid—you'd be one icy fucker if you weren't—but I also see you're curious. You sitting there thinking, If this crazy Mordovian don't pull this trigger, I've got to know why he points it at me in the first place. I see that in your eyes, man. I see it. You a type."

"Yeah, what type?"

"The type keep coming. What's that saying about size of the dog?"

"It's not the size of the dog in the fight, it's—"

"The size of the fight in the little dog. Yeah."

"Close enough."

"So, I've got to figure you already know where this crazy Amanda is."

"What makes you think she's crazy?"

"She stole from us. That makes her fucking cuckoo clock, man. And if you don't know where she is, I bet a bag of mice you're close."

"A bag of mice?"

"Old Mordovian expression."

"Ah."

"So where's she at, my friend?"

"Let me ask you something first."

"Shoot straight away."

"What does she have that you want so bad?"

"You playing with me, guy?"

"No."

"Making fun of Yefim?"

"Definitely not."

"Then why you ask such a asshole-stupid question like that? You know what we want."

"I honestly do not. I know you want Amanda and I know—"

"We don't want Amanda, man. We want what she took. Kirill looks bad, man. He looks like he can't find one little girl stole his property? The Chechens up the block? They're starting to laugh, guy. We probably have to kill a few just to close their mouths, not have to look at their rotting fucking teeth."

"So, what—?"

"The fucking baby! And the fucking cross! I need both. If that stupid card-junkie piece-of-shit doctor goes back to work and can find me another baby, I'll give that one to Kirill, he won't know the difference. But if I don't have that cross and *some* baby by this weekend? It's going to be a fucking blood-bath, guy."

"And you'll give me Sophie in exchange?"

"No, I won't fucking give you Sophie. We're not let's-make-it-a-deal here. Yefim say he wants the baby and the cross, you bring me the baby and the cross. Otherwise, they sell this soup in the little towns along the Black Sea? Only get it in these little towns. It comes in a red can. Parts of you will be in those cans. Parts of your family too, guy."

Neither of us said anything for a minute. The heel of my hand had turned dark red from clenching the phone and my pinkie had gone numb.

"You still there, my main man?"

"Go fuck yourself, Yefim."

He gave that a low, soft laugh. "No. I fuck you, man. I fuck you and your wife and your little girl in Savannah."

I looked out on the road. The tar was very black. It matched the tree trunks by the church. The clouds had dropped down the mountain and hovered just above the telephone wires that stretched the length of the road. The air was damp.

"You don't think we watch you?" Yefim said. "You don't think we have friends in Savannah? We have friends everywhere, guy. And, yeah, you got that big crazy Polack protecting your little girl so we lose a couple of guys taking them out. But that's okay—we get more guys."

I stood on the porch looking out on the road. When I spoke, the words came out clipped and harder than I intended. "Tell me about this cross."

"The cross," Yefim said, "is the Belarus Cross. It go back a thousand years, man. Some people call it the Varangian Cross, other people, they call it the Yaroslav Cross, but I always like Belarus Cross. No price on this thing, man. Prince Yaroslav, he pay the Varangians with this cross to kill his brother Boris in the unification war back in, like, 1010 or 1011. But then he miss the cross so much, after he become ruler of all Kievan Rus, he send some other Varangians against the first Varangians, and they kill them, bring the cross back to him. It was in the czar's pocket back in '17 when they put him against that basement wall and, *boom,* blow his brains out. Trotsky had it in Mexico with him when they ice-axed his head. That cross get around, man. Now Kirill get it, and he's showing it off at party on Saturday. All the big fish be there, man. Real gangsta. And he need that cross."

I finally trusted myself to speak. "And you think—"

"No think. I know. That little girl has it. Or that fucking card-junkie doctor. Oh, you tell him to get back to work. You tell him we need him so much we won't take a finger. We take a toe. He don't need a toe as much and he need his finger. So, yeah, he'll limp. People limp. Get me that cross, get me that baby, man. I'll—"

"No deal."

"I just told—"

"I know what you just told me, you fucking hump. You threaten my wife? You threaten my daughter? One thing happens to them, or my friend calls and says he saw one of you Stallone-in-*Nighthawks*-looking motherfuckers at the strip mall? I'll burn your whole fucking organization to the ground. I'll—"

He was laughing so hard I had to hold the phone away from my ear.

"Ho-kay," he said finally, still chugging out a trail of soft giggles. "Ho-okay, Meester Kenzie. You funny guy, my main friend. Funny, funny guy. You know where my cross is?"

"I might. You know where Sophie is?"

"Not anymore, but I can find her plenty fast." He chuckled again. "Where you come up with 'hump,' man? I never hear that."

"I don't know," I said. "Old tape, I guess."

"I like it. I can use it?"

"Help yourself."

"Say to some guy, 'You pay me money or else, you, you hump.' Ha."

"All yours."

"I find Sophie. You find cross. I'll call you later."

He laughed once more and hung up.

I WAS STILL SHAKING WHEN I got back into the house, the adrenaline swirling at the base of my skull so badly I got a headache.

"Tell me about the Belarus Cross."

Dre looked like he'd hit the flask a few more times while I was out on the porch. Angie sat in the armchair closest to the hearth. She looked so small, for some reason, so lost. She gave me a look I couldn't quite read but it was pained, even forlorn. Amanda sat at the far end of the couch, a video baby-monitor on the end table beside her. She'd been reading *Last Night at the Lobster* and she put it on the coffee table, spine bent, and looked at me.

"Who were you talking to?"

"The Belarus Cross," I said.

"You were talking to a cross?"

"Amanda."

She shrugged. "I have no idea what you're talking about. The what?"

I didn't have time for this. Which left me with two options—threat or promise.

"They'll let you keep the baby."

She sat up. "What?"

"You heard me. If this genius over here"—I nodded at Dre—"can come up with another baby pronto, they'll let you keep Claire."

She turned on the couch. "Can you?"

"It's possible."

"Fucking Dre," she said, "can you or not?"

"I don't know. There's one girl who's close. I mean, she *could be* in early labor or it could just be false labor. With the equipment I have at my disposal, it's an inexact science."

Amanda's jaw clenched and unclenched. She used both hands to pull her hair behind her head. She slowly twirled it into a ponytail and took a band off the side table and tied it off.

"So you talked to Yefim."

I nodded.

"And he was explicit."

"Couldn't have been clearer—give them the cross and *a* baby, and they forget all about you."

She'd pulled into herself, her knees up to her chest, bare feet clutching the couch cushion. Pulling the hair off her face should have made her features sharper and less vulnerable, but it managed to have the opposite effect. She looked like a child again. A petrified child.

"Did you believe him?"

I said, "I believe he believed it. Whether he can float it past Kirill and his wife, that's another issue."

"This all started because Kirill saw a picture of Sophie. That's one of the"—she looked down the couch—"services Dre provides, the pictures. Kirill and Violeta saw Sophie, and I guess she looked like Violeta's younger sister or something and, from that point, they wanted Sophie's baby, no one else's."

"So it might be more complicated than Yefim lets on."

"It's always more complicated," she said. "How old are *you*?"

I gave that a small smile.

Amanda looked down the couch at Dre, who sat there like a dog waiting for her to say "park" or "supper."

"Even if he could supply another baby, wouldn't we be doing the same thing—giving a child over to two psychopaths?"

I nodded.

"Can you live with that?"

I said, "I came here to find you and get Sophie out of their hands. That's as far as I've thought."

"How nice for you."

"Hey, Amanda? People who live in glass houses with kidnapped babies shouldn't throw stones."

"I know, it's just that it sounds so much like the kind of logic that sent me back to Helene twelve years ago."

"I'm not playing this record right now. You want to hash all that shit out at some quieter time, I'll be your Huckleberry. But right now we need to get them this Belarus Cross and, if possible, convince them we'll get them another baby."

"And if we can't?"

"Get them another baby?"

She nodded.

"I don't have a clue, but I do know the cross will buy us time. It's supposed to be on display in Kirill's house by Saturday night. If it's not there, I have no doubt they'll kill all of us, my family included. We get it to them, though, it'll buy us another couple of days on the baby issue."

Angie's eyes had widened and she glared at me.

"Sounds good to me," Dre said.

"I'm sure it does," Amanda said. She turned back to me. "What if they renege? All Yefim has to do is figure out where I am, and there's not too many places for me to hide. You found us in one morning. What's to stop him from getting the cross and then coming right up the road for the baby?"

"His word that he wouldn't is all I got to go on."

"And you'd take it—the word of an assassin who goes all the way back to the Solntsevskaya Bratva in Moscow?"

"I don't even know what that is," I said.

"A gang," she said, "a brotherhood. Think the Crips or the Bloods with military discipline and connections going all the way to the top of the Russian oil conglomerates."

"Oh."

"Yeah. That's where Yefim got his start. And you'll take his word?"

"No," I said. "I won't. But what's our alternative?"

After a couple of tentative yelps, the baby started crying full-force. We could hear her on the monitor and we could hear her through the door. Amanda slid off the couch and slipped on her flats. She took the monitor with her into the bedroom.

Dre took another drink from his flask. "Fuck-ing Russians."

"Why don't you slow down?" I said.

"You were right." He took another drink. "Earlier."

"About what?"

He ground the back of his head into the couch, his eyes rolling back toward the bedroom door. "Her. She doesn't like me very much, I don't think."

"Why's she with you, then?" Angie asked.

He exhaled up toward his own eyes. "Even Amanda, cool as she is, needs help with a newborn. Those first couple weeks?

You're going to the supermarket every five minutes—diapers, formula, more diapers, more formula. The kid's up every ninety minutes, wailing. Ain't much in the way of sleep or freedom."

"You're saying she needed a gofer."

He nodded. "But she's got the hang of it now." He let loose a soft and bitter chuckle. "I thought when we first met, you know, here's my shot—an innocent girl, untouched, uncorrupted, of *blazing* intelligence. I mean, she can quote Shaw, she can quote Stephen Hawking, she's so cool she can quote *Young Frankenstein,* get into a debate with you on quantum physics and the lyrics to 'Monkey Man' on the same night. She likes Rimbaud and Axl Rose, Lucinda Williams and—"

"This going to go on for a while?" Angie said.

"Huh?"

I said, "It sounds like you thought you could mold Amanda into your very own Nexus 6 model of every chick who dumped on you in high school."

"No, it wasn't like that."

"It was exactly like that. This version wouldn't take a shit on you, she'd adore you. And you could sit up all night and give her your rap about Sigur Rós or the metaphorical significance of the rabbit in *Donnie Darko.* And she'd just bat her eyes and ask where you'd been all her life."

He looked down at his lap. "Hey, fuck you," he whispered.

"Fair enough."

I could see the child I'd found after seven months, playing on a porch not far from here with an openhearted woman who'd adored her, and a bulldog named Larry. If I'd left her there, who would she be now? Maybe she'd be a basket case who remembered just enough of her life before she'd been snatched from a neglectful mother to know that her life here with Jack and Patricia Doyle was a lie. Or maybe she'd have very little memory of her time with a white-trash alcoholic in a three-decker apartment in Dorchester that smelled of carpet funk and Newports, so little that she'd live a well-adjusted life in small-town America and all she'd know of identity theft and credit card fraud and Russian killers from the Solntsevskaya Bratva would be things she picked up watching *60 Minutes*. Even if Amanda had never been kidnapped in the first place, with Helene for a mother, her chances of growing up a healthy, well-adjusted child were somewhere in the neighborhood of a hundred million to one. So the kidnapping had, in some demented way, exposed her to the knowledge that another way of life existed. One that wasn't her mother's life of fast food and full ashtrays. Of collection notices and ex-con boyfriends. After she'd glimpsed the world of this tiny mountain town, she'd decided to will her way back to it. And maybe, from that point on, will became her defining character trait.

"They won't just let this go," Dre said, "no matter what Yefim told you."

"Why not?"

"For starters?" he said. "Somebody's got to pay for Timur."

"Who's Timur?" Angie asked, coming over to the couch.

"He was a Russian."

"Yeah? What happened to him?"

"We kinda killed him."

CHAPTER TWENTY-ONE

S O YOU KINDA KILLED A RUSSIAN named Timur to get the
Belarus Cross."

"No," he said.

"No you didn't kill him?"

"Well, yes, but we didn't do it to get the Belarus Cross. We
didn't know shit about the Belarus Cross until we opened the
suitcase."

"What suitcase?" Angie sat on the edge of the couch.

"The one handcuffed to Timur's wrist."

I narrowed my eyes. "Whatchoo talkin' 'bout, Willis?"

Dre considered his flask but returned it to his pocket. He
played with a key chain instead, swinging the keys absently
around a hard plastic fob, which encased a picture of Claire.
"You heard of Zippo?"

"Sophie's boyfriend," Angie said.

"Yeah. Notice how no one's seen him around in a while?"

"It did come to our attention."

He lay back on the couch like he was in a shrink's office. He dangled the key chain above his head so that the picture of Claire swung back and forth over his face, the shadow passing over his nose. "There's an old movie memorabilia warehouse in Brighton, right along the Mass Pike. You go in there, you'd see an entire floor devoted to posters, half of them oversize European ones. Second floor is props and costumes; you want the NYU philosophy degree that Swayze had on his wall in *Roadhouse,* they got it there, not in L.A. Russians got all sorts of weird shit there—Sharon Stone's chaps from *The Quick and the Dead,* one of Harry's fur suits from *Harry and the Hendersons.* They also have a third floor no one goes to, because that's where the delivery and postdelivery rooms are." He wiggled his fingers. "I'm a doctor, lest we forget, and these babies can't be documented at a hospital. The moment they enter the system, they're traceable. So we deliver them at a movie memorabilia warehouse in Brighton and they're usually on a plane out of town three days later. Some special cases, they're out the door as soon as the cord is cut."

"Which was the case with Claire." Angie leaned forward, chin on her hand.

He held up one finger. "Which was *supposed to be* the case with Claire. But it wasn't just me and Sophie in the delivery room. Amanda was there and so was Zippo. I'd advised strongly against it. It was going to be hard enough to give the baby up without actually seeing her be born. But Amanda overruled me, as Amanda is wont to do. And we were all in there when Sophie gave birth." He sighed. "It was an incredible birth. So smooth. Sometimes it goes that way with young mothers. Normally it doesn't, but sometimes . . ." He shrugged.

"This was one of those times. So we're all standing there, passing this baby around, laughing, crying, hugging—I actually hugged Zippo, though I couldn't stand the kid in real life—and the door opens and there's Timur standing there. Timur was a giant, a bald, big-eared, face-only-a-blind-mother-could-love Chernobyl baby. You think I'm kidding but, no, he was literally born in Chernobyl in the mid-eighties. A mutant freak, Timur. And a drunk and a crank addict. All the positives. He comes through the door for the pickup. He's early, he's fucked up, and he's got a suitcase cuffed to his wrist."

I started seeing it now—five people walk into a room, two die, but four walk out. "So he's not taking no for an answer."

"Not taking 'no'?" Dre sat up and put the key chain in his jeans. "Timur crashes into the room, says, 'I take baby,' and goes to cut the umbilical cord. I swear to Christ—I never saw anything like it. He grabs the surgical shears, starts coming toward me with them, I'm holding the baby, we've all just been laughing and hugging and crying and here's this Chernobyl mutant coming at me with surgical shears. He's got them open and he's heading right for the umbilical cord, one eye closed 'cause he's so fucked up he's seeing double, and that's when Zippo jumps on his back and cuts his throat with the scalpel. I mean, just opens it from one side to the other." He covered his face in both hands for a moment. "It was the worst fucking thing I ever saw and I did my ER internship in Gary, Indiana."

I hadn't heard anything from the back bedroom in a while. I stood.

Dre didn't even notice. "Here's the best part. Timur the Chernobyl Mutant? Even with his throat cut, he flips Zippo off his back and as soon as Zippo hits the ground, Timur shoots him three times in the chest."

I stood by the bedroom door, listening.

"So now we've got this freak of nature with a cut throat pointing a gun at us, and we're all going to die, right? But then his eyes roll back to whites and he drops toward the floor and he's already gone by the time he lands."

I knocked softly on the bedroom door.

"We don't know what to do at first, but then we realize no matter what happens, they'll probably kill us. Kirill loved Timur. Treated him like his favorite dog. Which, when you think of it, he was."

I knocked softly again. I tried the door. It was open. I pushed it inward and looked in at an empty bedroom. No baby. No Amanda.

I looked back at Dre. He didn't seem surprised. "She gone?"

"Yeah," I said. "She's gone."

"She does that a lot," he said to Angie.

WE STOOD OUT BACK, LOOKING at a small yard and a strip of gravel that ran along the edge of the yard in a downward slope and ended at a thin dirt alley. Across the alley was another yard, much bigger, and a white Victorian with green trim.

"So, you had another car back here," I said.

"You're the private investigators. Aren't you supposed to check for stuff like that?" He took a snort of the clean mountain air. "It's a stick."

"Huh?"

"Amanda's car. A little Honda thing. She just dropped the emergency brake and rolled to the alley, took a right." He pointed. "She made the road in about ten seconds from there, would be my guess, and then she turned the engine over, popped it into first." He whistled through his lower teeth. "And a-way she went."

"Nice," I said.

"She does it a lot, like I said. She's half-jackrabbit. Anything bothers her, she just leaves. She'll be back."

"What if she doesn't come back?" I said.

He plopped down on the couch again. "Where's she going to go?"

"She's the Teenage Great Impostor. She can go anywhere."

He held up an index finger. "Correct. But she doesn't. This whole time on the run, I'm like you—I've been advocating foreign countries, islands. Amanda won't go for it. This is where she was happy once, this is where she wants to stay."

"It's a nice sentiment," Angie said, "but no one's that sentimental with their life on the line, and Amanda strikes me as far less sentimental than most."

"Yet"—he raised his hands to the sky—"here we are." He hugged his arms. "I'm cold. Heading back in."

He went back inside. I started to follow, but Angie said, "Hang on a sec."

She lit a cigarette and her hands shook. "Yefim threatened our daughter?"

"It's what they do to rattle you."

"But it's what *he* did. Yes?"

After a moment, I nodded.

"Well, it worked. I'm rattled." She took a few quick puffs off her cigarette, and for a time she wouldn't meet my eyes.

"You gave your word to Beatrice you'd find Amanda and bring her home. And you . . . baby, you'd break yourself in half before you'd break your word, which is what I probably love most about you. You know that?"

"I do."

"You know how *much* I love you?"

I nodded. "Of course. Gets me through more than you know, believe me."

"Back at ya." She gave me a shaky smile and took another shaky toke off her shaky cigarette. "So you have to honor your word. I wouldn't have it any other way."

I saw where this was going. "But you don't have to."

"Exactly. 'It's who you give your word to.'" She smiled, her eyes filling.

"You know how hot it is that you can quote *The Wild Bunch*?"

She gave me a faux curtsy, but then her face returned to something serious and addled.

"I don't care about these people," she said. "I mean, did you listen to that story in there? That turd isn't just a turd, he's a *monster* turd. He sells babies. In a just world, he would be getting raped in prison, not sitting in a warm living room in a pretty little town. And now my daughter's in *danger*? Because of them?" She pointed at the house. "It's not an acceptable risk-versus-reward equation for me."

"I know."

"Knowing that they *know* she's in Savannah? She's not going to sleep tonight without me."

I told her that I'd alerted Bubba and that he'd let me in on the backup he'd brought down South with him, but it didn't seem to do much to allay her fears.

"That's nice," she said. "It is. He's Bubba and he'd die protecting her. I don't doubt that. But, baby? I'm her *mother*. And I need to get to her. Tonight. No matter what it takes."

"Which is what I love most about you." I took her free hand. "You're her mom. And she needs her mom."

She laughed, but it was a torn, wet laugh, and she ran the heel of her hand under each eye. "Her mom needs her."

She draped her arms over my shoulders and we kissed in the bright cold, which made the smooth warmth of her tongue even warmer, even smoother.

When we broke the kiss, she said, "There's a bus station in Lenox."

I shook my head. "Don't be ridiculous. Take the Jeep and drive like, well, me. Leave the car in long-term parking at the airport. If I need it, I'll come get it."

"How will you get home?"

I put my hand on her cheek for a moment, thinking how outrageously lucky I was to have met her and married her and become a parent with her. "Have you ever, in your life, known me to have a problem getting where I need to get?"

"You are a marvel of self-sufficiency." She shook her head, the tears coming now. "But we're breaking you of that, you know, your daughter and me."

"Oh, I noticed."

"You did?"

"I did."

Her hug was crushing, her hands gripping the back of my head and neck like it was all that kept her from drowning in the Atlantic.

We walked around the front of the house to the Jeep. I handed her the keys. She got in and we traded another full minute of inappropriate public affection before I stepped back from the driver's window.

Angie put the Jeep in drive, looked out the window at me. "How come they can find our daughter in Georgia but they can't find one sixteen-year-old girl in Massachusetts?"

"A fair question."

"A sixteen-year-old girl toting a baby around a town with a population of, at best, two thousand?"

"Sometimes hiding in plain sight is the best cover."

"And sometimes if something smells it's because it's rotten, babe."

I nodded.

She blew me a kiss.

"As soon as you see our daughter," I said, "shoot me a photo of her."

"Love to." She looked back at the house. "I don't know how I did this for fifteen years. I don't know how you do it now."

"I don't think about it."

She smiled. "Sure you do."

I LET MYSELF BACK INTO THE HOUSE and found Dre plopped on the couch watching *The View,* Babs and the girls chatting about global warming with Al Gore. The nitwit blonde with the concentration-camp collarbones asked him to explain a study she'd read that linked global warming to cow flatulence. Al smiled and looked like he'd rather be getting a colonoscopy during a root canal. My cell phone vibrated—the restricted number again.

"It's Yefim," I said.

Dre sat up. "I have it."

"What?"

"The cross." He grinned like a little boy. He reached under the collars of his pullover and the henley beneath it. He pulled out a leather cord hung around his neck. A cross dangled from it, thick and black. "I gots it, baby. You tell Yefim—"

I held up a finger to him and answered the phone.

"Hello, Patrick, you hump."

I smiled. "Hello, Yefim."

"You like? I used 'hump' for you."

"I like."

"You got my cross, man?"

It hung against Dre's upper chest. It was black and the size of my hand.

"I have your cross."

Dre gave me a double thumbs-up and another idiotic grin.

"We meet, then. Go to Great Woods."

"What?"

"Great Woods, man. The Tweeter Center. Oh, hang on." I heard him place his hand over the phone and speak to someone. "I been told it's not called Great Woods or the Tweeter Center no more. It's called—what? Hang on, Patrick."

"The Comcast Center," I said.

"It's called the Comcast Center," Yefim said. "You know it, right?"

"I know it. It's closed now. Off-season."

"Which is why nobody will be around to bother us, man. Go to the east gate. You'll find a way in. Meet me by the main stage."

"When?"

"Four hours. You bring the cross."

"You bring Sophie."

"You bring baby, too?"

"Right now all's I got is the cross."

"That's a sucky deal, man."

"It's the only deal I got if you want that cross in Kirill's house by Saturday night."

"Bring the doctor, then."

I glanced at Dre, who stared at me with wide eyes and a childlike giddiness that I assumed was pharmaceutically generated.

"Who says I even know where he is?"

Yefim sighed. "You too smart not to know we know more than we say we know."

It took me a second to catch up to that sentence. "We?"

"Me," he said. "Pavel. We. You part of something, my friend, something you not supposed to understand yet."

"Really?"

"True. I'm playing her game, you play mine. Bring doctor."

"Why?"

"I want to deliver message to him in person."

"Mmmm," I said. "Not so sure I like that."

"Don't worry, guy, I'm not going to hurt him. I need him. I just want to tell him personally how much I would like to see him back on the job. You bring him."

"I'll ask him."

"Ho-kay," Yefim said. "I see you soon." He hung up.

Dre returned the cross to its hiding place beneath his pullover but not before I got a look at it. If I'd passed it in an antique shop, I would have guessed the price at fifty dollars, no more. It was black onyx, fashioned in the Russian Orthodox style, with Latin inscriptions carved into the top and bottom of the face. In the center was etched another cross along with a spear and a sponge above a small rise that I presumed represented Golgotha.

"Doesn't seem worth a bunch of dead people through the ages, does it?" Dre said before slipping it under his collar.

"Most of the things that people kill for don't."

"To the assholes doing the killing they do."

I held out my hand. "Why don't you give it to me?"

He gave me a smile that was all teeth. "Fuck you."

"No, really."

"No, really." He bugged his eyes at me.

"Seriously," I said. "I'll take it and I'll do the swap. No need for you to risk your ass out there with these kinds of people. It's not your thing, Dre."

His smile widened. "You might have everyone else buying your good-guy bullshit, but you're no different than anyone else. You get a chance to hold this in your hand? This artifact worth, I dunno, what van Goghs are worth? You'll *think* about doing the right thing, but then you'll just keep driving until you can find someone to fence it."

"So, why don't you?"

"What?"

"Steal it and fence it?"

"Because I don't know any fences, man. I'm a pill-popping degenerate gambler, I'm not fucking Val Kilmer in *Heat*. The first person I trusted to help me move this would shoot me in the back of the head as soon as I turned my back. You, though, you do know fences, I bet, and you do know people you can trust in the criminal world. You'd be halfway to Mexico with this thing if you could."

"Uh, okay."

"Your aw-shucks shtick doesn't fool me."

"Apparently not," I said. "Darn. Let me ask you—why does Yefim seem to know everything about us right now but yet he somehow can't find us?"

"What does he know about us?"

"He knows we're together. He even made a reference to this being Amanda's game, and all of us caught playing it."

"And you doubt that?"

AN HOUR LATER, WE SET OUT for the Comcast Center at Great Woods in Mansfield. As we walked out to Dre's Saab, he removed the key from his key chain and handed it to me.

"It's your car," I said.

"Given my substance abuse issues, do you really want me behind the wheel?"

I drove the Saab. Dre rode shotgun and stared dreamily out the window.

"You're not on just booze," I said.

He turned his head. "I took a couple Xanax. You know . . ." He looked back out the window.

"A couple? Or three?"

"Three, actually, yeah. And a Paxil."

"So pills and liquor, that's your prescription for dealing with the Russian mob."

"It's brought me this far," he said and dangled the photo fob of Claire in front of his blurry eyes.

"Why the hell do you have a picture of the kid?" I said.

He looked over at me. "Because I love her, man."

"Really?"

He shrugged. "Or something like love."

Half a minute later, he was snoring.

IT'S RARE YOU DEAL WITH ANY KIND of illegal swap where the party with the power doesn't change the meeting place at the last minute. It tends to root out the threat of law enforcement surveillance, because it's hard to set up audio bugs on the fly, and teams of black-clad federal agents weighted down with boom mikes, recorder bags, and infrared telephoto lenses are easier to spot when they're scrambling around in the background.

So, I assumed Yefim would call to change the meet at the last minute, but I still wanted to get a lay of the land in case he didn't. I'd been to the Comcast Center at least two dozen times in my life. It was an outdoor amphitheater cut into the woods of Mansfield, Massachusetts. I'd seen Bowie open for Nine Inch Nails there. I'd seen Springsteen and Radiohead. A year back, I saw the National open for Green Day and thought I'd died and gone to alt-rock heaven. Which is to say, I knew the layout pretty well. The amphitheater was a bowl with a long, high slope running down to it, and lower, wider slopes curving around in gradual swirls, so that if you continued to walk in a circle one way, you would eventually run out of road at the amphitheater itself. And if you walked in a circle the other way, you would eventually reach the parking lot. They set up the T-shirt kiosks on these slopes alongside the beer booths and the booths for cotton candy, baked pretzels, and foot-long hot dogs.

Dre and I walked around for a bit as a hesitant snow fell in the gathering dusk. Flakes appeared in the darkening air like fireflies, then melted on contact with whatever they touched— a wooden booth, the ground, my nose. At one of the wooden booths near a stand of turnstiles, I looked right and left and realized Dre was no longer with me. I turned back and walked up one slope and then down another, following my faint footsteps on the dampening pavement. I saw where his broke off and I used the last one I could make out as an arrow. I was walking past the VIP box seats toward the stage when my phone rang.

"Hello."

It was Amanda. "Where are you guys?"

"One could ask you the same thing."

"*My* location doesn't matter right now. I just got a call that they've changed the location of your meeting. What meeting is that, by the way?"

"We're at the Comcast Center. Who called?"

"A guy with a thick Russian accent. Any other stupid questions? He said Yefim is having trouble getting through to your cell."

"How'd the Russians get your number?"

"How'd they get *yours*?"

I didn't have an answer for that one.

"The meeting's changed to a train station," she said.

"Which one?"

"Dodgeville."

"Dodgeville?" I repeated. I vaguely remembered seeing the name on packages when I'd loaded trucks in college but I couldn't have pointed it out on a map. "Where the hell's that?"

"According to a map I'm looking at, go to 152 and head

south. Not far. They said only one of you can leave the car with the cross. So you have the cross, I take it."

"Dre does, yeah."

"They said bring the cross or they'll kill Sophie in front of you. Then they'll kill you."

"Where are—?"

She'd hung up.

I came to the bottom of the aisle, found Dre sitting on the edge of the stage, looking out at the seats.

"Meeting location's been changed."

He didn't seem surprised. "That's what you predicted."

I shrugged.

"Must be great," he said, "being right all the time."

"That's how I come off, uh?"

He stared at me. "People like you wear your self-righteousness like—"

"Don't blame me because you fucked your life up. I don't judge you for any of that."

"Then what do you judge me for?"

"Trying to get into the pants of a sixteen-year-old."

"In many cultures that's considered normal."

"Then move to one of those cultures. Here, it just means you're a douche bag. You don't like yourself? Don't put it on me. You don't like the way your life turned out? Welcome to the club."

He looked out at the seats, suddenly wistful. "I played a pretty mean bass in this band I had in high school."

I managed not to roll my eyes.

"All these things we could have been," he said. "You know? But you gotta choose a path, so you choose it, and you find yourself exiting med school knowing only one thing for certain—that you're going to be a subpar doctor. How do you embrace your own mediocrity? How do you accept that in any race, for the rest of your life, you'll arrive with the back of the pack?"

I leaned against the stage with him and said nothing. It was quite the view—all those seats. Beyond it, the great lawn of general seating rising into the dark sky under gently falling snow. Most nights in July, it would be full. Twenty thousand people chanting and screaming and swaying, pumping their fists toward the sky. Who wouldn't want to stand onstage and have that view?

On some minor level, I felt bad for Dre. He'd been told by someone—a mother, I assumed—that he was special. Probably told it every day of his life, even as the evidence mounted that it was a lie, however well-intentioned. And now here he was, first career in shambles, second career about to be, and probably unable to remember the last time he'd made it through a day without substance abuse.

"You know why I never had any qualms about brokering baby sales?"

"No, I don't."

"Because nobody knows nothing." He looked over at me. "You think the state knows any better about placing kids? You think anyone does? We don't know shit. And by we, I mean all of us. We all showed up at the same shitty semiformal and we hope that somehow everyone will buy that we are what we dressed up as. A few decades of this, and what happens? Nothing. Nothing happens. We learn nothing, we don't change, and then we die. And the next generation of fakers takes our place. And that? That's all there is."

I clapped him on the back. "I see a future in self-help for you, Dre. We got to motor."

"Where?"

"Railway station. Dodgeville."

He hopped off the stage and followed me up the aisle.

"Quick question, Patrick."

"What's that?"

"Where the fuck's Dodgeville?"

CHAPTER TWENTY-TWO

ODGEVILLE, AS IT TURNED OUT, was one of those towns so small I'd always thought it was just an extension of another town—in this case, South Attleboro. As far as I could tell, it didn't even have a traffic light, just one stop sign about six miles from the Rhode Island border. Idling there, I saw an RR sign to my left. So I turned left off Route 152, and after a few hundred yards, the train station appeared, as if dropped there, in an otherwise uninterrupted stretch of woodlands. The tracks ran straight into the forest—just a hard line that vanished into cowls of red maple. We pulled into the parking lot. Other than the tracks and the platform, there wasn't much to see—no stationhouse to protect against December's bite, no Coke machines or bathrooms. A couple of newspaper stands by the entrance stairs. Deep woods on the far side of the tracks. On the near side, the platform on the same level as the rails, and the parking lot we'd pulled into, which was lit with sallow white light, the snow spinning like moths under the bulbs.

My phone vibrated. I opened the text:

One of you bring cross to platform. One of you stay in car.

Dre had craned his head to look at the message. Before I could reach for my door, he'd reached for his and was out of the car.

"I got this," he said. "I got this."

"No, you—"

But he walked away from the car and out of the parking lot. He climbed the short steps to the platform and stood in the center. From where he stood, a strip of hard black rubber fringed in bright yellow paint extended across the track.

He stood there for a bit as the snow fell harder. He took two or three steps to the right, then four or five to the left, then back to the right again.

I saw the light before he did. It was a circle of yellow bouncing in the woods, a flashlight beam. It rose, then fell and rose halfway back up again before it slid left, then right. It made the same movement a second time—the sign of the cross—and this time Dre's head turned toward it and locked on. He raised one hand. He waved. The light stopped moving. Just hovered in the woods directly across from Dre, waiting.

I rolled down my window.

I heard Dre say, "No worries," and cross the tracks. The snow grew thicker, some of the flakes starting to resemble bolls of cotton.

Dre entered the woods. I lost sight of him. The flashlight beam vanished.

I reached for my door, but my cell vibrated again.

Stay in the car.

I kept the phone open on my lap and waited. It wouldn't be much of a task to simply hit Dre over the head, take the cross, and disappear into the woods with Sophie, the cross, and my peace of mind. My left hand clenched the door handle. I flexed the fingers, relaxed. Ten seconds later, I found myself clenching the handle again.

The cell phone screen lit up:

Patience, patience.

In the woods, the yellow light reappeared. It hovered, steady, about three feet off the ground.

My cell vibrated, but it wasn't a text this time, it was an incoming call from a restricted number.

"Hello."

"Hey, my . . ." Yefim's voice dropped out for a second. " . . . you at?"

"What?"

"I said where . . . ?"

The phone went dead in my ear.

I heard something thunk into the gravel on the near side of the platform. I peered out the windshield, but I couldn't see anything, with the hood of the Saab in the way. I kept looking anyway, because that's what you do. I gave the wipers a quick flick on and off and sloughed off the snow. A few seconds later, Dre appeared at the same spot in the woods where he'd vanished. He was moving fast. He was alone.

My phone vibrated. I heard a horn. I looked down and saw RESTRICTED NUMBER on my screen.

"Hello?"

"Where you?"

"Yefim?"

The windshield vanished behind a cloak of mud. The Saab shook so hard the dashboard rattled. The seat shimmied beneath me. An empty coffee cup tipped out of the cup holder and fell to the floor mat on the passenger side.

"Patrick? . . . you go . . . I no . . . stage."

I flicked on the wipers. The mud swept right and left, thinner than mud, I realized, as an Acela blew through the station. "Yefim? You keep dropping out."

"Can . . . hear . . . guy?"

I got out of the car because I couldn't see Dre anymore, noticed my hood was speckled with whatever had hit my windshield.

"I can hear you now. Can you hear me?"

Dre wasn't on the platform.

He was nowhere.

"I . . . fuck . . ."

The connection died. I flipped my phone closed, looked left and right down the platform. No Dre.

I turned back around and looked down the line of cars beside my own. There were six of them, spread out, but I saw the same liquid splashed across their hoods and windshields under the weak white lights. The Acela had vanished into the trees, going the kind of fast you thought only jets could go. The wet cars and wet platform glistened with something besides melting snow.

I turned my head, looked at the platform, turned again, looked at the cars.

Dre wasn't anywhere.

Because Dre was everywhere.

I FOUND A FLASHLIGHT AND TWO plastic supermarket bags in the trunk of Dre's car. I put the bags over my shoes and used the handles to tie knots around my ankles. Then I walked through the blood to the platform. I found one of his shoes down the track, tucked into the inside of the rail. I found what could have been an ear a few feet farther down on the platform. Or it could have been part of a nose. Apparently, an Acela going top-speed didn't run you over; it blew you up.

On my walk back up the tracks, I spotted a shoulder between the track and the woods. That was the last of Dre I ever saw.

I went to the spot where he'd entered and exited the woods. I shone my flashlight in there, but all I could see were dark trees with clumps of leaves pooled at their bases. I could have gone in farther, but (a) I don't like woods; and (b) I was running out of time. The Acela passed through Mansfield station, three miles up, and there was a chance someone would spot blood on the front of it or along the side.

Yefim, I could assume, had long since left and taken Sophie and the cross with him.

I walked back across the tracks and at first I didn't compute what I saw there. Part of me understood it enough to hold the flashlight beam in place, but the other half of me couldn't make sense of it.

I bent by the gravel between the tracks and the fence that rimmed the parking lot. I'd heard a thunk as it landed, as someone, for who knew what reason, tossed it from the woods to the other side of the tracks. And Dre had come rushing out after it and stepped into the path of over six hundred tons of steel traveling 160 miles an hour.

The Belarus Cross.

I pinched the top left corner of it and lifted it out of the gravel. It was speckled with evaporating snow that revealed it was as bloody as the windshields in the parking lot, as bloody as the platform and the trees and the stairs I descended to Dre's car. I popped the trunk and sat on the edge and removed the plastic bags and placed them in a third plastic bag. I found a rag in the trunk, and I used it to wipe off the cross as best I could. I tossed the rag into the plastic bag and tied off the handles. I took the bag and the cross up front with me and placed them on the passenger seat and got the hell out of Dodgeville.

CHAPTER TWENTY-THREE

THERE WAS ONLY ONE PEDIATRICIAN in a fifteen-mile radius of Becket, a Dr. Chimilewski, two towns over in Huntington. When Amanda pulled up in front of the office at ten the next morning, I stayed where I was and let her go inside and keep her appointment. I sat in Dre's car and replayed the conversation I'd had with Yefim on my way out of Dodgeville. He'd called me minutes after I left the train station and nothing we'd discussed made any sense yet.

When Amanda came out twenty minutes later, I was waiting with a cardboard cup of coffee that I offered to her. "I guessed cream, no sugar."

"I can't drink coffee," she said. "It aggravates my ulcer. But thanks for the thought."

She clicked the remote on her car to unlock the doors and came around me with the baby in the car seat. I opened the door for her.

"You can't have an ulcer. You're sixteen years old."

She snapped the car seat into its base in the backseat. "Tell that to my ulcer. I've had it since I was thirteen."

I stepped back as she closed the door on Claire.

"She okay?"

She looked through the window at the baby. "Yeah. She's just got that rash. No cause. They said it'll go away, just like Angie said. They said babies get rashes."

"Hard, though, right? All these things that could be real health scares turn out to be absolutely nothing, but you never know so you got to get it checked out."

She gave me a small and weary smile. "I keep thinking they're going to throw me out next time."

"They don't throw you out for being too careful about your child."

"No, but they tell jokes about you, I'm sure."

"Let 'em tell jokes."

She walked around to the driver's side, looked over the roof at me. "You can follow or just meet me back at the house. I'm not running anywhere."

"I've noticed."

I turned to walk toward Dre's Saab.

"Where's Dre?"

I turned back to her, met her eyes. "He didn't make it."

"He . . ." She cocked her head slightly. "The Russians?"

I said nothing. I held her gaze. I looked for something in her eyes that would tell me, one way or another, which side she was playing in this. Or was it all sides?

"Patrick?" she said.

"I'll see you back at the house."

IN THE KITCHEN, SHE MADE GREEN tea for herself and brought the cup and small pot out to the dining room with her. Claire sat in her car seat in the center of the dining-room table. She'd fallen into a deep sleep in the car and Amanda told me she'd learned no good came from pulling her out of the car seat and moving her to the bassinet once they were inside. It was just as easy and just as safe to leave her where she slept.

"Angie get back all right?"

"Yeah. She arrived in Savannah at midnight. Got to her mother's by half-past."

"She doesn't strike me as someone from the South."

"She's not. Her mother remarried in her sixties. Her husband lived in Savannah. He passed about ten years ago. By then, her mother was in love with the place."

She placed her teapot on a coaster and sat at the table. "So what happened at the train station?"

I sat across from her. "First tell me how we ended up at the train station."

"What? I got a call and they said the meeting site was changed."

"Who called you?"

"It could have been Pavel, could have been this other one they call Spartak. Actually, now that I think of it, it did sound more like him. He's got a higher voice than the others. But then what do I know for sure?" She shrugged. "They all sound pretty much the same."

"And Spartak or whoever said . . ."

"He said something like, 'We no like Comcast Center. Tell them meet at Dodgeville Station, half hour.'"

"But why call you?"

She sipped her tea. "I don't know. Maybe Yefim lost your—"

I shook my head. "Yefim never made that call."

"He had Spartak make it."

"No, he didn't. Yefim was waiting at the Comcast Center when Dre got himself vaporized by an Acela."

The teacup froze halfway to her mouth. "You want to repeat that one?"

"Dre got hit by a train going so fast that it liquefied him. There's probably a forensics team out there right now, bagging up the Dre scraps. But they're little scraps, I assure you."

"Why would he step in front of a . . . ?"

"Because he was chasing this." I placed the Belarus Cross on the table.

It sat between us for about twenty seconds before either of us spoke.

"Chasing it?" Amanda said. "That makes no sense. He had it with him when he left the house, didn't he?"

"And I assume he handed it over to someone, and then that someone threw it back over the tracks."

"So you think . . . ?" She closed her eyes tight and shook her head. "I don't even know what you think."

"I don't either. Here's what I know—Dre crossed the tracks into the woods and then someone threw this cross out of the woods and over the tracks. Dre came running out after it and ran into a really fast train. Yefim, meanwhile, claims he was never at the train station and that he never changed the original meeting place. Whether he's lying or not, and there's a fifty-fifty chance either way, that's his claim. We don't have Sophie, they don't have the Belarus Cross, and it's Christmas Eve. Friday. Dre was the last chance Yefim had of scoring another baby to give to Kirill and Violeta. So now Yefim wants the original deal back in place—that cross"—I looked down the table—"and that baby for Sophie's life, my life, the life of my family, and your life."

She fingered the cross a couple of times, pushing it up the table a few inches.

"What do the inscriptions mean, do you know? I can't read Russian."

"Even if you could," I said, "they're not in Russian. That's Latin."

"Fair enough. You know any Latin?"

"I took four years of it in high school but all I retained is about enough to read a building foundation."

"So, no idea?"

I held it in my hand. "A little. The one up top reads *Jesus, Son of God, defeats.*"

She frowned.

I shrugged and racked my brain a bit. "No, wait. Not *defeats. Crushes.* No. Wait. *Conquers.* That's it. *Jesus, Son of God, conquers.*"

"What about the bottom one?"

"Something about a skull and paradise."

"That's the best you can do?"

"I took my last Latin class ten years before you were born, kid. My best ain't bad."

She poured herself more tea. She held the cup in both hands and blew on it. She took a tentative sip and then placed the cup back down on the table. She sat back in her chair, her eyes on me, as calm as ever, this serious child, this marvel of self-possession.

"It doesn't look like much, does it?"

"It's the history that gives it its worth. Or maybe just someone deciding it's worth something, like gold."

"I never understood that mentality," she said.

"Me, either."

"I can tell you, though, that Kirill's already lost too much face over this to let any of us live. Certainly not me."

"You been reading the papers lately?"

She looked over the teacup at me and shook her head.

"Kirill's hitting his own product too much. Or he's just having a full-on mental breakdown. He might wrap one of his cars around a pole at a hundred miles an hour before he ever gets around to you."

"So, I'll just wait for that day." She grimaced at me. "And even if, let's say, everything goes according to this fairy-tale scenario that Yefim—Yefim, yes?—outlined for you?"

"Yefim, yeah."

"So, okay. We live, Sophie lives, your family lives. What about her?" She pointed down the table where Claire sat, strapped in her car seat, wearing a tiny pink knit hoodie and matching pink sweatpants, her eyes closed to slits. "They take her into their home, Kirill and Violeta, and pretty soon she's not just the *idea* of a baby. She's an actual baby. She cries at inconvenient times, she screams, she howls when her diaper's wet, and she shrieks—I mean, like an electrified banshee— when you change her top because she hates having anything covering her face and you can't remove a top without covering her face, at least not the ones I have on hand. So they take her, these psychotic children in middle-aged bodies, and let's say they get past all the inconveniences and total lack of sleep that go with having a baby in the house, twenty-four-seven. Let's give them the benefit of the doubt. You don't think Kirill, who's now lost massive face, power, and respect because he got his own black-market baby stolen from him and he couldn't get her back—you're telling me he's not going to resent that child? Kirill, who, as you said, is having some sort of psychotic meltdown lately? He's not going to come home some night, amped up on Polish vodka and Mexican cocaine, and bludgeon that baby when she has the temerity to cry because she's hungry?" Amanda threw back her entire cup of tea like it was a shot of whiskey. "Do you really think I'm giving my baby back to *them*?"

"It's not your baby."

"That social security card you saw yesterday? That wasn't mine. That was hers. I already have one with the same last name. She's mine."

"You kidnapped her."

"And you kidnapped me."

She'd never raised her voice, but the walls seemed to shake just the same. Her lips trembled, her eyes grew red, tremors raced through her hands. Outside of highly controlled fury, I'd never seen her show emotion.

I shook my head.

"Yes, you did, Patrick. Yes, you did." She sucked wet air through her nostrils and looked up at the ceiling for a moment. "Who were you to say where my home was? Dorchester was just where I was born. I was Helene's spawn, but I was Jack and Tricia Doyle's child. You know what I remember about that time when I was so-called *kidnapped*? For seven perfect months, I didn't feel nervous or anxious. I didn't have nightmares. I wasn't sick, because when you leave a house where your mother never cleans and there's roaches and roach bacteria everywhere and rotten food fermenting in the sink—when you leave a place like that, you tend to feel better. I ate three times a day. I played with Tricia and our dog. After dinner, every night, they dressed me for bed and then brought me to a chair by the fireplace—seven o'clock on the dot—and they read to me." She looked down at the table for a moment, nodding to herself in such a way I doubted she knew she was doing it. She looked up. "And then you came. Two weeks after you returned me to Dorchester, and a DSS caseworker had cleared Helene to raise me, you know what happened at seven o'clock?"

I said nothing.

"Helene had spent the day drinking because she got stood up on a date the night before. She put me to bed at five o'clock because she was too far in the bag to deal with me anymore. And then at seven o'clock—on the dot—she came into my bedroom to apologize for being such a bad mother, feeling all sorry for herself and confusing that with empathy for another human being. And while she was apologizing, she puked all over me."

Amanda reached out and pulled the small teapot to her. She poured the rest of it into her cup. She didn't have to blow on it as much this time.

"I'm—"

"Don't dare say you're sorry, Patrick. Spare me that, please."

A long, dead minute passed.

"You ever see them anymore?" I asked eventually. "The Doyles?"

"They're prohibited from having any contact with me. It's a provision of their probation."

"But you know where they are."

She looked at me for a moment, then nodded. "Tricia did one year in jail and got another fifteen probation. Jack got out two years ago, after ten years in prison for reading me bedtime stories and giving me proper nutrition. They're still together. You believe that? She waited for him." She looked at me with shiny, defiant eyes. "They live in North Carolina now, just outside Chapel Hill." She pulled her hair from its ponytail and shook it violently until it hung straight down beside her face again. From back in its shroud, her eyes found me again. "Why'd you do it?"

"Bring you home?"

"Bring me back."

"It was a case of situational ethics versus societal ones, I guess. I took society's side."

"Lucky me."

"I don't know that I'd do any differently now," I said. "You want me to feel guilty and I do, but that doesn't mean I was wrong. If you keep Claire, trust me, you'll do things that make her hate you, but you'll do them because you'll believe it's for her own good. Every time you say no to her, for example. And sometimes you'll feel bad about it. But that's an emotional response, not a rational one. Rationally, I know damn well I don't want to live in a world where people can just pluck a child out of a family they deem bad and raise a stolen child as they see fit."

"Why not? That's what the Department of Children and Families does. That's what the government does all the time when they take kids away from bad parents."

"After due process, though. After checks and balances and diligent investigation of the charges. You, on the other hand? One day your uncle Lionel snapped when your mother left you in the sun all afternoon because she was drunk. She took you home when she should have taken you to an emergency room, and Lionel came up to deal with your cries. He called a cop who was *known* for kidnapping kids he felt lived in unsafe environments, and they kidnapped you. No due process for your mother—"

"Don't call her my mother, if you please."

"Fine. No due process for Helene. No representation of her side of the story. Nothing."

"My uncle Lionel had watched Helene 'raise' me, for lack of a better word, for four years. I'd say she was the beneficiary of four years of due process and due diligence on his watch."

"Then he should have filed charges with DCF and asked a court for the right to raise you. It worked for Kurt Cobain's sister, and she went up against a celebrity with money."

She nodded. "Nice. When it comes to—what'd you call it?—societal ethics versus situational ones, Patrick Kenzie invokes the memory of Kurt Cobain to represent the interests of the state."

Ouch. Direct hit.

Amanda leaned forward. "Because here's what I heard about *you* many years later—I heard that the child molester you killed while you were looking for me? What was his name?"

"Corwin Earle."

"Right. I heard—from *impeccable* sources—that he didn't have a weapon when you shot him. That he posed no direct threat to you." She sipped her tea. "And you shot him dead. Shot him in the back, wasn't it?"

"The back of the neck, actually. And his hand was touching a weapon, technically speaking."

"Technically speaking. So, you come upon a child molester who poses no direct threat to you, at least not by the state's definition if they had investigated very hard, and you deal with this by firing one hell of a situational ethic into the back of his head." She raised her cup to me. "Well done. I'd clap, but I don't want to wake the baby."

We sat in silence for a bit and she never took her eyes off me. Her self-possession was, quite frankly, a bit scary. It definitely didn't fill me with feelings of warmth. And yet, I liked her. I liked that the world had given her a raw deal and she'd dealt with it by playing the world's game right up to the point where she raised her middle finger to it and walked away from the whole sham. I liked that she refused to wallow in self-pity. I liked that she seemed incapable of asking for anyone's approval.

"You'll never give that baby up, will you?"

"They could break every bone in my body, and I'd continue fighting them with whatever muscle I got left. Cut out my tongue or I'll never stop screaming with it. And if they lose sight of me for one second, I'll sink my teeth into their eyes."

"Like I said, you'll never give up that baby, will you, Amanda?"

"And you?" She smiled. "You would never let me fight the fight alone, would you, Patrick?"

"Maybe," I said. "Maybe not. But I'm not leaving Sophie out there to die or be shipped to the basement harem of some emir in Dubai."

"Okay."

"But Yefim's going to want a baby."

"We might be able to stall him on that if he gets the cross."

"Yeah, but he won't give us Sophie. He'll just let us live another day."

"That twit."

"Who?"

"Sophie. You know I sent her to Vancouver right after, well, after—"

"Dre told me all about the bloodbath with Timur in the birthing room."

"Ah. Yeah, so after that, I send Sophie to Vancouver with impeccable paperwork. I mean, flawless. The kind people pay six figures for. I rebirthed her."

"But the new birth canal led right back to the Russian mob."

"Yeah."

I watched her for a bit, looking for some kind of uncertainty, even a hair of it, to creep into those placid eyes. But it never happened.

"Are you ready—I mean, really ready—to give up all you're giving up here?"

"What am I giving up?" she asked. "You mean, like, Harvard and all that?"

"For starters."

She widened her eyes at me. "I've got five ironclad identities. One of them, by the way, is already enrolled in Harvard next year. And one is enrolled in Brown. I haven't decided which one I want yet. A real degree from either of those schools, or any school for that matter, is no better than a fake one. And in some cases, it's worse because it's less malleable. There's an eighth continent now, Patrick. It's accessed by a keyboard. You can paint the sky, rewrite the rules of travel, do whatever you want. No boundaries and no border wars because very few people even know how to find this continent. I do. Some other people I've met do. The rest of you remain here." She leaned forward. "So, yes, playing by your rules, I'm Amanda

McCready, an about-to-turn-seventeen high school dropout. According to *my* rules, though, Amanda McCready is just one card in a thick deck. Look at it like—"

She pushed back her chair, her eyes on the window that faced the street. She grabbed the bag at her feet and tossed it onto the table. I followed her gaze and saw a car out front, one that hadn't been there a minute before.

"Who is it?"

She didn't answer. She dumped her leather bag on the dining-room table and pulled out of the pile two sets of the weirdest-looking handcuffs I'd ever seen. There was no chain between the cuffs. The base of each cuff met the base of the other. They were encased in hard black plastic. One cuff was standard size. On the other end, it was tiny. Small enough to cuff a bird maybe.

Or a baby.

"What the fuck are those?" I crossed the dining room and threw the lock on the front door.

"Don't curse in front of the baby."

The top of someone's head passed beneath the dining-room window.

"Fine. What the heck are those?"

"High-security rigid handcuffs." Amanda struggled into her Björn. "They use them to transport terrorists on planes. I had these modified. They kick ass, right?"

"They're cool," I said. "How many doors into the house?"

"Three if you count the cellar." She unstrapped Claire from the car seat. The baby groaned and then huffed out several un-happy grunts. Amanda fit her legs into the holes of the Björn, slipped one flap over her shoulder, and buckled it as someone kicked in the back door.

Amanda snapped one cuff over her own left wrist, one over her right.

I pulled my .45, pointed it at the dining-room portico.

Amanda snapped one of the smaller cuffs over Claire's left wrist.

A window broke in the living room, followed a second or two later by the sounds of someone climbing through it. I kept my eye on the portico, but now I knew they could flank me.

"A little help?" Amanda said.

I came over to her and she held her right arm up so that the smaller cuff hovered beside Claire's left wrist.

"You bring game, sister." I snapped the cuff closed over Claire's wrist.

"In for a penny, in for a pound."

Kenny came through the portico at the end of the room with a shotgun leveled at us.

I pointed my .45 at his head, but it was a hollow gesture; if he pulled that trigger from this distance, he'd kill all three of us.

I heard the racking of another shotgun, to my left. I glanced over. Tadeo stood where the living room met the dining room at the base of the staircase.

"You just ejected a shell trying to make a cool sound," I told him.

He turned a bit red. "Still got one to put in your chest."

"Dang," I said, "that gun's almost as big as you."

"Big enough to cut you in half, homes."

"But the recoil will blow your ass into the front yard."

Kenny said, "Put your gun down, Patrick."

I kept my gun where it was. "You Mexican, Tadeo?"

He nestled the shotgun stock into his shoulder. "You damn right I am."

"I never had a Mexican standoff with an actual Mexican. There's something cool about that, don't you think?"

"Sounds racist to me, homes."

"What's racist about it? You're Mexican, this is a Mexican standoff. It'd be like going Dutch with someone from Amsterdam. Now if, because I'm Irish, you accused me of having a small dick and being a drunk, *that's* racist, but describing a standoff as a Mexican standoff as opposed to a plain old, you know, standoff, that seems a pretty victimless racial modification to me."

"You're stalling," Kenny said.

"I'm giving everyone time to calm down."

Helene came through the portico behind Kenny. She saw the three guns and took a big swallow, but kept coming into the dining room.

"Honey," she said in a syrupy voice, "we just want the baby."

"Don't call me honey," Amanda said.

"What should I call you?"

"Estranged."

Kenny said to Helene, "Just get the baby."

"Okay."

Amanda raised her wrists so Kenny and Helene saw the cuffs. "Claire and me? We're a package."

Kenny's face grew long and defeated. "Where are the keys?"

"Behind you in the handcuff-key jar." Amanda rolled her eyes. "Really, Ken?"

"I can kill you," Kenny said, "and just cut those cuffs off with a hacksaw."

"If it was 1968 and this was *Cool Hand Luke,* maybe," Amanda said. "You see any length of chain on these? You see anything you could cut?"

"Hey!" Helene yelled as if she were the voice of reason. "No one's killing anyone."

"Gosh, Moms," Amanda said, "what exactly do you think Kirill Borzakov is going to do to me?"

"He won't kill you," Helene said, patting the air for effect. "He promised."

"Oh, well, then," I said to Amanda, "you're fine."

"Right?"

"Patrick," Kenny said.

"Yeah?"

"You can't win this. I mean, you've got to know that."

"We just want the baby," Helene said again.

"And that cross on the table," Kenny said, noticing it for the first time. "Damn. Helene, pick that thing up, would ya?"

"Which?"

"The only Russian cross on the dining-room table."

"Oh."

As Helene reached for the cross, I noticed something odd in the pile of things Amanda had dumped from her leather bag—Dre's key chain. I experienced what Bubba likes to call a disturbance in the Force, and I was so baffled I almost said something to Amanda right then, but Kenny snapped my attention back the other way by tapping the barrel of the shotgun against the wall.

"Lower your gun, Patrick. Seriously, man."

I looked at Amanda, looked at the baby strapped to her chest and cuffed to her wrists. Claire hadn't made a peep since the second cuff went on her. She just stared up at Amanda with what, in a self-aware being, could have been considered awe.

"The gun's making me nervous too," Amanda whispered. "And I don't see how it helps us."

I flicked the safety on and raised my hand, the gun dangling from my thumb.

"Take his gun, Helene."

Helene came over and I handed her the gun and she placed it awkwardly in her handbag. She looked past me at Claire.

"Oh, she's so pretty." She looked back over her shoulder at Kenny. "You should see her, Ken. She's got my eyes."

No one said anything for a few seconds.

"How is it," Kenny asked, "you're allowed to vote and operate machinery?"

" 'Cuz," Helene said proudly, "this is America."

Kenny closed and opened his eyes.

"Can I touch her?" Helene asked Amanda.

"I'd kinda prefer you didn't."

Helene reached out anyway and squeezed Claire's cheek.

Claire began to cry.

"Great," Kenny said. "We gotta listen to that all the way back to Boston."

Amanda said, "Helene?"

"Yeah?"

"Could you do me a huge solid and grab that diaper bag and the little cooler of formula?"

"What're you going to do with me?" I asked Kenny. "Tie me to a chair or shoot me?"

Kenny gave me a confused look. "Neither. The Russians want all of you." He used three fingers to point at us. "And they're paying by the pound."

CHAPTER TWENTY-FOUR

THE ONLY TRAILER PARK INSIDE BOSTON city limits is on the West Roxbury–Dedham border, squeezed in between a restaurant and a car dealership on a strip of Route 1 that is otherwise zoned for commercial or industrial use. And yet, after decades of fighting off developers and buyout offers from the car dealership, the little trailer park that could remains pressed hard against a sluggish brown stretch of the Charles River. I'd always rooted for the place, taken a vicarious pride in the residents' resilience to yet more commercial sprawl. It would break my heart someday to drive past it and see a McDonald's or an Outback in its place. Then again, I doubted someone would take me to a McDonald's to kill me, but it looked highly likely that I might breathe my last in a trailer park.

Kenny pulled off Route 1 onto the entrance roadway and drove us due east toward the river. He was, I'd learned, still pissed about his Hummer. He ranted about it for half the drive.

How the cops had it impounded over in Southie and wouldn't believe his story that it was stolen and he was probably going to have his parole revoked over it if they could prove he'd been anywhere near it that morning, but most of all, what really killed him, was that he'd loved that car.

"One," I said, "I don't know how anyone could *love* a Hummer."

"Oh, I loved it, bitch."

"Two," I said, "why you beefing with me? I didn't shoot your stupid-looking car. Yefim did."

"You stole it, though."

"But it's not like I said, 'Let me take it through the bullet wash.' I was trying to find out where they were taking Sophie, and Yefim shot the shit out of your ugly car."

"It's not an ugly car."

"It's a hideous car," Amanda said.

"It's a pretty gay-looking car," Tadeo chimed in. "You man enough to get away with it, though, Ken."

Helene touched his arm. "I love it, honey."

"All of you, please," Kenny said, "shut the fuck up now."

We drove in silence for the last forty minutes. Kenny was driving a late-'90s Chevy Suburban, which probably got the same mileage as the Hummer but somehow managed to be only half as ridiculous to behold. Amanda, the baby, and I sat in back with Tadeo between us. They'd tied my hands behind my back with a length of rope. It was a pretty uncomfortable way to sit for a two-hour drive, and I got a crick in my neck that worked its way down into my shoulders and would, I was sure, stay there for days. Sucks getting old.

We got off the Pike and drove south on 95 for ten miles before Kenny pulled off onto 109 and drove east another six miles, then turned right on Route 1, and took a right into the trailer park.

"How much they paying you for this?" I asked Kenny.

"How about my life? That's a good one. Can you double it?"

"No."

"Didn't think so." He looked in the rearview at her. "Amanda."

"Yo, Ken."

"I always thought you were a sweet kid, for what it's worth."

"I die fulfilled, then, Ken."

Kenny snorted. "You're what we'd call a pistol in my day."

"I didn't know they had pistols in your day."

Tadeo laughed. "This bitch is cold." He turned to her. "That's a compliment."

"Never had a doubt."

We drove to the end of the main road. The trees and the river were the same light brown, and a riot of leaves salted with snow covered everything—the ground, the cars, the trailer roofs, the satellite dishes on top of the trailers, the tin carports. The sky was unblemished blue marble. A hawk flew in low over the river. The trailers sported wreaths and colored lights and the roof of one even sported a light display in the shape of Santa riding a golf cart, for some reason.

It was one of those days that, while cold, was so clear and bright that it nearly made up for the four more months of frigid gray we faced. The crisp air smelled like a cold apple. The sun was sharp and warm on my skin when Kenny stopped the Suburban and opened the back door and pulled me out.

Amanda, the baby, and Tadeo got out the other side and we all stood by a long double-wide trailer along the riverbank.

It was empty back here. No cars in front of the few nearby trailers, everyone probably at work or last-minute Christmas shopping.

The door of the trailer opened and Yefim stood there, smiling while he chewed some food, a sub sandwich in one hand, a Springfield XD .40 cal in his waistband.

"Welcome, my friends. Come, come." He waved us toward him and we all filed in.

When Amanda passed him, he raised an eyebrow at the cuffs. "Not bad." Once we were inside, he closed the door behind us, and said to me, "How you doing, hump?"

"I'm all right. You?"

"Good, good."

The inside of the trailer was a lot bigger than I'd imagined. On the back wall, in the center, was a sixty-inch TV screen. Two guys stood in front of it playing Wii Tennis, swinging their arms back and forth and jumping in place while their midget avatars ran back and forth across the screen. To the right of the TV was a sky-blue leather couch, two matching armchairs, and a glass coffee table. Past that, a thick black curtain was strung across the width of the room. On the sky-blue couch, Sophie sat with her mouth covered with electrical tape and her hands bound with a bungee cord. She glanced at all of us, but her eyes lit up when they fell on Amanda.

Amanda smiled back at her.

To our left was a kitchenette, and beyond that a small bathroom and a large bedroom. Cardboard boxes took up nearly every inch of free space—filling the shelves, stacked on the floors, crammed in the spaces above the kitchen cupboards. I could see them stacked in the bedroom and assumed they filled the space behind the black curtain—DVD players, Blu-Ray players, Wii, PlayStation, and Xbox players, Bose home theater systems, iPods, iPads, Kindles, and Garmin GPS systems.

We stood in the entranceway and watched the two men play virtual tennis for a moment with Sophie staring at us. She looked much better than she had the other day, like maybe they'd kept her meth-free and her body was starting to respond.

Yefim cocked his head at me. "Why you tied up, man?"

"Your friend Kenny."

"He's not my friend, man. Turn around."

Kenny seemed hurt by the comment. He gave Helene a look like, *You believe this shit?*

I gave Yefim my back and he cut the rope off my wrists, eating his sub the whole time, breathing through nostrils thick with hair.

"You look well, my friend. Healthy."

"Thank you. You too."

He slapped his heavy gut with his gun hand. "Ha ha. You a funny hump." His voice suddenly boomed. "Pavel!"

Pavel turned in the middle of his backhand and looked back at Yefim as his avatar spun and then fell on the court and the tennis ball bounced past him.

"You on the clock. Take their weapons."

Pavel sighed and tossed his remote onto a chair. His companion did the same. His companion was skinny as death, sunken cheeks and shaved head, Russian words tattooed on his neck. He wore a wife-beater that clung to his emaciated chest and black-and-yellow-striped sweatpants.

"Spartak," Amanda whispered to me.

Spartak took Tadeo's shotgun and Pavel took Kenny's.

"Other guns," Pavel said, snapping his fingers, his voice and gaze as flat as a dime. "Hurry."

Kenny handed over a Taurus .38 and Tadeo forked over a FNP-9. Pavel put the two shotguns and two handguns in a black canvas bag on the floor.

Yefim finished his sandwich and wiped his hands with a napkin. He burped and we all got a nice blast of peppers and vinegar and what I think was ham.

"I got to get to the gym, Pavel."

Pavel looked up from the bag as he zipped it closed. "You look fine, man."

"I feel I lack discipline."

Pavel took the bag over to the kitchen and placed it on the small countertop beside the stove. "You look fine, Yefim. All the ladies say so."

Yefim smiled broadly at that, his eyebrows raised as he mock-primped his hair. "I'm George Clooney, eh? Ha ha."

"You George Clooney with big Russian cock."

"That's the best George Clooney to be!" Yefim shouted, and he and Pavel and Spartak all roared with laughter.

The rest of us stood around looking at one another.

When Yefim stopped laughing, he wiped at his eyes and sighed and then clapped his hands together. "Let's go see Kirill. Spartak, you stay with Sophie."

Spartak nodded and pulled back the black curtain on another living room. This one was bigger than the one we were leaving, fifteen-by-twenty was my guess, and the walls were all mirrored. A long purple sectional formed a U. The sectional must have been custom-built, because its sides ran the length of the room. The center of the room was bare. Above our heads, and reflected in the mirrors, was a TV, this one playing a Mexican *telenovela*. Above the sectional were shelves, dozens of them, and all those shelves were filled with more Blu-Ray players and iPods and Kindles and laptops.

A thin man with a huge head sat beside a dark-haired woman in the center of the sectional. The woman had a kind of stricken madness in her face that drew you to her in helpless, morbid fascination. Violeta Concheza Borzakov had been beautiful once, but something had eaten away at her, and she was only thirty or thirty-two, tops. Her sunset skin was lightly dimpled all over, like the surface of a pond at the beginning of a light rain, and her hair was the blackest black I'd ever seen. She had eyes so dark they almost matched her hair, and something resided in them that was both frightened and frightening; a butchered soul lived back there, abandoned and agitated. She wore a charcoal newsboy cap, a black silk crewneck under a gray silk wrap, black leggings, and knee-high black boots. She watched us come like we were cuts at a steakhouse being wheeled to her on a cart.

Kirill Borzakov, meanwhile, wore a white silk sweatshirt under a white cashmere sportcoat, tan cargo pants, and white tennis shoes. His silver hair was cut tight to his huge skull and the pockets under his eyes came in layers of three. He smoked a cigarette with the kind of loud, liquid smacks that made you never want to smoke a cigarette, and flicked the ash in the vicinity of an overflowing ashtray by his right hand. Beside the ashtray was an open compact mirror that sported several small bumps of cocaine. His gaze was impersonal. It had been at least three decades since empathy had crawled in there and died. I got the feeling that if my chest burst open and Lenin himself stepped out of it, Kirill would continue smoking his cigarette and glancing up at the Mexican soap opera.

Yefim said, "Ladies and gentlemen, Kirill and Violeta Borzakov."

Kirill stood and walked around us, inspecting his collection of chattel. He looked at Kenny and Helene and then over at Pavel.

Pavel took Kenny and Helene by the shoulders and sat them down at the foot of the sectional on the left side. Kirill cocked his head at Pavel again, and a second or two later, Tadeo was pushed onto the couch beside Helene.

Kirill walked around me in a slow circle. "Who are you?"

"I'm a private investigator," I said.

A sucking noise as he took a drag off his cigarette and flicked the ash onto the faux-oak floor. "The private investigator who find the girl for me?"

"I didn't find her for you."

He nodded at that, as if I'd said something sage, and took my left hand in his. "You didn't find her for me?"

"No."

His grip was soft, almost delicate. "Who you find her for?"

"Her aunt."

"But not for me?"

I shook my head. "Not for you."

He gave me another nod as he wrapped his fingers around my wrist and ground his cigarette out in my palm.

I'm not sure how I managed not to scream. For half a minute, all I could feel was a fat ember burning through my flesh. I could smell it. My mind went black and then red and I flashed on an image of the nerves in my hand hanging like vines as smoke curled up them.

While he burned me, Kirill Borzakov looked into my eyes.

There was nothing to see in his. No anger, no joy, no thrill that comes with violence or the elation of absolute power. Nothing. He had the eyes of a reptile sunning itself on a rock.

I grunted several times and exhaled through gritted teeth and tried to block images of what my hand must look like by now. I flashed on my daughter, and for a moment that calmed me, but then I realized I'd brought her into this moment, this polluted violence and sickness, and I tried to remove the image of her from my head, tried to will her away from this depravity, and the pain pulsed twice as strong. Then Kirill dropped my wrist and stepped back.

"See if this aunt can make your skin grow back."

I flicked the dead cigarette butt from the center of my palm as Violeta Borzakov said, "Kirill, you're blocking the TV."

The coal was black now, on its way to ash, and the center of my palm looked like the top of a volcano—puckered and red, the burned flesh peeled back.

On the Mexican soap, the music swelled and a beautiful Latina in a white peasant top turned on her heel and stalked out of an earth-toned room as the lights went down. The next thing we saw was a commercial with Antonio Sabato Jr. hawking some kind of skin cream.

I would have paid a thousand dollars for that skin cream. I would have paid two thousand dollars for that skin cream and an ice cube.

Violeta took her eyes off the TV. "Why is the *bambina* still with the little girl?"

Amanda turned so they could see the handcuffs.

"What is this shit, Yefim?" Violeta sat up and leaned forward.

Yefim's eyes widened. He seemed frightened by her. "Mrs. Borzakov, we bring her to you as promised."

"As promised? You're weeks late, *pendejo*. Weeks. And do *you* bring her, Yefim, or was it these people?" She waved in the general direction of Kenny, Helene, and Tadeo.

"It was us," Kenny said from the couch. He gave Violeta a wave that she ignored. "All us."

Kirill lit a fresh cigarette. "You have your baby now. Go get her and be done with this."

Violeta slinked toward Amanda like a water snake. She peered at Claire and then sniffed her.

"Is she intelligent?"

Amanda said, "She's four weeks old."

"Does she talk?"

"She's four weeks old."

Violeta touched the baby's forehead. "Say 'Ma-*ma*.' Say 'Ma-*ma*.'"

Claire began to cry.

Violeta said, "Ssshhh."

Claire cried louder.

Violeta sang, "Hush, little baby, don't you fret. Momma's gonna make you a . . ."

She looked around the room at us.

"Mockingbird?" I tried.

She thrust out her bottom lip in a gesture of acceptance. "And if that mockingbird don't fly, Momma gonna buy you a . . ."

Another look for the room. Claire continued to wail.

"Corvette," Tadeo said.

She frowned at him.

"Diamond ring," Yefim said.

"That doesn't rhyme."

"And yet I am sure it is correct."

Claire's wailing hit a new pitch, the banshee-shrieking Amanda had mentioned.

Kirill, sitting on the couch, snorted a line of blow off the compact mirror and said, "Make her stop."

Violeta said, "I'm trying." She touched Claire's head again. "Sssssshhhhh." She hissed it, over and over—"Ssssssshhhhhhhh! Sssssssshhhhhh!"

This did not make things better.

Kirill winced and snorted another line. He placed a hand to his ear and winced harder. "Shut her up."

"Sssssssshhhhhhhhh! Sssssssssshhhhhhhh! I don't know what the fuck to do. You said you would hire a nanny."

"I *hire* the nanny. But I don't bring her here. Shut her up."

"Ssssssshhhhhhh!"

By now Tadeo and Kenny both had their hands over their ears and Pavel and Yefim made various faces of discomfort. Only Helene seemed oblivious, her eyes on the DVD players and the iPods.

I said to Amanda, "Pacifier?"

"Right pocket."

I held my hand by her pocket, looked at Yefim. "May I?"

"Shit, my friend, absolutely."

I reached into Amanda's pocket and pulled out the pacifier.

"Sssssssshhhhhhhhhh!" Violeta was screaming it now.

I pulled the plastic cover off the pacifier, movement that drove a spike into my burned palm. My eyes watered and widened, but I reached over Amanda's shoulder and plopped the pacifier into the baby's mouth.

The volume in the room immediately plummeted. Claire sucked the pacifier back and forth against her lips.

"Better," Kirill said.

Violeta ran both palms down her cheeks. "You have spoiled her."

Amanda said, "Excuse me?"

"You have spoiled her. This is why she screams like this. She will learn not to do that."

Amanda said, "She's four weeks old, you fucking moron."

"Don't swear in front of the baby," I reminded her.

She met my eyes and hers were bright and warm. "My bad."

"What did you call me?" Violeta looked back at her husband. "Did you hear her?"

Kirill yawned into his fist.

Violeta stepped in close to Amanda and stared at her with those ravaged eyes of hers.

"Cut it off," Violeta said.

"What?" Yefim said.

"Cut it off her."

"You cannot cut those cuffs," Yefim said. "Burn them off, maybe."

Kirill lit a new cigarette with the butt of an old one, squinting around the smoke. "Then burn them off."

"We'll end up burning the girl."

Violeta said, "Not if you cut off her hands."

Yefim said, "Mrs. Borzakov?"

Violeta kept her eyes on Amanda, their faces so close their noses almost touched. "We'll shoot her first. Then we cut off her hands. Then we find a way to take the handcuffs off the *bambina*." She looked back at her husband. "Yes?"

Kirill was looking up at the TV. "What?"

"*Escuche! Escuche!*" Violeta slapped her own chest. "I'm here, Kirill." She slapped her chest again, harder. "I exist." One more slap. "I live in your life."

"Yes, yes," he said. "What now?"

"We shoot the girl, cut off her hands."

"Okay, darling." Kirill waved toward the other end of the trailer. "Do it in the back bedroom."

Yefim reached for Amanda, who didn't so much as flinch.

"Let me," Violeta said.

Yefim's eyebrows shot up. "What?"

"I want to do it," Violeta said, her eyes never leaving Amanda's face. "She would prefer a woman do it. I know her."

"Let her do it," Kirill said to Yefim and waved a tired hand.

Through the entire conversation about her own murder, Amanda didn't make a sound. She didn't shake, she didn't blanch. She stared at the two of them, unblinking.

Helene said, "What? Wait a minute. What's going on here?"

Helene's bag was still at her feet. They'd never checked her for a weapon, and my .45 was in there. It would take me four steps to reach the bag. Then I'd have to reach in, thumb off the safety, and point it at someone. I figured that even in the most optimistic scenario, Pavel and Yefim would empty a good two dozen rounds into me before I cleared the gun from the bag.

I stayed where I was.

"What's going on?" Helene said again, but no one listened to her.

Violeta kissed Amanda's cheek and ran her hand over Claire's head.

"Mrs. Borzakov?" Yefim said. "You ever fire this gun before?"

She went over to Yefim. "What gun?"

"This one," he said. "It's a forty-caliber automatic."

"I like revolvers."

"I don't have a revolver right now."

"Okay." She sighed and brushed her hair back off her shoulders. "Show me this gun."

Yefim put the gun in Violeta's hands and showed her where the safety was. "It pulls a bit to the left," he said. "In this space? It will be loud."

Helene said to Kenny, "You promised no one would get hurt."

Kenny said to Kirill, "Yeah, Mr. Borzakov. We had, like, a deal."

"No deal with you." Kirill waved his hand. "Pavel."

Pavel pointed a Makarov pistol at Helene and Kenny. "Take them in back, too, Kirill?"

"Yes," Kirill said. "What did you do with the other girl?"

Pavel gestured at the baby. "Baby's mother?"

"Yeah."

"She no bother, boss. She's in the living room. Spartak take care of her, soon as I tell him."

"Good, good."

Yefim finished showing Violeta how to use the gun. "You got it now?"

"I got it."

"Are you sure, Mrs. Borzakov?"

She let go of the gun. "I'm sure, I'm sure. You think I'm stupid, Yefim?"

"Tiny bit, yes." Yefim tilted the muzzle up and pulled the trigger. The bullet entered Violeta's head in the soft skin under the palate. It exited the top of her head and followed a starburst of blood and bone into the ceiling. Her newsboy hat disappeared behind the couch. Her knees buckled left, then right, and she fell on the sectional and slid from there to the floor.

Kirill started to get off the couch, but Yefim shot him in the stomach. Kirill let loose a sound I'd once heard a dog make when it was hit by a car.

Spartak came through the curtain with a revolver extended and Pavel shot him in the temple as Spartak was in mid-stride. Spartak took a half-step with his brains dripping pink and red down the mirrored wall, and then he fell face-forward on the floor by my foot, his mouth open and huffing.

After a few seconds, no more huffing.

Pavel swung his arm and pointed at Kenny's chest.

"Wait," Kenny said to Pavel. "Hold on."

Pavel looked over at Yefim. Yefim flicked his eyes to Amanda. After a second or two, he looked back at Pavel and blinked once.

Pavel fired a round into Kenny's chest and Kenny jerked in place like he'd been hit with a cattle prod.

Helene screamed.

Tadeo said, "No, no, no, no, no," his eyes clenched.

Kenny raised an arm and looked around, his eyes wild and so terribly afraid. Pavel took one step forward and fired another round into Kenny's forehead and Kenny stopped moving.

Helene curled into a fetal position on the sectional and screamed herself into silence, her mouth open and soaking wet, the spittle dripping off her chin, but no sound coming out as she looked at Kenny lying dead as dead got on the carpet beside

Spartak. Pavel trained his gun on her but didn't pull the trigger. Tadeo dropped off the couch and landed on his knees and started praying.

Kirill pawed the couch like he was trying to find the remote in the dark. He grunted, over and over, the blood slopping all over his white sweater and tan pants. He opened his mouth and gulped at the air, his eyes on the ceiling as Yefim put one knee on the couch beside him and pressed the muzzle of his Springfield XD against Kirill's heart.

"I loved you like a father, but you go become a fucking embarrassment, man. Too much shit up your nose, I think. Too much vodka, eh?"

Kirill said, "Who will work with you if you kill your own boss? Who will trust you?"

Yefim smiled. "I got approval from *everyone* on this—the Chechens, the Georgians, even that crazy Muscovite there in Brighton Beach? One you said could never run the show? He runs the show, Kirill. And he agree—you got to go."

Kirill held both hands over the hole in his abdomen and arched his back from the pain.

Yefim gritted his teeth and then sucked his lips in against them.

"Let me tell you, Yefim. I—"

Yefim pulled the trigger twice. Kirill's eyes snapped back into his head. He exhaled, the sound impossibly high-pitched. His eyes remained back in his head, only the whites showing. When Yefim came off the couch, the smoke exited Kirill's mouth and the hole in his chest at the same time.

Yefim walked over to Amanda. "We let your mother live?"

"Oh, God," Helene shrieked from her fetal position on the couch.

Amanda looked at Helene for a long time.

"I guess. Don't call her my mother, though."

"What about little Spanish guy?"

"He probably needs a job."

"Hey, little fellah," Yefim said. "You want a job?"

"Nah, man," Tadeo said. "I'm so fucking done with this shit. I just want to go work with my uncle."

"What's he do?"

Tadeo's accent suddenly disappeared. "He sells, like, insurance?"

Yefim smiled. "That's worse than what we do. Hey, Pavel?"

Pavel laughed. It was surprisingly high-pitched, a giggle.

"Ho-kay, little man. When you leave here, you go sell insurance. I think we done killing for the day, then. Pavel?"

Pavel nodded. "My fucking ears hurt, man."

Yefim looked up at the ceiling. "Shit-ass construction, these things. Too much tin. *Boom boom*. Now that I'm king, Pavel? No more trailers for us."

Pavel said, "George Clooney no king."

Yefim clapped his hands together. "Ha! You right there. Fuck George Clooney, eh? Maybe someday he get to *play* a king, but he'll never *be* a king like Yefim."

"You know that is sure, boss."

Yefim reached into his jacket pocket and came out with a small black key. He stepped up to Amanda and said, "Hold out your wrists."

Amanda did.

Yefim unlocked Amanda's right handcuff and then the baby's. "Man, look at her. She's sleeping."

"She doesn't seem to mind loud noises," Amanda said. "This kid, I swear, every day's a surprise."

"You telling me." Yefim unlocked the left cuffs. "You got her?"

"I got her."

"Hold her tight."

"I'm holding her. She's in a Björn, Yefim."

"Of course. I forget." Yefim pinched the handcuffs at their centers and pulled them away from Amanda and the baby.

Amanda rubbed her wrists and looked around at the carnage. "Well . . ."

Yefim held out his hand. "Pleasure, Miss Amanda."

"You're no slouch yourself, Yefim." She shook his hand. "Oh, the cross is in Helene's purse."

Yefim snapped his fingers. Pavel threw him the purse. Yefim pulled out the cross and smiled. "My family, before we end up in Mordovia two hundred years ago? We live in Kiev." He raised his eyebrows at me. "True. My father, he tells me we're descended from Prince Yaroslav himself. This is a family heirloom, man."

"From a prince to a king," Pavel said.

"Oh, you too kind, man." He rummaged in the bag and then looked at me. "Whose gun?"

"That's mine."

"It was in the bag the whole time? Pavel!"

Pavel held up his hands. "Spartak supposed to check woman."

They both looked down at Spartak as his blood ran under the sectional. After a few seconds they looked at each other and shrugged.

Yefim handed me my gun like he was handing me a can of soda, and I put it in the holster behind my back. Four people had just been killed in front of me, and I felt nothing. Zip. That's what twenty years of swimming in shit had cost me.

"Oh, wait." Yefim reached into his back pocket and pulled out a thick black wallet. He rummaged around in it for a bit and then handed me my driver's license. "You ever need something, you call me."

"I won't," I said.

He narrowed his eyes at me. "You go sell insurance like the little man?"

"Not insurance."

"What you do, then?"

"Going back to school," I said and realized I meant it.

He raised his eyebrows at that and then nodded. "Good idea. This is no life for you anymore."

"No."

"You're old."

"Right."

"You have kid, wife."

"Exactly."

"You're old."

"You said that already."

He held the cross out for me to see. "Beautiful, eh? Every time someone die for it, it gets more beautiful, I think."

I pointed at the Latin on the bottom. "What's that mean?"

"What you think it means?"

"Something about heaven or paradise. Eden, maybe. I don't know."

Yefim looked at the bodies on the couch and on the floor by his feet. He chuckled. "You like this, man. It means, 'The place of the skull has become paradise.'"

"Which means what?"

"I always thought, dying isn't death. Where you see a skull, that guy? He already in paradise. Forever, my friend." He scratched his temple with his gun sight and sighed. "You got Blu-Ray?"

"Huh?"

"You got Blu-Ray player?"

"No."

"Oh, man, you crazy. Pavel, tell him."

Pavel said, "You not watching movies unless you watch the Blu-Ray. It's the pixels. Ten-eighty dpi, Dolby True HD sound? Change your life, man."

Yefim waved his arms at the boxes stacked above Kirill's corpse. "I like the Sony, but Pavel swears by JVC. You take two. You watch both with your wife and daughter, tell me which you like best. Hey?"

"Sure."

"You want PlayStation 3?"

"No, I'm good."

"iPod?"

"Got a couple, thanks."

"How about a Kindle, my friend?"

"Nah."

"You sure?"

"I'm sure."

He shook his head several times. "I can't give those fucking things away."

I held out my good hand. "Take care, Yefim."

He clapped both my shoulders hard and kissed me on both cheeks. He still smelled of ham and vinegar. He hugged me and pounded his fists on my back. Only then did he shake my hand.

"You, too, my good friend, you hump."

CHAPTER TWENTY-FIVE

ALL IN ALL, IT WAS an interesting Christmas Eve.

We were delayed getting out of the trailer park, because both Helene and Tadeo soiled themselves when Yefim and Pavel shot four people to death in the time it took to light a cigarette. Then Tadeo fainted. It happened just after Yefim and I discussed Blu-Rays and Kindles. We exchanged our Russian man-hug and heard a thump and looked over to see Tadeo lying on the floor of the trailer, breathing like a fish that had ridden a wave into shore but forgot to ride it back out.

"You ask me," Yefim said, "I'm not sure this little man can handle the insurance business."

We stood by the Suburban for a minute—Amanda, the baby, Sophie, and me. Sophie shivered and smoked and looked at me apologetically, either for the smoking or the shaking, I couldn't tell. Pavel had told us to stay put and then he'd gone back inside the trailer. When he returned, he carried two Blu-Ray players.

Inside, someone fired up a chain saw.

Pavel handed me the Blu-Ray players. "You enjoy. *Do svidanya.*"

"*Do svidanya.*"

I went to the back of the Suburban and then called to Pavel as he reached for the door of the trailer. "We don't have the car keys."

He looked back at me.

"Kenny had them. They're still in one of his pockets."

"Give me minute."

"Hey, Pavel?"

He looked back, one hand on the door.

"You have any ice in there?" I held up my scorched palm.

"I take a look." He went back into the trailer.

I put the Blu-Ray players on the ground at the back of the Suburban, and my phone rang. I read the caller ID: ANGIE CELL. I flipped the phone open as fast as I could and walked away from the Suburban toward the river.

"Hey, babe."

"Hi," she said. "How's Boston?"

"It's nice here right now. The weather." I reached the river-bank, stood watching the brown Charles slosh along, ice chips surfing along the top every now and then. "Thirty-eight, maybe thirty-nine degrees. Blue sky. Feels more like Thanksgiving. How's it there?"

"It's about fifty-five. Gabby loves it, man. All the squares, the horse-drawn carriages, the trees. She can't get enough."

"So you're going to stay?"

"Hell, no. It's Christmas Eve. We're at the airport. We board in an hour."

"I never gave you an all-clear."

"Yeah, but Bubba did."

"Oh, really."

"He said it was just as easy to shoot Russians in Boston."

"A solid point. All right, then, come home."

"You done?"

"I am done. Hold on."

"What?"

"Hang on a sec." I crooked the phone into the space be-tween my ear and my shoulder, never as easy to do on a cell as it is on a home phone. I pulled my .45 Colt Commander out of the holster at my back. "You still there?"

"I'm here."

I ejected the clip, then jacked the round out of the chamber. I pulled back on the slide and disengaged it from the grip. I tossed the slide in the water.

"What're you doing?" Angie asked.

"I'm throwing my gun in the Charles."

"No, you're not."

"I am." I tossed the clip in, watched it sink beneath the sluggish current. I flicked my wrist and the grip followed. I was left with one bullet and the frame. I considered both.

"You just threw your gun away. The .45?"

"Yes, ma'am." I tossed the frame up and out in an arc and got a respectable splash when it hit.

"Honey, you're going to need that for work."

"No," I said. "I'm not doing this shit anymore. Mike Co-lette offered me a job in his freight company and I'm going to take him up on it."

"You're serious?"

"Know what it is, babe?" I looked back at the trailer. "When you start out doing this, you think it's just the truly horrible shit that's going to get you—that poor little boy in that bathtub back in '98, what happened in Gerry Glynn's bar, Christ, that bunker in Plymouth . . ." I took a breath, let it out slowly. "But it's not those moments. It's all the little ones. It's not that people fuck each other over for a million dollars that depresses me, it's that they do it for ten. I don't give a shit any- more whether so-and-so's wife is cheating on him, because he probably deserved it. And all those insurance companies? I help them prove a guy's faking his neck injury, they turn around and drop coverage on half the neighborhood when the reces- sion hits. The last three years, every time I sit on the corner of the mattress to put my shoes on in the morning, I want to crawl back into bed. I don't want to go out there and do what I do."

"But you've done a lot of good. You do know that, don't you?"

I didn't.

"You have," she said. "Everyone I know lies, breaks their word, and has perfectly legitimate excuses for why they do. Except you. Haven't you ever noticed that? Two times in twelve years, you said you'd find this girl no matter what. And you did. Why? Because you gave your word, babe. And that might not mean shit to the rest of the world, but it means everything to you. Whatever else happened today, you found her twice, Patrick. When no one else would even try."

I looked at the river and wanted to pull it over me.

"So I understand why you can't do it anymore," my wife said, "but I won't hear you say it didn't matter."

I kept looking at the river for a bit. "Some of it mattered."

"Some of it did," she said.

I looked at the bare trees and the slate sky that stretched behind them. "But I'm all the way out. You okay with that?"

"Absolutely," she said.

"Mike Colette's having a good year. His distribution warehouse is thriving. He's opening a new warehouse off Freeport next month."

"And you, having worked your way through college in the freight business . . ." she said. "And that's where you see yourself in ten years?"

"Huh? No, no, no. That where you see me?"

"Not at all."

"I thought I'd get my master's. I'm pretty sure I could secure some kind of financial aid, a grant, something. My grades were pretty stellar back in the day."

"Stellar?" She chuckled. "You went to a state college."

"Cold," I said. "Still counts as stellar."

"And what will my husband become in his second career?"

"I was thinking a teacher. History maybe."

I waited for the sarcastic assessment, the playful dig. It didn't come.

"You like that idea?" I asked her.

"I think you'd be great," she said softly. "So what'll you tell Duhamel-Standiford?"

"That this was my last lost cause." A hawk glided low and fast over the water and never made a sound. "I'll be waiting at the airport."

"You just made my year," she said.

"You made my life."

After I hung up, I looked out at the river again. The light had changed while I'd been on the phone and now the water was copper. I perched the last remaining bullet on the end of my thumb. I peered at it for a bit, squinting until it looked like a tall tower built along the riverbank. Then I flicked my middle finger off the center of my thumb and fired it into the copper water.

"MERRY CHRISTMAS," JEREMY DENT said when his secretary put me through. "You done with your charity case?"

"I am," I said.

"So we'll see you the day after tomorrow."

"Nah."

"Huh?"

"I don't want to work for you, Jeremy."

"But you said you did."

"Well, then, I guess I led you on," I said. "Doesn't feel good, does it?"

He was calling me a very bad name when I hung up on him.

AT THE SOUTHWESTERN TIP of the trailer park, someone had arranged a few benches and potted plants to create a sitting area. I walked over to it and took a bench. It wasn't the rear patio at The Breakers or anything, but it wasn't bad. That's where Amanda found me. She handed me the car keys and a small plastic bag filled with ice. "Pavel put your DVD players in the back."

"That's one considerate Mordovian hit man." I placed the ice over the center of my palm.

Amanda sat on the bench to my right and looked out at the river.

I reached across and placed the Suburban keys on the bench beside her. "I'm not driving back to the Berkshires."

"No? What about your Blu-Rays?"

"Keep 'em," I said. "Have a high-def fest."

She nodded. "Thanks. How're you going to get home?"

"If memory serves," I said, "there's a bus station on Spring Street, the other side of Route 1. I'll take it to Forest Hills, catch the T to Logan, meet my family."

"That's a sound plan."

"You?"

"Me?" She shrugged. She looked out at the river again for a bit.

After the silence had gone on too long, I asked, "Where's Claire?"

She cocked her head back toward the Suburban. "Sophie's got her."

"Helene and Tadeo?"

"Last I saw Yefim, he was trying to get Tadeo to fork over extra cash for a pair of Mavi jeans. Tadeo's still shaking, he's all, 'Just give me the fucking Levi's, man,' but Yefim's like, 'Why you wear Levi's, guy? I thought you were classy.'"

"Helene?"

"He gave her a sweet pair of Made Wells. Didn't even charge her."

"No, I meant—is she still puking?"

"She stopped about five minutes ago. Another ten minutes, she'll be good for the car."

I looked back over my shoulder at the trailer. It looked pale and innocuous against the brown water and the blue sky. Across the river stood an Irish restaurant. I could see patrons eating lunch, staring blankly out the windows, no idea what lay inside that trailer, awaiting the chain saw.

I said, "So, that was . . ."

She followed my gaze. Her eyes were wide with what I'd guess was residual shock. She might have *thought* she knew what it was going to be like in there, but she really hadn't. A strange, fractured half-smile/half-frown tugged the corners of her mouth. "Yeah, right?"

"You ever see anyone die before?"

She nodded. "Timur and Zippo."

"So you're no stranger to violent death."

"No expert, either, but I guess these young eyes have seen a few things."

I zipped my coat up an inch and raised the collar as late December drifted off the river and snaked into the trailer park. "How'd those young eyes feel when they saw Dre blow up in front of them?"

She remained very still, bent forward just a bit, elbows resting on her knees. "It was the key chain, right?"

"It was the key chain, yeah."

"The idea of him, dead or alive, carrying a picture of my daughter in his pocket? It just didn't sit right with me." She shrugged. "Oops."

"And you knew the Acela's schedule, I'm sure, when you threw the cross back over the tracks."

She laughed. "Are you serious? Whatever you think happened in those woods, do you honestly believe people walk around all conscious of their motives all the time? Life's a lot more sideways than that. I had an impulse. I threw the cross. His dumb ass chased it. He died."

"But *why* did you throw the cross?"

"He was talking about quitting drinking so he could be the man I needed. It was gross. I didn't have the heart to tell him I don't need a man, so I just threw the damn cross."

"Not bad for a story," I said, "but it doesn't answer the original question—why were we there in the first place? We weren't trading anything for Sophie. Sophie wasn't even in those woods that night."

She remained unnaturally still. Eventually, she said, "Dre had to go. One way or the other, he'd served his purpose. If he'd just walked away, he'd still be alive."

"You mean if he'd just walked away to anything but the path of a fucking Acela."

"Yeah. That."

"What if I'd been with Dre?"

"But you weren't. That wasn't accidental. Since the day Timur and Zippo died, and I ended up with Claire and the cross in my possession?" She shook her head slowly. "Nothing's been accidental."

"But if everything hadn't gone according to plan?"

She turned her palms up on her knees. "But it *did*. Kirill never would have allowed himself to be led to a place like this if everything didn't look perfectly logical in a very logically fucked-up way. Everybody had to play their parts to a T. In my experience, the only way that ever happens is when people don't know they're playing parts."

"Like me."

"Come on." She chuckled. "You *suspected*. How many times did you ask why I'd made myself so easy to find? We had to make it easy—the combined intellect of Kenny, Helene, and

Tadeo couldn't solve a *TV Guide* crossword. I had to make sure the bread crumbs were croutons."

"So how soon after Timur died did Yefim find you?"

"It took him about six hours."

"And?"

"And I asked him how he felt about having a boss so sloppy he'd send a moron like Timur to pick up something as priceless as the Belarus Cross. That got the wheels turning pretty quick."

"So the plan was always to make Kirill desperate enough and embarrassed enough that a palace coup would look inevitable from the outside."

"We refined it as time wore on, but that was the general objective. I got the baby and Sophie, Yefim got everything else."

"And what about Sophie? What happens next for her?"

"Well, rehab for starters. And then maybe we'll go visit her mom."

"You mean Elaine?"

She nodded. "That's her mom. It's all about nurture, Patrick, not nature."

"And what about your nurturer?"

"Beatrice?" She smiled. "Of course, I'm going to see Bea. Not tomorrow, but soon. She's got to meet her grandniece. Don't you worry about Bea. She never has to worry about anything for the rest of her life. I've already got a lawyer working on Uncle Lionel's early release." She sat back. "They're going to be fine."

I watched her for a bit, this almost-seventeen-year-old going on, what, eighty?

"You feel remorse about any of this?"

"Would that help you sleep? To know I feel remorse?" Amanda pulled one leg up on the bench and propped her chin on her knee and peered across the space between us. "For the record, I don't have a hard heart. I just have a hard heart for assholes. You want crocodile tears, I don't have them. For who—for Kenny and his rape jacket? Dre and his baby mill? For Kirill and his psycho-bitch wife? For Timur and—"

"What about yourself?" I said.

"Huh?"

"Yourself," I repeated.

She stared back at me, her jaw working, but no sound leaving her mouth. After a time, her jaw stopped moving. "You know what Helene's mother was?"

I shook my head.

"A gin-soaked mess," she said. "She went to the same bar for twenty years to smoke and drink herself into an early grave. When she died, no one from the bar went to her funeral. Not because they didn't like her, but because they'd never learned her last name." Her eyes clouded for a moment, or it could have been the reflection of the river. "*Her* mother? Pretty much the same. Not a McCready woman I know of ever graduated high school. They all spent their lives dependent on men and bottles. So twenty-two years from now, when Claire's going off to grad school, and we're living in a house where roach-races aren't our primary form of entertainment and the electric has *never* been shut off, and collection agencies don't call every night at six? When *that's* my life, then you can ask me how many regrets I have about my lost youth." She pressed both palms together above her knee. Seen from a distance, she might have appeared to be praying. "Until then, though, if it's okay with you? I'll sleep like a baby."

"Babies get up every couple hours and cry."

Amanda gave me a gentle smile. "Then I'll get up every couple hours and cry."

We sat there for a few minutes with nothing to say to each other. We watched the river. We huddled into our separate coats. Then we both stood and walked back to the others.

HELENE AND TADEO SHIFTED IN PLACE by the front of the SUV, listless, in shock. Sophie held Claire and kept looking at Amanda like she was going to found a religion in her name.

Amanda took Claire from Sophie and looked at her motley crew. "Patrick is going to take off for public transportation. Say bye to him."

I got three waves, Sophie's accompanied by another apologetic smile.

Amanda said, "Tadeo, you said you're over at Bromley-Heath, right?"

Tadeo said, "Yeah."

"We'll drop Tadeo first, then Helene. Sophie, you're at the wheel. You're sober, right?"

"I'm sober."

"Okay, then. We've got to make one stop. There's a Costco up Route 1 a couple miles. They got kids' stuff."

"This ain't time to shop for toys," Tadeo said. "Man, it's Christmas Eve."

She grimaced at him. "We're not getting her toys. We're getting her a car seat base and a car seat. Drive all the way back to the Berkshires without one? Damn, man." She ran a hand over Claire's fine brown hair. "What kind of mother do you think I am?"

———

I WALKED TO THE BUS STATION. I took the bus to the subway. Took the subway to Logan Airport. I never saw Amanda again.

I met my wife and daughter in Terminal C of Logan. My daughter did not, as I'd always imagined she would at a moment such as this, run into my arms in slow motion. She hid behind her mother's leg in one of her extremely rare shy moments and peeked at me. I came to her and kissed Angie until I felt a tug on my jeans and looked down to see Gabby peering up at me, her eyes still puffy from the nap she'd taken on the plane. She raised her arms.

"Up, Daddy?"

I picked her up. I kissed her cheek. She kissed mine. I kissed her other cheek and she kissed my other cheek. We leaned our foreheads together.

"Miss me?" I asked.

"I missed you, Daddy."

"You said that with such formality. 'I missed you, Daddy.' Was your grandma teaching you how to be a proper lady?"

"She made me sit up straight."

"Horrors."

"All the time."

"Even in bed?"

"Not in bed. Know why?"

"Why?"

"That would be silly."

"It would," I agreed.

"How long's this cute-fest going to drag on?" Bubba appeared out of nowhere. He's the size of a young rhino standing on its hind legs, so his gift for sneaking up on people never ceases to amaze me.

"Where were you?"

"I stashed something on the way in, so I had to pick it up on the way out."

"I'm surprised you didn't smuggle one through security."

"Who says I didn't?" He jerked his thumb at Angie. "This one has luggage issues."

"One little bag," Angie said, spreading her hands the length of a bread loaf. "And another little bag. I did some shopping yesterday."

"To baggage claim," I said.

IT WAS LOGAN, SO THEY CHANGED the baggage carousel location twice, and we trekked back and forth through the claim area. Then we stood with a bunch of other people, everyone jostling to get closest to the belt, and watched as nothing happened. The belt didn't move. The little siren light didn't spin. The clarion bell that announced incoming luggage didn't sound.

Gabby sat on my shoulders and tugged at my hair and occasionally my ears. Angie held my arm a little tighter than usual. Bubba wandered over to the newsstand and next thing we knew he was chatting up the cashier, leaning into the counter and actually smiling. The cashier was toffee-skinned and in her mid-thirties. She was small and thin but even from a distance she had the look of someone who could kick some major ass if pissed off. Under Bubba's attentions, though, she lost five years in her face and began to match him smile for smile.

"What do you think they're talking about?" Angie said.

"Weaponry."

"Speaking of which, you really threw it in the Charles?"

"I did."

"That's littering."

I nodded. "But I'm a big recycler, so I'm allowed the occasional eco-sin."

She squeezed my arm and put her head to my chest for a moment. I held her tight with one arm. The other was deployed keeping my daughter safe on my shoulders.

"You shouldn't litter," Gabby said, her upside-down face suddenly an inch from mine.

"No, I shouldn't."

"So, why did you?"

"Sometimes," I said, "people make mistakes."

That must have satisfied her, because her face rose back up from mine and she returned to playing with my hair.

"So what happened?" Angie said.

"After I talked to you? Not too much."

"Where's Amanda?"

"Beats me."

"Boy," she said, "you risk your life to find her and then you just let her go?"

"Pretty much."

"Some detective."

"Ex-detective," I said. "Ex."

ON THE RIDE BACK FROM THE AIRPORT, the girls razzed Bubba about flirting with the cashier. Her name, we learned, was Anita, and she was from Ecuador. She lived in East Boston with two children, no husband, and a dog. Her mother lived with her.

"That's scary," I said.

"I dunno," Bubba said, "those old Ecuadorans can cook, man."

"You're already thinking about dinner with the parents?" Angie said. "Dang. You name your first child yet?"

Gabby squealed at that. "Uncle Bubba's getting married."

"Uncle Bubba's not getting married. Uncle Bubba just got some digits. That's it."

Angie said, "You'll have somebody to play with, Gabby."

"I'm not having a kid," Bubba said.

"And dress up."

"How many times do I—?"

"Can I babysit her, too?" Gabby said.

"Can she babysit her?" Angie asked Bubba. "Once she's old enough, of course?"

Bubba caught my eyes in the rearview. "Make them stop."

"You can't make them *stop*," I said. "Man, have you guys met?"

We emerged from the Ted Williams Tunnel onto 93 South.

Angie sang, "Bub-ba and A-ni-ta sit-ting in a tree," and my daughter joined in, "K-I-S-S-I-N-G . . ."

"If I gave you my piece," Bubba asked, "would you shoot me?"

"Sure," I said. "Hand it up."

We came out of the dark of the tunnel into the late-afternoon traffic as the girls sang and clapped their hands to the beat. Traffic was light, because it was Christmas Eve and most people had either not gone to work or had left early. The sky was purple tin. A few flakes of snow fell, but not enough to accumulate. My daughter squealed again and both Bubba and I winced. It's not an attractive sound, that. It's high-pitched and it enters your ear canals like hot glass. No matter how much I love my daughter, I will never love her squealing.

Or maybe I will.

Maybe I do.

Driving south on 93, I realized, once and for all, that I love the things that chafe. The things that fill me with stress so total I can't remember when a block of it didn't rest on top of my heart. I love what, if broken, can't be repaired. What, if lost, can't be replaced.

I love my burdens.

For the first time in my life, I pitied my father. It was such a strange sensation that I allowed the car to drift over the white lines for a moment before I made a correction. My father was never lucky; his rage and hatred and all-consuming narcissism—all of it unfathomable, even now, twenty-five years after his death—had robbed him of his family. If I'd squealed like Gabriella in the back of a car, my father would have backhanded me. Twice. Or he would have pulled the car to the side of the road and climbed back there to give me a beating. Same with my sister. And when we weren't around, my mother. Because of this, he died alone. He'd demeaned my mother into an early grave, my sister refused to return to Boston when he was terminally ill, and when, at the hour of his death, he'd reached across the hospital bed for me, I let his hand hang in the air until it fell to the sheets and his pupils turned to marble.

My father never loved his burdens because my father never loved anything.

I'm a deeply flawed man who loves a deeply flawed woman

and we gave birth to a beautiful child who, I fear sometimes, may never stop talking. Or squealing. My best friend is a borderline psychotic who has more sins on his ledger than whole street gangs and some governments. And yet . . .

We left the expressway at Columbia Road as the day finished furling up into a sky which was now the color of plum skin. The snow kept falling weakly, as if it couldn't commit. We turned left on Dot Avenue as lights came on in the three-deckers and the bars and the senior citizens' home and the corner stores. I'd like to say I found a sublime beauty in it all, but I didn't.

And yet.

And yet, this life we'd built filled our car.

I saw our street in the distance, and I didn't want to pull up in front of our house and let this moment empty from the car. I wanted to keep driving. I wanted everything to stay exactly as it was right now.

But I did turn.

When we got out of the car, Gabby grabbed Bubba's hand and led him toward the house so she could take him down to the cellar. Last year we'd answered her incessant queries about how Santa could enter a house with no chimney by assuring her that in Dorchester, he came through the cellar. So she'd enlisted Bubba to help her lay out the milk and cookies.

"Beer, too," Bubba said as they reached the house. "He likes beer. And he doesn't turn his nose up at vodka."

"Watch that," Angie called as we went to the back of the Jeep for the luggage. "That's my child you're corrupting."

A snowflake fell on my cheekbone and instantly melted and Angie wiped at it with her finger. She kissed my nose. "Great to see you."

"You too."

She took my burned hand in hers, looked at the large Band-Aid I'd placed across the palm. "You okay?"

"Sure," I said. "Don't I look okay?"

She peered into my eyes, this gorgeous, volatile, hyper-passionate woman I've been in love with since second grade. "You look great. You just look, I dunno, pensive."

"Pensive."

"Yeah."

I pulled Angie's bags out of the back. "Something occurred to me today while I was sitting by the river, throwing away a five-hundred-dollar gun."

"What's that?"

I closed the hatch. "My blessings outweigh my regrets."

She cocked her head and gave me a crooked smile as the snow found her hair. "Really?"

"Really."

"Then you won, babe."

I sucked in a breath of snow and cold air. "For now."

"Yeah." She held my gaze. "For now."

I slung one bag over my shoulder and lifted the other with my right hand. My injured left hand I closed over my wife's and we walked up the small brick path to our home.

ACKNOWLEDGMENTS

SPECIAL THANKS TO:

Lieutenant Mark Gillespie of the MBTA Police and Chris Sylvia of Foxborough Terminals Co. Inc.

Ann Rittenberg, Amy Schiffman, Christine Caya, and my Midtown family—Michael Morrison, Brianne Halverson, Seale Ballenger, and Liate Stehlik.

Angie, Michael, Sterling, and Tom for the early reads.

And Claire Wachtel for deworming the dog and sending it to the groomers.